About The Author

Tricia Heighway started writing in 2008. She writes both prose and poetry, and has explored writing in many genres, but loves comedy writing above anything else.

Tricia was born in Leicester but brought up in Bournemouth. She sang, acted and daydreamed her way through school, which was also the last time, until two years ago, that she wrote anything. Despite dreams of being the next Olivia Newton-John, she trained as a nurse. Now she is writing full time (or, at least, that's what she tells people), she much prefers the new day job to the old one.

She lives in north Hampshire with her husband, two teenage children, an elderly cat, and a selection of gerbils.

Tricia was a finalist in the Brit Writers' Awards 2010.

Paddytum is her first novel.

D1157396

PADDYTUM

Tricia Heighway

To Megan (or should
I call you Foggie?
Hope you enjoy reading
this, curled up with
a cup of tea!
love
Tricia
x

Paddytum
Tricia Heighway

First Published in the UK in September 2010 by Hirst Publishing

Hirst Publishing, Suite 285 Andover House, George Yard, Andover, Hants, SP10 1PB

ISBN 978-0-9566417-3-1

Copyright © Tricia Heighway 2010

The right of Tricia Heighway to be identified as the author of this work has been asserted by him in accordance with the Copyright, Designs and Patents Act 1988.

All rights reserved. No part of this publication may be reproduced, stored in or introduced into a retrieval system, or transmitted, in any form, or by any means (electronic, mechanical, photocopying, recording or otherwise) without the prior written permission of the publisher. Any person who does any unauthorised act in relation to this publication may be liable to criminal prosecution and civil claims for damages.

A CIP catalogue record for this book is available from the British Library.

Cover by Glyn Heighway

Printed and bound by Good News Digital Books

Paper stock used is natural, recyclable and made from wood grown in sustainable forests. The manufacturing processes conform to environmental regulations.

This book is sold subject to the condition that it shall not, by way of trade or otherwise, be lent, re-sold, hired out, or otherwise circulated without the publisher's prior consent in any form of binding or cover other than that in which it is published and without a similar condition including this condition being imposed on the subsequent purchaser.

www.hirstbooks.com

Author's Acknowledgments

A lot of people encouraged me to complete this novel, but my first thanks need to go to the *Paddytum Massive* on Protagonize.com, the birthplace of this story. So, I give huge thanks and virtual hugs to:

Marc Aucoin, Alexa, Burndtree, Eric Rountree, Robert Jadah, Megan Little, Trevor Kozma, Chris McIntyre, Jim McWhinnie, Ana Cristina Simon, Kirsten Hansen, Andy Montgomery-Hurrell, Charley Robson, Jonty Stern, Dan Mason, Nick Bouton, Roseanna Cooke, MelBelle, Seldom, Ritu Acharya, Cathryn Mullen, Briony Singh, Monica Manning, Kai Poynting, Maria Nikkel, Mary Cafferty, April Schoffstall, Parker Smith, Tammy Meulemeester, Edgar Sylvestre, Craig Cignarelli, Charlotte Perry, Ben Dunsmuir, Jordan Rockerbie, Grace Feehan and Jess Harrison.

Thanks to my family – my husband, Glyn, and my gorgeous children, Paddy and Lucy, for supporting my efforts and joining in with the squees when good things happened, and ignoring my exasperated hair-tearing when they didn't. Also, to my mother, Bridie Hutchinson, for always asking 'how's the writing going', even when it wasn't.

I am also indebted to the late Sir William Schwenck Gilbert for the loan of some of his lyrics and snatches of dialogue. (I'd thank Sir Arthur Sullivan too but it's not an audiobook.)

This book is a work of fiction. Names, characters, places, organisations, and incidents are either products of the author's imagination, or are used fictionally. Any resemblance to actual events, organisations, places, or persons, living or dead, is entirely coincidental.

ONE

At one thirty three in the afternoon on the second Wednesday in May, something happened which was to change Robert Handle's life forever. At the time, he didn't realise it would be a change for the better.

Rob was lying on his bed, in his room, in the house where he had lived for forty-one years and two weeks, munching his way through a family-size bag of Maltesers (made for sharing), when his mother called up the stairs, as usual, to tell him his lunch was ready.

'Yeah, okay,' he said.

At first, he thought the tiny sigh he heard had come from one of the characters in the Australian daytime soap he was watching on the TV/DVD combo set in the corner of his bedroom. So he ignored it. The next sound could not be ignored.

'Well, go on then!'

He looked at the television set. The two characters on the screen were in the middle of a passionate snogging session, so what he had just heard didn't fit. Besides, the voice was definitely English, a deep, velvety drawl. It must be someone in the street below, or in the garden next door. He shrugged, and put his hand back into the bag, drawing out another Malteser. He had it halfway to his mouth when the voice came again, this time louder; it sounded very annoyed.

'Disgraceful!'

He dropped the Malteser in shock. It bounced off his chest, rolled across his duvet cover and plopped onto the rug. Rob sat up and looked around.

'Get your fat bottom off this bed and get down those stairs to your mother!' This time he had no doubt that the voice was here in the room with him. It was right beside him, in fact. He turned his head slowly and looked at his teddy bear.

'Paddytum?'

He knew it couldn't be. He felt beyond foolish addressing the stuffed toy. He had spoken to it over the years, but never with any expectation of a reply.

'Right! For starters, you can stop calling me that. It was fair enough when you were three years old and had trouble with the name, but you have now been capable of pronouncing it correctly for at least thirty-six years. Be so kind as to do so.'

Rob stared at the toy. He rubbed his eyes. He stared at it again. It was motionless. But the voice, which sounded like a cross between George Sanders and Jeremy Irons, with a smattering of Alan Rickman thrown in, was emanating from it. Of that, he was certain. He cleared his throat.

'Padding—'

'Well, it's true your mother tried to make me look like *him*. She couldn't afford a real one. But the lovely little duffle coat she made for me is long gone, and you threw my red Wellington boots into a duck pond when you were six. And goodness only knows what happened to the hat—'

Rob didn't dare shift his eyes from the toy throughout this diatribe, his mouth hanging slightly open. Nothing had moved. Not a tuft of fur so much as rippled. The bear wasn't even facing him while it was, apparently, speaking. Am I hallucinating? he thought. He looked at the packet of Maltesers. Maybe they were off.

'But I do not wish to be called that. I never much liked the name. It is far more fitting for a railway station than a bear. Please call me Frederick.'

This was seriously not right. Rob stood, and backed away from the bed. 'How are you doing that? I mean, you're a stuffed toy. You don't have lungs, or vocal cords, or a tongue, and your mouth is just a line of stitching—'

'I do not require any of those things, Robert. You are hearing my voice through the power of telepathy.'

'What? In my head, you mean? I knew it was a hallucin—'

'No it isn't. My voice and my thoughts are real. And it's high time you started listening to me.'

'This is mad.' Rob picked up the remote and turned up the volume on the television, where the previously loved-up couple were now shouting at each other. Good. It would drown out this

8

... whatever it was. If he ignored it, it would go away. He sat on the bed again, and started to lift his feet up.

'NO!' The shout made Rob jump, and he dropped the remote. He shrank back against the headboard. The voice went on, slow, deliberate and firm. 'Go downstairs, you lazy, ungrateful wretch, and eat the lunch your poor, long-suffering mother has so kindly prepared for you.'

Rob crept over to the bedroom door, never taking his eyes off the bear. He slipped through, and closed the door quietly behind him. With a sense of surreal detachment, he descended the stairs to the kitchen on shaky legs.

His mother was sitting at the kitchen table, thumbing through a magazine, and sipping at her mug of tea.

'Hello dear,' she said, turning a page. 'Did you have a good sleep?' He didn't reply, and she looked up. 'Are you all right, son? You look a bit peaky.'

'I'm—I'm ok, Ma. Just feeling a bit—under the weather.'

'Oh dear. Well, have your lunch. I expect you're just hungry.'

'Yeah,' he said. 'Probably that's it.' He picked up the plate of sandwiches, and his mug of tea, as he always did, and carried it back upstairs, as he always did.

He didn't see, but his mother looked disappointed, as she always did.

Rob loitered on the landing, holding his plate and mug. He was missing his favourite soap, but he didn't want to go back in the bedroom. What if that voice started up again? But surely that had been due to low blood sugar or something. He had conveniently forgotten he'd ploughed his way through half a bag of Maltesers, and his blood sugar was anything but low.

He balanced the plate on top of the mug, and inched the door open. He listened. Nothing. He peeped in, and walked to the bed. He picked the bear up by one ear, and inspected the fur on its back and front, looking for signs it might have been tampered with, and then dropped it on the floor.

'Charming!'

Rob flinched, and the plate fell off the top of the mug, spilling the sandwiches on to his duvet cover, and splashing tea on his slippers.

'Pick me up. And what are you doing back here? This is a bedroom, not a dining room. You're supposed to eat downstairs.'

Rob lifted Paddytum up, this time by his arm, and placed him gently back on the bed. Then he scooped the sandwiches back onto the plate and slunk away toward the bedroom door again.

'Oh, you might as well stay, just this once. Your mother is right. You do look pale. I suppose this must have been a shock. Perhaps I should have taken a—gentler approach.'

Rob put the plate on top of his chest of drawers, his loss of appetite due to more than just an overdose of chocolate. His head was spinning and he felt faint, but he wondered how the bear knew what his mother had said. He sat on the bed, fighting the urge to lie down and put a pillow over his face.

'The thing is, Robert, I've been meaning to talk to you for ages.'

In the background, someone said 'Oh no!' and the soap's theme music started. Rob tried to tune the voice out, and his eyes drifted back to the television. As the credits rolled, the announcer reminded him it was a medical programme next. He enjoyed those. With any luck, there would be a feature on schizophrenia.

'Turn off the television, Robert,' the voice said. 'I can hardly hear myself think over that racket.'

Rob obeyed. The external sound now gone, he could hear his own heartbeat thudding in his ears. He perched on the edge of the bed, looking at his bear.

'This can't go on, Robert. You're wasting your life. It's time you heard a few home truths.'

TWO

Rob lifted Paddytum onto his lap. It was weird enough having a conversation with an inanimate cuddly toy, but at least the bear was facing him now.

'Paddytum ...'

'Frederick.'

'Oh no, do I have to? It's hard enough getting my head around the idea that you're talking, without having to cope with a different name.'

'Very well, you may continue to address me by that name. For now.'

Rob scanned the pile of soft toys at the foot of his bed. 'Can Sharp talk, too?' He inclined his head in the direction of a saggy, scruffy-looking, jointed brown bear.

'Ah. Well, I suppose you had better be told. Sharp is dead.'

'Dead? How? What happened?' How bizarre, he thought, that he should be shocked to learn of the death of something he had not, until now, considered to be alive.

'Oh, he died many years ago. Luckily, he drowned.'

'Luckily? How can it be lucky to drown?'

'Well, it was that time your mother put him in the washing machine after you were sick on him at your seventh birthday party. I say it was lucky he drowned, because it spared him the ordeal of the 600-rpm spin-cycle. That would have been altogether more traumatic and distressing for the poor thing. To be honest, Robert, you should have thrown him away long ago. That bit of wire sticking out of his foot is dangerous.'

'Was that how the wire started poking out? I'd forgotten. Ma still doesn't know about it, you know.'

'Yes. You discovered it a few days after the washing machine incident. That's when you started calling him Sharp.'

'Oh yeah! He was Tommy before that.' He knew this conversation wasn't really happening, but Rob was beginning to enjoy it. He knew it wouldn't last, so he might as well go along with it. 'Maybe I should bury him, though, if he's dead, like you say.'

'While you're at it, Robert, you can get rid of Action Man, too.'

'What? Is he dead as well?'

'Sadly not. It's just that I'm sick of sharing a bed with the frightful naked creature. Just why is he called Action Man, anyway? He hasn't got any … man-bits.'

'How about Pandy? Does he talk? Or is he dead?'

'*Sh*e is a pand*a*, not a pandy. And yes, she *can* speak. But she doesn't bother speaking to you, because you wouldn't understand Mandarin. Tell me, Robert—just *why* are you hanging on to all of these toys anyway?'

Rob looked at Paddytum. Because you're my only friends? He didn't say it out loud, and he wondered if the telepathy worked both ways. 'Its because—it's because I thought I could pass you all onto my kids some day?'

The bear gave a scornful laugh. 'Oh? And just how and where do you intend to obtain these future progeny, eh, Robert? Are they going to come down the chimney with Father Christmas? Or will the stork perhaps bring them?'

Rob was silent. The bear had a point.

'Robert, you are forty-one years of age. You have never had a job—'

'No, I have—it's just that—'

'—which has lasted more than forty-eight hours,' the bear interrupted. 'You have no friends, and you have never had a girlfriend—'

'Yes I have!' Rob butted in. 'I've got a few, actually.'

'Robert, if you're talking about those questionable females you talk to all night in Internet chat rooms, that doesn't count. Some of them probably aren't even female. I'm willing to bet that at least one of them is a forty-five year old police sergeant on the lookout for chat-room paedophiles.'

Rob gaped at the bear. 'How dare you!' he spluttered 'I won't have that. I never speak to anyone under the age of eighteen.'

'Yes, well, probably most of these *young women* you speak to every night, are forty-something, bored, desperate housewives. I wonder how disappointed they'd be to find out that the *twenty-eight* year old *fitness*-mad *stockbroker* with whom they've wasted many of the small hours chatting away—' Rob opened his mouth to protest. 'I can see the laptop screen, Robert. I *know* what you tell these women,' Rob closed his mouth. '—is an eighteen-stone unemployed slob in his early forties!'

'That's harsh, Paddytum,' Rob muttered,

'At this point, harshness is what is required, Robert,' Paddytum said, but his tone was more gentle. 'I want to help you.'

'Well, you can't,' Rob said. 'Nobody can. I'm a failure, a hopeless case. Do you know why I've never had a job, or a girlfriend, or a—life?'

'Yes, Robert, I know exactly why. It's because you're frightened.'

'No,' Rob said, his voice not far above a whisper. 'I'm not frightened. I'm absolutely bloody terrified.'

'Robert—' Paddytum said. 'Have you ever thought about the future? Your future, I mean?'

Rob rested his head back on the pillow. 'I try not to think about it too much.' He closed his eyes, and sighed. 'But I tell myself that when the right girl comes along—'

'WHAT?' Rob could have sworn he felt the bear move on his lap, and his head shot up off the pillow. 'What right girl? Oh, is Miss Right going to fly past your bedroom one day in a helicopter, perhaps, and swoop down and whisk you away to her fairytale castle in Disneyland?'

'I'm just unlucky—' Rob muttered.

'I have news for you, my boy. You have to make your own luck in this world.'

'Perhaps Ma should have encouraged me more—'

This time, the voice almost deafened him. 'Don't you DARE blame your mother, or anyone else, for your predicament, young man. That poor woman spends all day, every day, tending to your every need. And what does she get in return? Not gratitude. And certainly not company!'

Rob sat up. 'That's not fair. I help her with the housework sometimes. I go shopping—'

'Oh, *right*. You help her,' Paddytum said, venom in every syllable. 'You wash up the occasional mug. You run the vacuum round every week or so. Reluctantly. *When* she asks you. Oh, and if going *shopping* means dragging yourself across the road to the corner shop once in a while, to stock up on family size bags of Maltesers, then yes, I suppose you do go shopping.'

Rob sighed. 'I told you I was hopeless.'

'Robert, there is hope, if you do as I say,' Paddytum said. 'You're an intelligent chap. You could have gone to University. Your parents were so proud when you got a place. If only ...' he paused. 'But that's water under the bridge, and there's no point in dwelling on things that can't be undone. The point I'm making is that you have the capacity to *learn*. Which means you also have the capacity to *un*learn this terrible defeatist attitude you have to yourself and to life.'

Rob raised an eyebrow. 'So, what are you saying, Paddytum?'

'Robert,' Paddytum said, his voice booming with grandeur. 'I, Frederick, from this moment on, shall be your mentor.'

14

THREE

Maureen Handle lingered outside her son's bedroom on her way downstairs, listening at the door, as she had a few times since yesterday.

The boy was talking to himself again.

Not that it was anything new to hear Robbie's voice from behind his door. She had become used to hearing it from the bedroom for many years, more or less since ... *it* ... had happened. But yesterday she had noticed a difference, and what was different was the tone of his voice. Instead of the miserable muttering and moaning she usually heard, her son sounded almost animated. In fact, a couple of times she'd thought she was hearing one side of a heated discussion. And, last night, when she got up to go to the loo, she thought she heard him talking in his sleep. That was something new, and it had sounded different again, as if he were reciting something, like a poem, or lines from a play. Well, perhaps that was what it was; he'd enjoyed poetry and literature at school. Or was the poor lad finally cracking up? She craned her neck toward the door. What was he saying now? It sounded as if he were in a normal conversation. If you could call it that.

She had spent the past twenty-three years worrying about her Robbie. Would he ever get a job? Would he ever find a nice girl and settle down? She shook her head, smiling to herself. Settle down? That was definitely the wrong phrase in Robbie's case. Goodness, if he settled any further, he'd mummify. Settling down was what young men did who spent every night out on the town with their mates. Settling down was what they did when they'd sowed their wild oats. Maureen wondered if Robbie had ever had any to sow.

It really was a worry. She wasn't getting any younger, after all. They'd had only each other for the past two decades, since the thing had happened which had rocked both their lives. The man at the University – the Dean – had been most understanding when she'd phoned him to explain the circumstances. Of course, he'd said, after offering his condolences, there was absolutely no

15

problem with deferring Robert's University place until after the funeral.

But a week after they'd buried Eric. Robbie said he still didn't feel ready, and then a month later, the same thing. By the time six months had slipped by, she was deep into the depression which had seized her after the funeral, so when the infinitely patient Dean wrote to her to say it made more sense now for Robert to take up his place in the next academic year, she had filed the letter away 'somewhere safe' and then forgotten it. And so had Robbie, it seemed. By the time she emerged from the cloud created by her little pills, back to the real world, she realised her son had dismissed his dreams of academia and preferred the sanctuary of his bedroom. Part of her had hoped Robbie, always a shy lad, would step into his dad's shoes and become 'the man of the house', but it never happened. Instead, he had withdrawn even further.

She blamed herself. Nowadays, she supposed she would have been able to send him to some kind of therapist. Grief counselling, they called it, didn't they? She'd had nowhere to turn to for help, back then. There had been no male relatives on the scene, to give her lad a stern talking-to. But somewhere in her fogged brain had lingered the thought that he would eventually pull himself together and start living his life. She realised now that the transition from 'there's plenty of time' to 'it's too late' had slipped past them both unnoticed. Now, all she could do was look after him and, as she had always done, protect him from the world. Whenever the notion that it suited her for things to remain this way nudged her in the arm, she shoved it firmly out of the way and reminded herself that it was Robbie who needed her, and not the other way round.

But he shouldn't. Not still. Not at his age. She cringed. It's not my fault. I've been a good mother to him.

On Monday, Wednesday and Saturday mornings, she worked at *Crafty Notions*, a tiny shop on the outskirts of Fleesham, owned by a pair of friends from her tailoring days. From there, she ran a small side-business, undertaking dressmaking commissions, like costumes for dance school productions and theatre groups, as well as alterations and repairs, and helped out in the shop, which sold embroidery threads and fabrics, patterns and yarns. The

16

arrangement suited her, because it meant she could measure and discuss requirements with her small but loyal clientèle on the premises, and then carry out the work here at home in her time off. Her earnings, and Robbie's Jobseekers' Allowance, were sufficient to cover the utility bills – Eric's life insurance had paid off the mortgage – and to keep them fed and clothed. They needed little else.

But even though money was not an issue, she knew that a man needed a job. It would give him a sense of self-worth, and besides, what was going to happen to Robbie after she'd gone? Her health was good. Her brow furrowed as she realised it was probably better than her son's. She shook her head to dislodge the thought that she might even outlive him. If he could just hold down a job he might start to meet people, maybe even find a nice girl.

Was it too late for that, though? Barbara and Joan from work both knew she had a grown-up son at home, but neither of them ever asked about him – as if he were a guilty secret who shouldn't be mentioned. As if he were retarded. Well, she supposed he was, in a way. She cringed again. Robbie was socially retarded.

If he had a job, it would give them something to talk about in the evenings. He had no conversation, because all his days were exactly the same. They had just fallen into the routine of sitting in front of the TV in the evenings with trays on their laps, until they both went to their own rooms, she to sleep, and Robbie to do whatever it was he did into the small hours. No wonder he slept until lunchtime every day.

She pressed her ear to the door, straining to hear. The talking had stopped, and she noticed something else. Silence. Now, that was odd. There was always some sound coming from Robbie's room, from the TV or a DVD, or the music that came from those computer games he played late into the night when the telly was finished.

Maureen went downstairs, filled the kettle and flicked the switch. She started to butter bread and slice cheddar for their lunchtime sandwiches. Still deep in thought, she poured water onto the tea bags in their matching mugs, and then turned to go to the kitchen door to call Robbie down. She gave a little start when she saw him standing in the doorway.

17

'Oh! You're there,' she said, her hand to her chest. She went back to the worktop and picked up the sugar bowl, ready to pile the usual four spoonfuls of sugar into Robbie's mug.

'Not for me, Ma,' he said.

She stopped, with the spoon poised on its journey between bowl and mug, and a few grains scattered on the worktop. She looked over at him. He was sitting at the kitchen table. He pulled the plate of sandwiches toward him.

'Oh,' she said. She couldn't remember the last time Robbie sat with her for lunch. He always, without fail, took his sandwiches upstairs to his room, and stayed there until dinnertime. She put the mug of unsugared tea in front of him, and sat opposite him with her own plate and mug.

'Thanks, Ma,' He took a bite of the sandwich, and then lifted one corner of the bread. He peered inside. 'Is this butter?'

'Yes, love. Why? Is there something wrong with it?'

'No,' he said. 'No, it's fine. But could we get some low-fat spread? And wholemeal bread, instead of this white stuff? And can we have ham tomorrow, instead of cheese? It's lower in fat.'

Well, this is a change, she thought. She had been making cheese sandwiches for Robbie's lunch for as long as she could remember. Past attempts to give him something different had met with resistance.

'You going on a diet, love?' she asked.

'Well,' he said, patting his ample belly, 'I've put on a bit of weight, lately.' Something of an understatement, she thought. He'd been steadily piling it on since his father went. She had never said anything about it, because she didn't want to hurt his feelings. In the early days, she thought it was just comfort eating, a reaction to his grief. But he hadn't grown out of it; he'd just grown. Secretly, it was one of the things that worried her most. He was into his forties now, and must be a prime candidate for heart disease; she'd watched the medical programmes.

As if he'd read her thoughts, he said, 'There was this thing on telly the other day about reducing your fat intake. Cholesterol and that. Would probably do us both good, Ma.' He smiled at her. When had she last seen him do that?

She flashed him a cautious grin.

'So,' he said, after a slug of tea, 'How *are* you, Ma?'

'I—I'm fine, thanks, son,' she answered, bemused. 'Um ... are *you* ... all right?'

His eyes were roaming the kitchen, almost as if he'd never been there before. 'Where's the key to the shed, Ma?' he asked.

'It's on the hook, there,' she said, pointing to the wall by the back door. Why?'

'Well, I noticed the grass is getting a bit long,' he said, and continued, as if it wasn't anything unusual, which it most decidedly was, 'I thought I'd mow the lawn after lunch. And maybe do a bit of weeding.'

Maureen had just taken a sip of her tea, and she nearly choked on it.

'Oh. Oh! That would be a great help, Robbie,' she said, not quite believing what she'd just heard. 'Thank you, love.'

'Right, that's what I'll do then.' He nodded, twice, and took another bite of his sandwich.

His mother looked at him. A stranger was sitting at her kitchen table, but she wasn't going to argue. This wouldn't last, so she'd better make the most of it while it did.

He finished eating and drinking, and surprised her again by taking both plates and mugs to the sink and washing them up. Her mouth was still open as her eyes followed him upstairs.

I won't see him now till dinner, she thought.

But he was back downstairs in minutes, dressed in a pair of old jeans, a T-shirt, and wearing a pair of strong boots. He was also, for some reason, carrying one of his old teddy bears – the very scruffy brown one he used to call Tommy. He unhooked the shed key, and went out to the garden, whistling. A few minutes later, she looked through the kitchen window. Sure enough, there he was, pushing the electric mower up and down the lawn, for the first time since his teens. He even looked happy to be doing it.

Maureen watched him for several minutes. What on earth had come over her Robbie? Then she got on with a bit of housework, resisting the urge to stop every few minutes to watch the spectacle. When she looked again he'd finished the mowing and was cleaning the mower. He put it away, then knelt at the edge of the lawn and started to pull weeds out of the flowerbed. She put her hand to her forehead. No fever.

The next time she looked, he had the garden fork, and was digging a hole in the soil in front of the shed. As she watched, he carefully laid the brown bear in it, and squatted for a few moments, before filling it in again. Maureen had no idea what all that was about. Perhaps he *was* cracking up.

She watched him put the tools away, and then went into the living room so he wouldn't suspect she'd been spying on him, and sat at the sewing machine to work on her current project. He opened the door, a few minutes later, flushed and smiling, and wiping his forehead with the hem of his T-shirt.

'All done, Ma,' he said, cheerfully. 'I'm off for a shower.'

'Thank you so much for doing that, love' Maureen said. 'I expect you've worked up an appetite now, with all that hard work.'

'Actually, Ma—' he said. 'Could we have a salad tonight?'

He left the room. Maureen sat, staring at the doorway as she heard him climbing the stairs.

Rob towelled his hair dry as he crossed the landing into his room. 'Ah, that's better,' he said, as he closed the door. 'I worked up quite a sweat.' He readjusted his bathrobe and swung his legs up on the bed.

'I'm proud of you, Robert,' the bear replied. 'See. That wasn't too difficult, was it?'

'No. To tell you the truth, I even enjoyed it.' He looked at Paddytum, and grinned. 'I just hope she didn't see me burying Sharp.'

'Oh, she saw you, all right. The look on her face was rather comical.'

Rob sat bolt upright. 'What? How do you know that?' He frowned. 'I've been meaning to ask you – the other day you said my mother was right about me looking pale. How did you know what she said, when you were up here and we were down in the kitchen?'

'Ah, You will perhaps discover that, when the night wind howls in the chimney cowls, and the bat in the moonlight flies,' Paddytum said, laughing. Rob wrinkled his brow.

'What does that mean? What are you on about?' He stood and took off the robe, throwing it down on the bed in disgust. 'I just don't get you. I want you to go away now; you're not real, anyway. You're a figment of my imagination, and you're not even a nice one. I preferred it when you were just an old bear sitting on my bed minding your own business. Maybe my mum *should* have me locked up. It'd be better for everyone.'

'Now, stop that, Robert. I'm sorry. I realise all this is difficult for you, but just … bear with me.'

Rob stared at him. His face cracked in a smile, and he roared with laughter.

'What? What's so amusing?'

'Nothing.'

'Oh, I see. Now, we need to talk about the next step in your … rehabilitation.'

'Rehab, is it?' Rob said, still laughing. 'I'm not some druggie pop star, you know. Honestly Paddytum, you're cracking me up.'

'Just try to keep a lid on the hilarity, Robert. This is serious.'

Rob took a breath and sat down, fixing a solemn expression onto his face, but could not control an occasional twitch at the corner of his mouth. 'Okay, what's this next step then?'

'You need to get a job. As soon as possible. It's the single most important stage of this journey we're taking together.'

Rob's face immediately straightened, and he groaned. 'I know. But I don't think you realise how difficult that's going to be. I reckon I'm pretty much unemployable now. Who's going to give someone my age a chance? They'd just consider me a bad risk.'

'Robert, you'll find something. If you look for a job, you at least have a chance. Admit it, you've given up looking, haven't you?'

'I always have a quick look when I go to the Jobcentre.'

'With the emphasis on "quick", no doubt. That's no good at all. You have to be proactive – start buying papers, circle the jobs. I know! Join an agency. When did you last buy a local paper and have a look at the jobs section?'

Rob was silent.

'I thought not. Promise me you'll start looking, Robert. Tomorrow.'

Rob looked at the bear. 'Okay. I've got nothing to lose, I suppose.'

'No. Nothing at all,' the bear said. 'And everything to gain.'

Rob sat on the top deck of the bus, his stomach fluttering. His fingers stole into the pocket of his fleece, and fingered the card. Whatever had he been thinking? He'd ring the phone number on it as soon as he got home, and cancel the bloody thing.

He let himself into the empty house. His mother wouldn't be back from *Crafty Notions* for a while yet. He went into the kitchen and put away the groceries he'd bought on the way home from the *Let's Get Personnel* recruitment consultancy. How pleased she'd been the first time he'd offered to do the shopping, on his first visit to the agency two weeks ago. How pleased would she be to discover what he was doing tomorrow? Ecstatic, probably.

But he wasn't going to tell her, because he wouldn't be going.

Rob paused at the hall table, and his hand hovered over the telephone receiver. He pulled the card with the library details out of his fleece pocket, and looked at the name and number. Ah. He hadn't noticed before, but there was also an e-mail address. Much easier. That way, he wouldn't have to speak to anyone. He went up to his bedroom.

As soon as he opened the door, Paddytum started.

'How did it go, then, Robert?' the bear asked.

Rob ignored him. He sat on the floor and booted up his laptop. He didn't even look at the bed, where his mentor was waiting for a response. Mentor? Tormentor, more like. He opened up his e-mail program, and clicked on *new message*, then, holding the card from the agency, began to type the library address into the bar. He made sure the screen was angled away from the bed, so that the annoying furry sticky-beak would not be able to see.

'Coward!' Paddytum shouted. 'There's no point in trying to hide it from me, you pathetic yellow-belly! I can read you as easily as a large print book, Robert Handle.'

Rob stopped typing, and looked at the bed. He sighed, heavily. 'What?'

'You did as I asked today, didn't you? You went into the agency, instead of just standing outside. You looked at the jobs they had on offer. And you even managed to get an interview somewhere, didn't you? And now you're cancelling it,' Paddytum said. 'Well? Aren't you?' Rob heard real anger and frustration in the bear's voice.

He looked at the half-typed address, his fingers resting lightly on the keyboard. He continued to type the address, one-fingered, one letter at a time. He was determined to get this done. Who did this stuffed toy think he was, trying to run his life?

'What is it, anyway?' Paddytum asked. 'This job you're about to throw down the toilet?'

Rob placed the cursor in the message box, and began typing: *Dear Miss Jenkins, Unfortunately I will be unable—*

'Answer me, Robert.' The low pitch of Paddytum's voice chilled him to the marrow. Given the choice, he preferred the shouting. He stopped typing and looked at the bear.

'If you must know, it's at Fleesham Public Library. I've been given an interview tomorrow morning,' he muttered, his heart sinking at the thought. 'Library Assistant. Putting books back on shelves, mainly. Very low paid. A dogsbody, really. Not for me at all.'

'*Really?* How demeaning, Robert,'

Oh no, Sarcasm Alert. He'd become accustomed to the warning tone in Paddytum's voice, and had come to dread it. The bear didn't disappoint.

'And the job you were hoping for was … what, exactly, Robert? Professor of Neurological Surgery at a top London Teaching Hospital? Future Nobel Prize-winning Nuclear Physicist? Prime Minister of Burkina Faso? How terrible that those … those Philistines at *Let's Get Personnel* are not able to recognise your enormous potential and were only willing to offer you the chance of this sickeningly humble position. Oh, you poor fellow, you must be mortified.'

Rob cringed. Paddytum had out-sarcasmed himself this time. And where was Burkina Faso? 'And that's supposed to make me change my mind, is it?' He recommenced his typing *—to attend for interview at—*

'Right. Please yourself, then. If you do this, Robert, I'm done with you. You're on your own, my friend. Just as you were before.'

Rob stopped typing, and stared at the monitor, almost seeing the bear's words flashing in the centre of the screen. *On your own.* They echoed in his head. *As you were before.* He closed his eyes, and a single tear slid down his cheek. He blinked, refocused on the screen, and clicked the cross in the top right-hand corner of the e-mail box. *Do you want to save changes to this message?* He clicked *NO*, and closed the laptop lid, then went to sit on the bed, next to Paddytum.

'Paddytum, I *want* to go, but I'm really scared, mate,' he said.

'I know that, Robert. But it's a job. It's a start!' The voice was gentler now. 'You had the courage today, for the first time, to go for it. You just need to summon up a tiny bit more tomorrow. Please, please, don't throw away this chance.'

'What's the point?' Rob said. 'I probably won't get it anyway.'

He heard Paddytum sigh. 'Well, no. With *that* attitude, you probably won't.'

There was a long silence. Rob rubbed his hand over his face.

'Wait a minute, Robert,' Paddytum said. 'I have an idea.'

Rob waited. And what Paddytum said next made him roar with laughter.

'I could come with you.'

'What?' Rob gasped. 'Oh yeah! That's bound to get me the job, isn't it, if I turn up to a job interview carrying a bloomin' teddy!'

'No, wait. They don't have to see me,' Paddytum said.

'You're not going to tell me you have the power of invisibility, as well as speech, are you?' Rob said, wiping his eyes.

'Just calm down, and listen a minute, will you,' Paddytum said. 'You can put me *in* something. A carrier bag. Just make out you've been shopping on the way to the interview. It wouldn't be out of the question, would it?'

Rob considered this. 'And— you'd, like, talk me through it? During the interview, and that?'

'Well, if need be, Robert. It could be that my input won't be needed. I'd be there for moral support. But should you get stuck for a reply to any of the questions, I could perhaps give you the odd—prompt.'

Rob pictured himself, turning up at the library, carrying a bag. Would anyone think it looked odd? Surely it was feasible that someone might nip to the shops on the way to an interview.

'You know, this could work! Paddytum, mate, you're a bloody genius!' He stood and went to the bedroom door.

'Where are you going?'

'I thought I'd have a look for a newish-looking carrier bag in the kitchen drawer. If I take an old one it won't convince anyone. I'm sure I've still got that big one from the sports shop, that I got with my last pair of trainers.'

'No need for that, Robert. You'll have a brand new bag,' the bear said, a touch of mischief in his voice.

Rob frowned. 'Will I? How's that, then?'

'Yes, of course. Just look at how much weight you've lost in just two weeks. You need to go out this afternoon, and buy yourself a new suit.'

Rob looked down at his trousers, and slipped his hand under the waistband. Paddytum was right. In fact, all his clothes were becoming looser since he'd started eating more healthily and doing more around the house. He'd even taken to having a walk to the park and back, after dinner each night – his own idea. And the bear was right. He didn't have a decent suit, except for that one of his dad's in his wardrobe. But he hadn't slimmed down quite enough to be able to fit into that, yet.

He heard the front door opening, and went to the top of the stairs.

'Ma!' he called. 'Fancy coming into town with me this afternoon? I'm going clothes shopping!'

FIVE

Rob sat on one of the hard plastic chairs in the entrance to the library, the glossy white paper carrier bag on his lap. It looked suitably pristine and bore the name of a well-known men's' clothing chain. He wiped his sweaty palms on the knees of his new smart blue suit trousers. Paddytum was chanting a mantra of advice in his head, and it was really starting to annoy him.

'Remember to shake her hand: don't sit down until she invites you; smile; don't laugh at everything you say; don't laugh at everything *she* says; make plenty of eye contact—'

'Stop it!' Rob hissed. 'You're making me more nervous.'

'Only trying to help,' Paddytum said, sounding affronted. 'I'll keep my opinions to myself then, if they're not going to be appreciated.'

'It's just that—it's like a barrage, and I'm trying to calm myself down and I can't, with you in my head the whole time,' Rob said.

'Oh, pardon me for existing,' Paddytum said, his voice soaked in acid.

Rob heaved a sigh. He was grateful to the bear, but he wished he wasn't so—spiky, sometimes.

'Look, Paddytum,' he said under his breath. 'I'm very pleased that you're here, really I am. And I'm really happy that you're helping me. But—but I'm nervous enough already, without having to try and remember all that stuff you're saying.'

At that moment, a door opened, to the side, and a young woman called his name. He stood, holding the bag to his chest, not knowing what to do or say. The voice in his head had nothing to offer, and he felt panicky. What if he had offended Paddytum so much he wasn't going to help after all? What if he was sulking now?

'Put your hand out,' Paddytum said.

Rob closed his eyes briefly, in relief, and extended his hand. The woman took it in hers. A dainty hand. A firm grasp. She smiled up at Rob. He became painfully aware that this was the first physical contact he'd had with any female, apart from his mother, since he had slow-danced with Karen Pitkin at the Sixth Form Disco the week he left school. His face burned.

'Hello. Rachel Jenkins,' she said, letting go of his hand. 'Library Manager. Would you like to follow me?' He looked down at Rachel. Did she have to be so petite and pretty? He'd expected 'Miss Jenkins' to be a raddled old spinster in her sixties, but instead, she was this—little packet of loveliness. She couldn't have been more than five feet two, and slim as a *Lladró* figurine, with large blue eyes, fringed with impossibly long black lashes. Her dark brown glossy hair, tied in a ponytail, swung as she led him into her office.

She seated herself at the desk, and he was about to sit in the chair opposite, when the voice in his head said, 'Wait to be asked.'

'Do sit down, Mr. Handle,' she said. He detected a slight lilt in her voice. Welsh? Irish, maybe? He obeyed, putting the bag on the floor at his feet.

'Been shopping,' he said, laughing nervously.

'Irrelevant,' Paddytum scolded, in his head. 'No need to draw attention to it.'

'Sorry,' Rob said, feeling his face colour.

Rachel Jenkins raised a well-shaped eyebrow, and said, 'That's fine, no need to apologise. Now, lets see.' She looked down at a sheet of paper in front of her. 'Let me tell you a little about the job, first, um ... Robert. And then you can tell me all about yourself.'

He waited for the voice. None came, so he nodded and forced a look of what he hoped was intelligent attentiveness onto his face. At least he could now feel the flush leaving his cheeks.

'As a Library Assistant, you'll be helping me and the other librarians. Your main duties will entail sorting and shelving returned materials: that is, books, CDs, computer games and DVDs, and maintaining the shelves in correct order. How does that all sound?'

'That's what I understood, really, from the job description,' he said, listening for a comment from the bear. None came. I must be doing all right, he thought.

Rachel continued. 'Later, as you gain experience, you will be expected to deal with simple enquiries from the library customers, or to direct them to ourselves, and there'd perhaps be a spot of database work, eventually. How are your computer skills?'

Rob's mind went blank. He was suddenly tongue-tied. His eyes drifted to a wide oblong of one-way glass behind Rachel's head, looking out into the library. He saw one or two posters on a notice board opposite the window, and focused on them, while he tried to calm down. Any moment now, he would have a panic attack, he was sure.

'You're computer literate. Tell her,' Paddytum said quickly. It broke his trance and Rob looked back at Rachel, and replied.

She nodded. 'Good. So, tell me how you feel about ... interacting with customers.' She picked up the sheet of paper and studied it, clearing her throat. 'I understand that this is your ... first job, in a little while?' Her voice was gentle, but Rob felt a tremor start in his hands, and the blush was back with a vengeance. It was the question he'd been dreading since the moment he left the agency.

He looked down at his shaking hands, his head bowed. He knew that this was the moment when he'd blow the whole thing. He was horrified to realise he was about to cry. He blinked, and got ready to stand and walk out. It had been a stupid idea.

'Tell her the truth.'

'What?' Rob said, looking up. His gaze wandered toward the window again. Rachel repeated her question. He looked back and she was watching him, her face concerned. She probably thinks I'm a bit simple, now, Rob thought. Or a complete nutter.

'You have nothing to lose. Tell her the truth, Robert. Trust me,' Paddytum's voice was firm, but kind. Rob took a deep breath. Here goes nothing, he thought.

'Well, Miss Jenkins,' he began. He waited for Paddytum to prompt him. Then he realised that he was on his own for this part. He looked down, started fiddling with his fingernails.

'Take your time, Robert.'

He took another deep breath, and looked straight into Rachel's denim-blue eyes. 'The thing is, I'm just very, very shy,' he said. 'I always have been, even at school. I did well; I was one of the brightest boys in my class, all my teachers said so. I could have gone on to Uni. I applied, and I got all the right A Level grades, and several good offers.' He looked down at his fingers again. 'But

28

something happened and I sort of lost all my confidence and ended up not going. It's the reason I never lasted long in a job, and then I suppose I sort of stopped … even looking for one. Well, not as hard as I should have anyway.' It sounded pathetic even to him.

'Because of your shyness?' Rachel asked gently. Rob nodded, not daring to look up. 'What would you have done, if you'd gone to University? I mean, what course?'

He looked at her. She was smiling, and seemed genuinely interested in his reply.

'English. English Lit, probably,' he said. 'I love reading. I used to read a lot. I even used to read a book while I was walking home from school,' he chuckled. 'Bumped into a few lampposts, I can tell you, because I wasn't looking where I was going.'

Rachel laughed. 'I used to do that, too. A dangerous pursuit. You'd be at home here, then,' she said.

'Looking good, Robert!' Paddytum said.

Rob crossed his fingers in his lap. At that moment, he wanted nothing more in his life than to get this job.

'I forgot to say; there will also be some minor repair work, on the books. But we'll train you in that,' Rob's heart was beating very fast. She'd said *will* not *would*. He clenched his fists, feeling excitement building.

'Oh, that's okay,' he said with another nervous laugh. 'I'm very good with my hands.'

Paddytum groaned. 'That was ill-judged, Robert, but never mind.'

Rachel was studying his face, and smiling. 'You know, I don't see why we shouldn't give you a chance, Robert. A month's trial; how does that sound?'

'Oh! Oh, that sounds marvellous. Brilliant. Fantastic.' He was being given a chance. And he'd be working with this—this angel. He stood up, and took a step to the side, putting his hand out to shake Rachel's. 'Thank you. Thank you so much.'

Then he looked down, and saw that his foot had caught the paper carrier bag as he stood, pushing it over to Rachel's side of the desk. He watched in horror as, in slow motion, it tipped over, spilling its fuzzy haired occupant onto the carpet, at Rachel's feet.

Rachel looked at Paddytum, then at Robert, and then back at Paddytum again. When she finally looked back up at him, he could see, in that look, all his hopes sliding away, slithering under her office door, and carrying his precious but all too short-lived self-esteem with them.

SIX

Rob froze with his hand still extended. He opened his mouth, but could not think of a single thing to say.

Then, Paddytum's voice, loud, in his head:

'Story Time.'

What? What did that mean? Was the bear asking him to make something up? His outstretched hand was starting to shake, and he dropped it to his side.

'Story Time, Robert. Look!' The bear sounded excited, impatient. 'Look at the poster!'

Rob peered through the window at the notice board inside the library. Ah! Oh dear. He understood. But he hoped Paddytum didn't mean what he thought he did.

'Oh,' he said. Rachel had picked Paddytum up and was studying the bear's face, as if *he* would tell her what was going on.

'Story Time,' he said.

Rachel looked at him, an eyebrow raised. 'Sorry?'

'Well, I um ... learned ... before I came ... that you have Story Time for Toddlers on Tuesday and—' he squinted hard at the poster, 'Thursday mornings.' He gestured at Paddytum, who was now being cuddled by Rachel. 'This is Pad—um—Frederick. And I brought him with me in case I could do something—um, with him, at that. What with today being a Tuesday.' He couldn't quite believe what he was suggesting. He didn't think, for one moment, Rachel would be convinced, either. Not after he'd just finished telling her about his crippling shyness.

'You mean, tell the children a story, and use this bear as a sort of—prop?' Rob nodded slowly, holding his breath and really hoping she'd turn him down.

She sat down again, with Paddytum on her lap facing him, peeping over the top of her desk. He seemed, to Rob, to be daring him.

'It's probably a silly idea. Forget I said it,' Rob said.

'Oh no, no, it's not silly at all,' said Rachel, caressing the bear's ear between her index finger and thumb. 'I think it's a very good idea, and how clever of you to think of it. I'm very impressed that you went to the trouble to research our activities here. Not many applicants for this sort of post would go to as much trouble, but—' She placed a finger on her chin, and studied Rob's face, her head tilted to one side. 'I wonder ...' She looked at her watch. 'Today's session is in about half an hour. Did you have something in mind?' Rob was about to say no, when Paddytum spoke again.

'Yes. You do. I do, anyway. Say yes. Trust me.'

Rachel was waiting for his reply. Her face gave nothing away. Was she trying to catch him out? Could he really trust Paddytum? He hadn't let him down so far, but Rob needed time alone with him.

'Yes, I sort of—do.' *Actually, I don't have a clue.* 'But, I need to sort of—work something out. On my own.' *So I can talk to the damn bear and ask him what the hell he's playing at.* 'Rehearse, sort of thing.' *But really, I'd rather go home.* But if he did, he knew he'd be nagged and lectured by this bear for the rest of the day. For the rest of his life, probably. To carry on with this farce might well be the lesser of two evils.

'Well, we have a staff room, if you'd like a short time in there. You can get yourself a coffee, too, if you like,' Rachel said, standing. She led Rob out into the library, still clutching Paddytum to her chest. She stopped at the counter, to murmur a few words to a stern-looking bespectacled woman, who lowered her chin to look at him over the top of her bifocals. The woman nodded once to him as she listened to Rachel, and Rob raised one hand in a little wave. She frowned at him. Oh dear, this was going to end in tears; he was sure of it.

Rachel stepped into a section of the library Rob took to be designated for children, judging from the bright red rug and yellow beanbags on the floor, and the brightly coloured posters tacked to the walls. She scooped up half a dozen large-format picture books from a green plastic table, and tucked them under one arm.

He followed her past her office and down another short corridor, to an airy room furnished with two small red sofas and a low table. The end of the room was lined with a unit containing a sink and a worktop, which held a tray with a kettle, assorted mugs, a jar of coffee, and a box of tea bags.

32

'Help yourself to a drink. Milk's in the fridge. Sorry, there's no sugar. None of us takes it,' Rachel said. She pointed to the small fridge under the worktop.

'That's all right. Neither do I,' Rob said. *And I wouldn't have the co-ordination to make a cup of coffee anyway,* he thought.

Rachel put the picture books on the table. 'Have a look through these, and pick one or two you and ... Frederick, would like to read to the children.' She checked her watch again. 'I'll come and get you in, say ... twenty minutes? Would that be okay?'

'Yeah. Yes, fine,' Rob said. Rachel handed Paddytum back to him, and then left, closing the door behind her.

Rob dumped Paddytum onto one of the sofas, and, suddenly parched, grabbed a mug and filled it with water from the cold tap. He gulped it down, then refilled the mug, and started to pace up and down. The urge to flee from the room, past the library staff, and run all the way home, leaving the damn bear here, was strong.

'Robert. Sit down,' Paddytum said. 'We don't have very long. We can do this. Trust me.'

Rob sat, setting the mug on the table. 'Trust you? Trust you? Trust you to help me make a complete ass of myself, you mean.' He sighed, and put his head in his hands. 'I don't. Want. To do. This, Paddytum,' he muttered through his fingers. 'Please don't make me.'

'It'll be fine. I just want to try something. Put me on your lap.' Rob took his hands away from his face and sighed, picking Paddytum up. 'Now, put your hands either side of my head.' Rob obeyed. 'Now, empty your mind.'

Rob took his hands off the bear's head. 'Oh, come on! What are you going to do? Hypnotise me?'

'No. Better than that,' Paddytum said, cheerfully. 'Put your hands back, and visualise a white space.'

Not expecting anything, Rob put his hands just below Paddytum's ears. He felt very stupid. A picture of Mr Spock doing a soft-toy version of the Vulcan mind-meld popped into his head. He tried to make his mind go blank, but the Star Trek image came back, and he snorted with laughter.

'Robert! You're not trying,' Paddytum said,

'I'm sorry. It's just so silly, though.' He took a deep breath and forced a solemn expression onto his face. 'Okay. I'll try, really hard.' He rubbed his hands, and then placed them back on either side of Paddytum's head. He pictured a high white wall. Pure white, going on for miles. Nothing but white.

Then Paddytum spoke. And something amazing happened.

SEVEN

Rob had almost no time to react. He was aware, for a split second, of a tingling in the angle of his jaw on the right side, and then his mouth opened and his lips and tongue moved.

'*Speak the speech, I pray you, as I pronounc'd it to you, trippingly on the tongue,*' he said.

Only he didn't say it, Paddytum did. At least, the voice issuing from his mouth was closer to the bear's velvet tones than to his own. His immediate response was to clap both hands over his mouth, to stop any more of these strange words pouring out, and he half-rose from the seat, looking at the door, his eyes wide and anxious. The bear toppled off his lap, and onto the floor.

'Pick me up,' he heard loudly, this time in his head. 'I was just getting into that!'

He stood with his bottom hovering over the seat. The voice had shocked him with its loudness, and he half expected the door to open and Rachel to come rushing in. He picked Paddytum up cautiously, scared to touch him again. It had been such a weird feeling – as if he had lost control of his own vocal equipment.

'What was that?' he asked, his voice shaking.

'Shakespeare, of course. I'm surprised at you, Robert,' Paddytum said. 'You did that play at school. It's from *Hamlet*. Come on. Put your hands back on my head. I want to have another go.'

Rob's curiosity got the better of him, and he slowly placed one hand either side of Paddytum's head, and braced himself. Again, he felt that odd, though not unpleasant, tingle in his jaw, but this time he was also aware of his diaphragm lowering, forcing air into his lungs, and the inhaled air being expelled evenly past his vocal cords, as his mouth opened, letting out, in a booming voice, '*Now is the winter of our discontent, Made glorious summer by this son of York …*'

Rob pulled his trembling hands an inch or two from Paddytum's head, fearful he would have to hear or rather, recite, the entire speech if he did not. The voice differed subtly from the voice he had been hearing in his head. Although it was undoubtedly the voice of the bear, it sounded quite a lot like ... him, too. Not surprising, he thought. The bear was using *his* vocal cords; and moving *his* tongue against *his* teeth, and forming the words with *his* lips. The voice sounded like Rob doing an impression of Paddytum.

'Am I never to be permitted to soliloquise?' The voice asked, in his head again, and laughed. Rob had the feeling this, too, was a quote, but it didn't sound like Shakespeare this time. How did the bear know all this stuff? He's probably heard it on the telly, he thought. 'Why did you take your hands away? We need to practise. You have a fine set of pipes, my boy, but your diction is a little ... flabby. We shall have to try an exercise or two; repeat after me: The tip of the tongue, the teeth and the lips. The tip of the tongue, the—'

'Stop!' Rob hissed. 'What's the point of all this. You're not planning to quote Hamlet at these toddlers, are you? You'll frighten the life out of them.'

'Actually, Robert, that second one was from *Richard III*. No, of course not. I was just trying out—the apparatus. However, I have always been fond of The Bard. And I did sound rather impressive, if I say so myself. No, I do have something in mind, and it does not involve Shakespeare.'

'That's all very well, Paddytum. But you seem to be forgetting something.' He leaned forward and took two of the big picture books from the top of the pile Rachel had given them. 'How am I supposed to hold your head, and one of these things, at the same time? And we still have to choose a couple, remember?'

'Oh dear, oh dear, Robert,' Paddytum said, 'How many times do I have to tell you that you need to trust me? All will be well. You'll see.'

At that moment, the door opened, and Rob jumped. Rachel stood in the doorway, smiling.

'Oh good, you've picked out a couple of books. Lovely! The children have started arriving. Are you—and Frederick—ready?'

Rob followed Rachel out into the library, hoping the wobbly feeling in his knees wasn't too obvious, and trying to ignore the urge to go to the loo. He was starting to wish his parents had bought him a trike for his third birthday, instead of this monstrous teddy bear.

As if Paddytum had read his thoughts, he said, 'Don't you get any ideas about chickening out of this Robert, It's going to go really well.' Rob did not miss the note of excitement in the voice. What on earth—surely the stupid bear wasn't actually looking forward to this?

In the Children's Library, a crowd was gathering. Rob felt his spirits sinking at the sight of, he reckoned, about seventy small boys and girls and an equal number of mums. And one dad, who looked at Rob, then at the bear, and then back up at Rob again, with a look of disdain.

'There are hundreds of them,' Rob muttered.

'I hardly think fifteen counts as hundreds, does it?' the voice in his head said.

Rob looked again. It must have been his nerves, giving him double vision, or quadruple double vision. He did a quick head count. Yes, there were only about fifteen toddlers, who were filing over to an incomplete circle of tiny red plastic chairs. The gap in the circle was closed by one of the huge, squashy yellow beanbags. Did Rachel expect him to sit on that? He looked over at her. She was watching the children as they took their seats, and saying hello to a few, who were obviously Story Time 'regulars'. He hoped they'd be a sympathetic audience. He also hoped at least a couple of the mums knew how to perform CPR, for he was sure he was about to have a heart attack or maybe a stroke. He was thankful he'd put on clean underpants this morning; it'd be less embarrassing when he was carted off to hospital.

'Right, children,' Rachel announced, 'We have a special guest for Story Time today.' She looked up at Rob, and smiled, and he clutched Paddytum tighter. 'This is Mr Handle.' Fifteen pairs of toddler eyes looked up, not at Rob, but at Paddytum. Well, that was a relief, anyway. Rachel saw where they were looking, and continued, 'and his bear, whose name is Frederick!'

One little girl with her hair in a high ponytail opened her eyes wide, and cried out, 'He looks like my brother's Paddington Bear, only he's very scruff-ty, isn't he? And he hasn't got no coat no more. And he's lost his hat.' The little lad sitting on her right giggled.

37

Rob cleared his throat. He wasn't used to talking to children, especially ones this young, but it might help to break the ice. 'He— he used to be a Paddington, too. Bu—but he told me he wants to be called Frederick now.'

A couple of the mums exchanged glances, and the dad glared at him and placed his hand on his little boy's head, as if to protect him from the lunatic with the teddy, but when Rob looked at Rachel, she was beaming. The children were lost in a torrent of giggles.

'Don't be silly! Toys can't talk!' a little boy wearing a Doctor Who T-shirt piped up amidst the merriment.

Rob was about to reply that of course the boy was right and he was only pretending, when his left arm was seized by a strong spasm, as if he'd been electrocuted. It started to rise to chest height, lifting Paddytum up in front of him. This is it, he thought. This is my coronary. Goodbye cruel world, it was nice while it lasted. He just had time to remember from one of his daytime TV programmes that one of the first symptoms of a heart attack or angina was pain in the left arm, when his right arm started to rise, too, and came to rest just behind Paddytum's right ear. He tried to force both arms down again, but, before he had a chance to panic at not being able to move them, his jaw started to tingle, and he knew what was coming. Or rather, he didn't, and that was the scary part. As his mouth opened, he thought oh no oh no oh no please don't I'll faint on the spot Paddytum please—

'*I think you'll find you're wrong about that, young man!*' Paddytum thundered, through Rob's open mouth. '*I, Frederick, can talk. In fact I can speak very well indeed, thank you very much!*'

Silence. Cringing inside, Rob looked down at fifteen gaping toddler mouths. He dared to raise his eyes to their parents. Fifteen adult mouths were open too. But the looks of surprise were morphing into looks of amusement. Even Glaring Dad cracked a smile. Rob sneaked a sideways glance at Rachel, whose expression was of pure delight. And maybe just a touch of admiration.

High-ponytail girl whispered, 'Ooh, can you really talk? Or is it batteries?'

'*Batteries! My goodness me, the very thought,*' Paddytum said, and Rob was sure he felt a shudder. '*Yes, young lady. It is indeed I whose voice you hear.*'

Two girls sitting next to each other were whispering in each other's ears and nodding, and then one of them spoke up. '*We* think it's the man, doing the voice,' she pointed at Rob.

'Him? *You think* HE*'s speaking for* me? *I don't think so, little maid! His voice is insignificant and paltry,*' Rob wondered how the bear expected three-year-olds to understand such vocabulary, but all eyes were fixed on Paddytum, who continued, '*while I,* Frederick, *am eloquent and elocuted, and thus, am qualified to address you all.*'

All the adults were laughing now, including Glaring Dad, who had lost his glare and looked at Rob as if he wouldn't mind asking him to come for a pint sometime.

And Rachel. She had her hands clasped together and was smiling up at him.

'Well, I suppose we'd better get started, then, hadn't we? Mr Handle—' She touched Paddytum on the head, 'That is, if it's all right with you, Frederick?' She winked at Rob.

'*Miss Jenkins,*' Paddytum said, in a rather more flirtatious tone than Rob liked, '*It will be my pleasure. But first, might we have a quiet word?*'

What? For half a second Rob thought Paddytum wanted to go off somewhere with Rachel and talk to her on his own, until he remembered the bear couldn't talk without him. Then Paddytum murmured something, just in his head this time, as he followed Rachel into a corner. Yes. Perfect.

'Um— Rachel,' he said, 'as you can see, I have my hands full, with Frederick,' And you don't know the half of it. 'So, would you mind holding the books up for me? If you could sit on the beanbag, we—I can sit on a chair—' He eyed the small plastic ones with trepidation. 'Perhaps a normal sized one?'

'Oh, yes, that's fine, Robert. Actually I was about to suggest that anyway.' She laughed. 'And I wouldn't have expected you to sit on a kiddie chair,' she said, her eyes twinkling. She picked up a chair with a padded seat and carried it over to the circle of children. She placed it next to the beanbag, which she arranged to make more room, before sinking gracefully into it. As Rob took his seat, Previously-Glaring Dad gave him a matey wink. One of the mums was smiling at him as if he were a long-lost brother. Fine. He hoped they'd all still be in a good mood when this was over.

He looked down at Rachel, who was holding up the first of the two books. Two books, he thought. How hard could it be? And thin books, at that. It wasn't as if he had to read them all three volumes of *The Lord of the Rings*. OK, he thought, here goes.

The angle at which Rachel held the book made it easy both for him to read the words and for the children to see the pictures. The front cover of this one showed an improbably bright yellow duckling with a dayglo orange beak almost as big as its face.

Rob read the title out loud, 'The Duck Goes Quack'.

The tingle in his jaw took him completely by surprise and he almost fell off the chair as his mouth flew open and Paddytum's voice bellowed out.

'*Oh dear, that* really *won't do!*' He sounded furious. All eyes were suddenly on the bear. Including Rob's. Rachel was looking at Paddytum too.

'What's the matter, Frederick?' he said, as nobody else seemed willing to ask. Thankfully, his voice sounded like his own.

'*It's preposterous! The Duck Goes Quack, indeed! I mean, really! Do the people who write these books honestly think you young ladies and young gentlemen are nincompoops?*'

The children gazed up at the disgruntled bear, waiting for more.

'*Children, how many of you here did* not *know that ducks go quack?*'

The children all looked around at each other, shaking their heads, and then gazed back up at Paddytum. Not a single hand went up.

'*Case proven!*' Paddytum said, and one of the mums snorted with laughter. '*Now, put your hands up if you'd like to hear a proper story.*'

Sixteen hands flew above fifteen heads. One of the boys had both hands up.

'*Then I shall begin—*'

Rob slid his eyes over to Rachel, expecting her to be annoyed at this departure from her normal Story Time format. Her smile had not faltered, although there was a touch of bemusement in her eyes. She shrugged, put the book down on lap, and settled back to listen.

'*Once upon a time, in a land far away—*'

Rob didn't think he'd ever heard the story Paddytum told before but, for a few minutes, he was transported back to a time when he was much, much younger, maybe the age of these children, when someone had told him a tale very like this one. He saw himself in soft jersey pyjamas with little trains all over them, tucked up in bed, his thumb in his mouth, eyes drooping, feeling happy and warm and cosy under crisp blue sheets and furry blankets. The memory faded, and he looked round at the children as Paddytum spoke. As *Paddytum* spoke. Because he was almost unaware that it was his own mouth moving. From time to time, a child made fleeting eye contact with him, but most of the time, not a gaze strayed from Paddytum. At one point, he caught Rachel's eye, but she too returned her glance to the bear immediately.

When Paddytum had finished, Rachel stood, and said, 'What a wonderful story! Children, would you like to thank Mr Handle and Frederick?'

A chorus of thank-yous followed, and a couple of the mums started a round of applause, which was quickly taken up by the children and Rachel.

'Are you going to do Story Time every week, Mr Bear?' Doctor Who T-shirt asked.

Rob waited for a reply from Paddytum, but, apart from a pleasant residual tickle along his jaw, there was no forewarning tingle. Perhaps the bear was allowing him to decide. 'Um, I don't know.' He looked at Rachel.

'Well, that *would* be lovely … but only if Frederick wants to.' She raised an enquiring eyebrow at Rob. 'Does he?'

Still no jaw-tingle. 'I'll have to ask him, and get back to you later,'

Rachel laughed. 'That's fine. Now, children, shall we have a few songs, before you go?'

As Rachel led the children in *'The Wheels on the Bus'* and *'Old MacDonald'* and *'Row, Row, Row Your Boat'*, Rob sat and thought about what had just happened. He didn't know what to make of it. How could a bear be sentient? Was this really happening? And if it were, could it be that Paddytum was just his own subconscious. Was he some sort of Guardian Angel? Or maybe Rob was possessed? Perhaps he should go and see a priest. Or a psychiatrist.

He realised that the singing had finished and the children were starting to leave. A few of them waved. To Paddytum.

Rachel walked over to where he was still sitting, and he got to his feet.

'Well, that was a surprise!' she said. 'You're very talented, Robert. And as for your Frederick here—' She reached out and patted the bear on top of his furry head, 'He's quite a character, isn't he?'

Rob felt his face burning, to the tips of his ears. He changed the subject, more from embarrassment than modesty. 'So anyway, the job, is that still … er, okay?'

'Yes, of course it is. We'd love to have you, and if you can spare Frederick for the odd Story Time, that's a bonus. The job is subject to a CRB check, of course, because we have access to names and addresses, and because of the contact with minors. But that's just a formality.' She walked him to the door. 'I'll pop an offer letter in the post to you this afternoon, and then we'll give you a call was soon as we hear back from the CRB. So,' she said, 'do you think the job will suit you?'

Once again, Rob half-expected Paddytum to prompt him, but he hadn't said a word since finishing the story. Rob wondered if something was wrong. It looked as if it was going to be up to him to decide. 'Of course. I think it's just perfect. And thank you very much for giving me the opportunity.' He put his hand out, and Rachel clasped it briefly.

'Oh, hang on a minute, Robert,' she said, holding up one finger, 'Is it Robert? Or are you a Bob?'

'Rob's fine.'

'Rob. Good. You left your bag in the staff room. I'll just fetch it.'

Rob laughed, 'Thanks. I would look a bit silly sitting on the bus with a teddy, wouldn't I?'

She grinned before disappearing down the corridor again.

Formerly-Glaring Dad was standing by the children's library, watching his toddler reading a flap book. He sidled over to Rob.

'Here, mate. You played a blinder with that teddy-bear act. D'you do kids' parties?' He moved out of earshot of the child, and said, out of the side of his mouth, 'It's his fourth you-know-what soon and we're looking for an entertainer, like. Do you have a card, or something?'

Rob laughed. 'Sorry, I don't. I work here. At the library.' It felt good, saying that.

Rachel came back, and he put Paddytum back in the carrier bag and went outside, after thanking her again. He headed for home. He had a lot to tell his mum.

EIGHT

Rob stood outside the library, looking up at the blue, cloudless sky, and decided he should walk home. He was beginning to enjoy exercise, and it would give him time to think about everything that had just happened.

After a few minutes he began to feel uneasy. Why was Paddytum being so quiet? He would have expected the bear to be talking non-stop, boasting about his triumphant début as a storyteller and a showman. He lifted the carrier bag to chest level. 'Paddytum?' he whispered. 'Frederick?'

No reply. Where was he?

Rob stopped dead, in the middle of the pavement. Oh my God, what if he was still in the library? Not the bear itself, of course, but whatever part of it was sentient. Rob suspected it didn't stay put in the stuffed body the whole time. What if it had found somewhere else to dwell, preferring to be surrounded by books and people than hang about in Rob's bedroom. Two or three of those kiddies had been clutching their own cuddly toys: bears or rabbits. What if, horror of horrors, Paddytum was now on his way home with one of those poor children, soon to be terrorising the poor little scrap with his sarcasm?

Should he go back? Not all the toddlers had left when he had. If he were lucky, Paddytum might still be in there.

No, that was just silly; what was he going to do? Stand in the middle of the library and call out the bear's name? He'd be thrown out, and the job would be gone for good. He'd just have to wait, and hope for the best. He carried on walking. Paddytum would probably come back when he was good and ready.

Besides, perhaps this was the end of it. No more Paddytum. He might have decided his work was now done. Rob was eating healthy food, steadily losing weight, and now had a job.

Oh! Rob stopped again. What would happen if Rachel asked him to repeat the Story Time thing? He couldn't do it on his own. Rachel had offered him the job before Paddytum had performed his party piece, so his employment was not dependent on that, but it could be awkward if she ever asked him for a repeat performance. He had to admit he'd enjoyed the looks of admiration from the kids and their parents and, let's face it, from Rachel, too, but while it was happening he had been terrified, because he hadn't known what the bear would come out with next.

So, if Paddytum had really gone for good, how would he deal with this problem? Should he say some accident had befallen 'Frederick', and that he wouldn't now be able to offer this service? No, that sounded lame.

How did he even feel about the possibility that Paddytum might not be around any more? He'd started to enjoy his company and conversation. Over the past couple of weeks, he had almost completely stopped watching television during the day, with the exception of a daily half-hour after lunch when he joined his mother for their favourite soap. Instead, he now helped around the house, doing housework, small DIY repairs, and gardening, Even in the evenings, more often than not, he left the television turned off and chatted to the bear instead. What would he do now?

Sudden weariness and melancholy engulfed him. Whether it was due to the excitement and traumas of the morning, or the thought that he'd lost his new friend for good, he could no longer face walking the rest of the way. He headed for the next bus stop, taking frequent glances behind him to see if there was a bus coming. He spotted one in the distance just as he reached the bench, and plonked himself down with a long sigh. It was only a few stops and he'd feel guilty riding such a short distance, but he didn't have the strength to go any further.

The single-decker bus was almost empty apart from a couple of elderly ladies sitting separately. He took a seat right at the back and lifted the carrier bag onto his lap. His happy anticipation at breaking the news to his mother was overshadowed by the worry that he might have lost Paddytum's company forever. He wasn't convinced his mum would be impressed with his news anyway, having seen him fail so often before. So many times, he hadn't even turned up for the interview, and she had put her foot down the last time he'd asked her to phone and tell them he couldn't come because he'd been stricken with a sudden mystery virus.

Other times, he'd set off but had stayed on the bus past the stop he needed, and gone to sit in a café somewhere, nursing a cup of tea until enough time had passed for him to go home. Once or twice he'd made it as far as the interview location, and then chickened out of going inside, turning away to wander aimlessly through the streets until he could get away with going home to tell his mother, when she asked, 'It all went quite well'. It was too easy to get away with it. These days, employers didn't send rejection letters so, when he heard nothing after a week or two, Maureen was never any the wiser.

He hadn't ducked out of every interview. Sometimes he gathered enough courage to go though with it. He had even been successful at one or two. He started each new job thinking this time it would all be different; this time he would stick it out. This time he wouldn't take it to heart when the boss, or the other staff, told him he was doing this or that thing wrong, and *we don't do it that way here*, and *don't you know anything?* He'd survived a whole two days of it once – his personal best. The main problem was, he was so fraught with terror on the first day of every new job that, however patiently and kindly someone showed him how to do something, it just didn't go in. And then, when he didn't have the courage to ask, he carried on making mistakes, and ended up being told off. So, he had stopped looking.

But he just knew this library job would be different. It had to be, or all Paddytum's work would be in vain. He just wished he would come back.

He peeped into the bag again. The bear didn't look any different from the way he had when he'd arrived at the library this morning, but he knew Paddytum wasn't in there. He didn't know how he knew this, any more than he knew how he'd got there in the first place. He lowered his head to the bag, and whispered.

'Where are you, mate? Where have you disappeared to?'

The senior citizen sitting a few seats in front of Rob turned to look at him, and then gathered up her shopping and moved to sit a few rows further down the bus, raising her eyebrows at the other elderly lady across the aisle, indicating with her head toward the back seat. The other woman turned her head to look, too. Oblivious to their stares, Rob was still talking, quietly, into the bag.

'Thank you for helping me, mate. I couldn't have done it without you. And I understand if you think it's time to go, because you think I don't need you any more, but I reckon I still do, Paddytum. Just for a little bit longer. I'll miss you so much if you go away now.' He lifted Paddytum out and cuddled the bear to his chest, his eyes closed.

One of the women raised her finger to her temple, making a circular motion. 'Shouldn't be allowed, that sort of person, on public transport with normal people, should they?' she whispered to her fellow passenger across the aisle. The other woman swivelled round to stare at Rob, whose eyes were still closed.

'Oh, I don't know. He seems harmless enough to me. Care in the Community, I expect. Poor thing. It's very sad, really.'

A few minutes later, Rob made his way down the bus, not noticing that both pensioners shrank away from him toward the window as he passed.

NINE

Rachel Jenkins waved Marjorie off before going back to her office to tidy away few bits and bobs. It had been a long day, and she'd be glad to get home to her flat. She smiled as she thought back to the beginning of the day and that most unusual interviewee. Not to mention his extraordinary interview.

Robert Handle. Rob. His application form still lay on her desk and she picked it up now, and scratched her head as she reread it properly. With his employment history – or lack of it – most prospective employers would have dismissed him with a 'We'll let you know', but she'd decided to give him a chance. Someone had to. There was an unworldliness about him that was refreshing.

Young man? She smiled. He was forty-one: five years older than her. Somehow he'd seemed younger. Not surprising, really, when it seemed he'd shut himself away from the world. He hadn't really lived, had he? But she had a feeling there was more to him than met the eye. And she'd always been a sucker for lame ducks and lost puppies.

She thought back to the moment he'd walked in. A tall guy, carrying perhaps a little too much weight, but with his large frame it didn't seem too excessive. A nice face. She smiled again. A very nice face, Kind, grey-green eyes that crinkled at the corners when he smiled. His suit had looked new – she wondered if it had been bought especially for the interview. How sweet, if so: to buy a smart suit for - let's face it - a pretty lowly post. He'd seemed intelligent enough. What a shame he hadn't taken up his University place all those years ago. She wondered what his life had been like.

She looked at the form again. *Next-of-Kin: Mother, Mrs M Handle.* Same address. Well, that wasn't such a big deal these days, with housing so expensive and mortgages difficult to get. The poor guy was on Job Seekers' Allowance, so who would give him a mortgage? No wonder his self-esteem was low when he was still living with his mother in his forties. His mum. Or his parents, perhaps? No clue here if his father was around.

And that performance with the teddy bear. Who could have seen that one coming? She'd strained to hear that quiet, hesitant, almost apologetic voice all through the interview, and then, when the bear 'spoke', it was as if a completely different person had turned up. Was Rob like those comedians and actors who play brash and ebullient characters in their professional life and are shy and self-effacing, even reclusive, in private? She wondered if he knew how clever he was to have effected such a transformation. Did he realise how charismatic that bear character was, and how transfixed the children had been? She laughed. Never mind the children, she had been fascinated too. And, she had to admit, oddly attracted. She had been rather drawn to him even during the interview. It can't just have been that he brought out her maternal, protective side. There was definitely something about him. Good looking, though it was obvious he didn't know it. If he were to lose some weight he'd be quite a hunk.

What was she thinking? Shame on you, Rachel Jenkins, it would definitely be a Bad Idea to get involved with a colleague, particularly one with whom she would be in a supervisory role. She'd have to watch that when he started work. Perhaps it was a rebound thing. After all, it hadn't been long since Paul. And she was off men, all men, for the foreseeable future. Even sweet, shy men. Collecting a lame duck was a definite no-no. She gave her head a shake to rid it of the thought, feeling her ponytail flick onto one shoulder, then the other.

She pulled the keyboard of her PC toward her and opened up the word processing program, then drafted a formal offer of employment, printed and signed it, and then hand addressed an envelope. As she stuck the stamp on, it occurred to her to deliver it by hand. His address wasn't too far out of her way. No, silly, that would be most unprofessional, and, although she could argue that she would be saving the County Council the cost of a stamp, she had to admit to herself that the real reason was curiosity. She wanted to see where he lived, and maybe, to see him again. Oh, for goodness' sake, she was off again! She'd be working with the guy soon enough.

She placed Rob's application form in a manilla folder and tucked it into the filing cabinet drawer where she kept all her Staff and Human Resources information. She left her office, making sure the public entrance was locked as she passed it, before going out through the staff door at the side of the building. She made a detour to the post box outside the sub-post office next to the library, before getting into her little blue Toyota.

Fifteen minutes later, she was unlocking the door to her flat.

'Hello, Miss Sparrow!'

She put her hand up to her chest. 'Oh, hello. You made me jump!' Bill, her neighbour. It was beginning to disconcert her how he seemed to be permanently hanging around the landing like the smell of cabbage in a school dining room. Whenever she arrived home, or left in the morning, his door would crack open and out he'd come, his grin stretching his snakebite lip piercings. She wished now she hadn't told him such a lot about herself, like where she worked, where she used to live, but she'd been chatting to him in a new-neighbourly sort of way, just after she moved in, and didn't see any harm in it at the time.

Anyway, what could she do? Could you put in a harassment complaint just because a neighbour said hello to you a lot and called you a sparrow? She could always move from the flat, she supposed, but she really wasn't keen on the idea; she'd only been here two months, since she and Paul split up. She'd only just got it looking nice and she'd spent a fortune on having the whole place rewired. She planned to move eventually, into her own house, as soon as she had enough saved for a deposit, but it would be a year or two before she was in that position.

'Just back from work?' Bill asked, leaning in his doorway.

She nodded. Of course she'd been at work; where else would she have been?

He licked his lip, giving her a glimpse of his tongue stud, and she shuddered. How could people stand to have something put through their tongue? It was bad enough when you accidentally bit it. And the other body decorations, too. To her, facial piercings always made people look threatening, even girls. She didn't mind the odd hole or two in ears; she had pierced ears herself. Even a nose piercing could look attractive as long as it was discreet. But this guy looked like one of those earring holders in Claire's Accessories. As well as the snakebites, he had a big ring through his eyebrow, and sometimes wore a spike in the middle of his lower lip, and one of those horrendous things in each earlobe that stretched them into big holes though which you could see daylight.

'Been stamping books all day, have you?'

She smiled and let herself into her hall. She wondered what he did all day. She didn't think he worked. She'd only ever seen him wearing black bondage trousers with zips and buckles all over them and a ripped black T-shirt which showed off his illustrated arms, because, as well as the piercings, he went in for body art in a big way. A few of his tattoos looked like DIY jobs, but some were obviously done by a proper tattoo artist. Was he a Goth? Or an Emo, she never had known the difference between those two. He must be a bit old for that kind of thing. Dyeing his hair black was no way to disguise how much it was thinning, and made the bald patch at the back and the receding hairline more obvious. He must be in his mid-forties at least, by the look of him. Either that or he'd had a particularly hard life.

She slipped her shoes off in the hall, padded along the carpeted corridor to her bedroom, and slid her feet into her blue furry moccasins. She sighed. Tuesday was a *FLOATS* night, and Thursday too. She only had an hour to chill out before she needed to go out again. She half wished she were back in the chorus for this production. At least she'd only need to do one night a week. Still, it was one of those activities where it always seemed like a chore before she set off, but once she was at the church hall where *FLOATS* did all their rehearsals, she loved every minute. They were a nice bunch, too. Even nicer than the am-dram group she'd belonged to back home in Swansea. She didn't know what she'd have done without *FLOATS* to cheer her up and help her get over her homesickness in the first few weeks after coming to live in Hampshire, when Paul had taken the new job in Fleesham. Ironic, really, that he'd moved somewhere else now, but she wouldn't dream of returning to Wales. She loved her job; she loved being part of *FLOATS*. All she needed now was a decent place to live.

TEN

When Rob went up to his room after dinner, his heart sank at the sight of the bear on the bed, but still no voice in his head. No nightly chat to look forward to, then. It was starting to look as if his fears were being confirmed and Paddytum wouldn't be back. Perhaps he should try talking to him anyway. Like you're supposed to with people who are in a coma. No, it would just make him more miserable, if the bear didn't respond.

He wasn't at all tired, his head still buzzy from the adrenaline that had built up in his system during the interview. He turned the television on and flicked through a few channels, but nothing interested him. He wouldn't be able to concentrate. Perhaps reading would relax him. As a child, he'd read in bed every night, often dropping off to sleep with the book on his chest, and then he'd find it on the bedroom floor the next morning, his place always lost when it closed as it hit the floor.

He padded over to the bookcase on which the TV stood. The tops of the books were thick with dust. When had he stopped reading, anyway?

'You know damn well when you stopped,' he said, knowing what Paddytum would say if he were around. Of course he remembered. At first he hadn't had the heart to pick up a book. But then he discovered that reading leads to thinking, and thinking hurts too much. He'd replaced books with television, and video games and, later, the Internet.

He ran his finger along the spines. Most were children's books. Had he been as unwilling to let go of these as he was of his toys? Clinging to his childhood because it had been the last time he was happy? In his teens he'd started to turn to Science Fiction, anything from HG Wells to John Wyndham. He didn't think he could cope with Douglas Adams tonight. Not in the right mood at all. At the end of the shelf was a clutch of newer volumes – all paperbacks. He pulled three of them out. *Boost Your Self-Esteem in 28 Days; How to Stop Worrying and Start Living; Life's Too Short to Be a Loser*. He'd bought them all online, when he went through a phase, a few years back – probably the year he hit thirty – of wanting to haul himself out of his rut. It hadn't worked. Most of the books had exercises to do, to be worked through day by day. But they all involved interacting with other people: going out and doing things, talking to strangers, taking risks. Oh, he'd started off with good intentions, and would read a chapter, and resolve to follow the advice, but by the following morning he'd have lost his nerve, and finally the books were relinquished, abandoned in the bookcase with all the rest.

Perhaps the time was right, now, while he was in this period of change. He had a job, and this time it was one he was confident he'd keep. Perhaps these books could help him keep up the momentum. If he were to start reading them now, he could give himself ... what was it they called them on those talk shows? Coping strategies, yes, that was it. He'd teach himself some strategies to help him cope with life as a working man.

He settled back on the bed and took the top book from his small pile. He read the first words: *What are you doing with your life?* He groaned, and closed the book. No good. It just reminded him of Paddytum. Something else, then.

His eyes strayed to his laptop. Even looking at it made him feel guilty. He hadn't been online for ages, not since Paddytum had turned up. Someone to talk to, that was what he needed, not reading. The hours always flew by when he was in the chat-room. Just what he needed to take his mind off things. He glanced at Paddytum and his lips turned up in a sheepish smirk. At least he wouldn't get told off.

He booted up the laptop and opened his browser. The first bookmarked page took him straight to the *HantsSingles* site, and he clicked on 'Chat'.

Twenty or so people were in the room. He scanned the list for his friends. Uh-oh, *BigGirl76* – she never knew when to shut up and went on and on and on about her hair extensions and her boobs and how she'd found a new tanning salon, and how she was planning to have her implants replaced with larger ones as soon as she'd saved enough money. You'd have to change your ID to *BiggerGirl76*, he'd told her, but she hadn't much liked that.

Ah, here was one he knew: *FoxyFrankie*. She always seemed nice, and didn't go on and on about herself the whole time like some of the others. She was a local, if he remembered rightly. She'd even gone to Fleesham Downs Comprehensive, like him, though he hadn't recognised the names of some of the teachers she'd mentioned.

He ignored all the 'Hi Robster' messages in the main room and clicked on *FoxyFrankie*'s avatar, inviting her into Private Chat.

Robster582:	*Hiya Frankie*
FoxyFrankie:	*rob! how ya doing? where ya been? missed you*
Robster582:	*Been away. Working.*

Rob hesitated with his hands poised over the keyboard. He'd already told one lie. Paddytum wouldn't approve of this, but discounting that, he could imagine the bear's voice telling him to come clean and tell her the truth, that he wasn't a stockbroker at all. That he hadn't been anything else either, except unemployed, all those other times he'd spoken to her. That he wasn't a member of a gym and didn't work out from 6am every day before driving his Aston Martin into town. Perhaps he could do it gradually. He took a deep breath.

Robster582:	*Had bad news last week*
FoxyFrankie:	*oh dear what was that?*
Robster582:	*Made redundant.*
FoxyFrankie:	*oh no!*

Rob smiled to himself, despite the guilt-induced hammering of his heart. Yes, that should do it. He grinned as he thought of something else.

Robster582:	*Had to sell the Aston. Couldn't afford to run it any more*
FoxyFrankie:	*oh dear poor you! your lovely car*
Robster582:	*Yeah. Gutted. Stroke of luck tho. New job ☺*
FoxyFrankie:	*another stockbroker thing?*
Robster582:	*No, I'm going to be working as a librarian.*
Robster582:	*Fancied a bit of a change.*
FoxyFrankie:	*coming down in the world tho?*
Robster058:	*It's a job. Tide me over, won't it?*

FoxyFrankie:	*so you'll have more time now*
Robster582:	*For what?*
FoxyFrankie:	*meeting up :) fancy it?*

Rob's heart started to bang against his chest wall. Whenever any of his 'chat girls' had suggested this in the past he'd always made an excuse: going away, too busy, ask me again sometime. What would Paddytum tell him to do? Surely he'd be just a little bit impressed if Rob summoned the courage to say yes.

There was a snag, though. He looked down at his belly. This woman would realise as soon as she saw him that he wasn't the fitness-freak he'd always claimed to be. He stood, and paced to the window, then turned his head to look at the bear. 'What should I do, mate? Should I go for it?'

No voice spoke up to tell him not to. Paddytum just carried on looking into the distance.

He sat back down, clenched his fists, and stretched his fingers out, blowing out his breath before returning them to the keyboard.

Robster582:	*Sorry about that. Dodgy connection*
FoxyFrankie:	*was about to log off. thought I'd scared you off lol*
Robster582:	*Not at all. So, about meeting up, I'd like that.*

He typed it quickly and screwed his eyes tight shut as he pressed the ENTER key. Then he opened them again. The cursor was still blinking. Was she thinking about it? Had he scared her off?

| FoxyFrankie: | *great. when?* |

Now, that was a tricky one. No point in rushing into it.

Robster582:	*Two weeks' time? Going on a course for new job.*
FoxyFrankie:	*ok*
Robster582:	*A meal somewhere?*
FoxyFrankie:	*sounds good to me*
Robster058:	*Call you nearer the time? What's your number?*
FoxyFrankie:	*got a pen?*

Rob tried to slow down his breathing. What had he done? He scribbled down the phone number, the digits blurring as he started to feel light-headed. He prayed she wouldn't ask for his number. He took a few slow, deep breaths and the fogginess cleared.

Robster582:   *Ta. Give you a call couple of days before?*
FoxyFrankie: *ok hun i'll look forward to it*

They chatted for a few minutes more and then said goodbye, and he logged out and closed the laptop down. When he'd put it away he lay back on the bed with Paddytum beside him, and closed his eyes.

'I'm going to regret this, mate. I can feel it in my bones.' He waited for the bear to tell him he was wrong, that it was the obvious next step in his metamorphosis. But Paddytum wasn't saying anything. Rob sighed and got up, and began to get ready for bed. He was sure sleep would be a long time coming, but exhaustion from the events of the day overtook him, and he drifted into a dreamless sleep.

ELEVEN

Rob awoke feeling refreshed, and with a euphoria which, for a few seconds, he couldn't pin down. Then he remembered. He was an employed man. Almost. He turned his head to look at Paddytum, and remembered the other thing that had changed, and his elation gave way to despondency. Paddytum was no longer a part of his life. He had reverted to being just another cuddly toy – inanimate and mute.

Rob sat up, wondering why, underneath the euphoria and disappointment, there lurked a feeling of unease. Then he spotted his laptop, on top of the chest of drawers. Oh bloody hell. Frankie. He put his hands up to his face and groaned. Perhaps it was just as well Paddytum had gone. He'd never hear the end of it if he found out.

Rob's mum patted his cheek as she passed him at the breakfast table. 'It's so good to see you looking happy, son,' she said. 'Such a load off my mind that you're looking forward to starting a job, instead of looking like it's the end of the world that you've been offered one.'

He poured muesli into his cereal bowl, and splashed skimmed milk onto it. 'I know. But that's what it used to be like, Ma. I don't know what's been up with me all these years. But I think I'm getting there.'

She put her hand on his shoulder, and looked into his eyes. 'Yes, I think you are, love. I don't know what's changed, but I couldn't be happier for you.' She kissed the top of his head.

Rob spooned cereal into his mouth. They were both getting used to the taste of skimmed milk, low fat spread, and all the other reduced fat alternatives they now used. The other day, she had told him, she'd made herself a cup of tea at work, using semi-skimmed milk. 'I didn't like it,' she said.' It tasted far too rich.'

Rob gazed out of the kitchen window into the garden. The sun glinted off the roof of the shed, and the grass looked lush, but neat from its most recent trim. It would need mowing again soon, and he was surprised to find himself actually looking forward to doing it. All those years, he thought, of my mum doing it herself – of her doing *everything* herself. I've been such a bad son.

'Robbie? What's the matter?' He looked up. His mother looked concerned. 'You look ever so sad, all of a sudden. Are you missing him?'

Rob froze. How did she know about Paddytum? Then it dawned on him that she meant his father.

'No. I mean, yes, of course I do, Ma. But that's not why I'm sad. I'm just really sorry. How I've treated you – I let you carry on doing everything for me and never, ever said thank you. I've been an ungrateful sod, haven't I?'

'Come on.' She pulled him to his feet, and put her arms around him. He couldn't remember the last time his mother had given him a hug like this, and it felt strange, towering over her petite frame. 'You don't need to be sorry, my lovely boy. It's partly my fault.' He started to protest but she raised a finger to his lips. 'Yes it is. I was too wrapped up in my own grief to notice how much you were withdrawing into yourself. Or, rather, I noticed, but by the time I did, I didn't know how to get you out of it. Anyway, I'm just glad you're back.'

Rob smiled. He looked into her face, and frowned. 'Ma, we never talk about Dad, do we? Not since the day he—' He stopped, shocked at the look on his mother's face. It was as if a curtain had fallen. But there was something else he had to ask. It had bothered him for years. 'Mum? Why are there no photos of Dad anywhere?' His mother flinched, as if he'd slapped her. 'Is it because it's too painful a reminder?'

She pulled away from him and went to the sink, and started to run water into it, her back to him. Then she turned round, and her eyes glimmered with angry tears.

'Rob, there's something you don't know about your father. I should have told you years ago.'

Maureen remembered the day Eric died as though it were yesterday. But some of the details were blurred, as though seen through a net curtain. For instance, she could remember the name of the police sergeant who came to the door late that night, but could not recall the colour of his hair. She remembered that the female officer held her pen in her left hand to write in her notebook, but not her name or how tall she was. She remembered that, when the doorbell rang, she was watching a documentary on insurance fraud and trying not to worry too much that Eric wasn't home yet even though he'd phoned two and a half hours ago to say he was just about to board the train, but she couldn't remember what meat was in the casserole she'd taken out of the oven an hour earlier to stop it drying up.

She knew, even before she got up off the sofa to answer it, that it would be the police with bad news. But she *knew* it only in the way she had always *known* before, on the handful of occasions Eric had been late home from work, or Robbie late from school, that some terrible thing had befallen them. The difference was that, in the past, she'd always been wrong.

So, when the doorbell rang this time, Maureen knew, but she also knew she'd be wrong again. Only, this time, she wasn't.

Robbie was upstairs in his room, reading and listening to music, and he didn't appear when the visitors came. The female officer asked if there was anyone else in the house to sit with her, because they had bad news.

'No, just my boy,' Maureen said, gripping the arm of the sofa. The police officers must have assumed she meant a child, and exchanged a look of pity.

And then they broke the news that a man they believed to be her husband had been found badly injured on a train, the stopping service from Waterloo Station to Poole.

Maureen didn't ask them then about the injury or how it had happened. She didn't even begin to wonder about that until she was sitting in the police car. Her brain was still trying to process the information that came straight afterwards. Eric had died in the ambulance.

They told her someone would need to identify him. But he wasn't even at their local hospital. The guard had pulled the communication cord as soon as he found Eric lying on the floor of the carriage, bleeding onto the grubby, shoe-scuffed rubber floor, and the train had stopped about twenty miles from Fleesham.

59

'Where had your husband been today, Mrs Handle? There was an overnight bag on the seat next to him. Would that have been his?'

'Yes. Yes, he left yesterday morning.' She stopped. He hadn't been here last night. He'd been alone in a strange hotel bedroom in London. Would she have held him closer the night before he left? Would she have made her goodbye kiss at the front door more tender, had she known it was their last? That was silly. Had she known, she would never have let him go to the stupid conference.

'Mrs Handle?' The WPC's left hand was poised above her notebook.

'He went to a conference. *AGO*.'

'I'm sorry?' The sergeant was frowning. 'Ago?'

'The Association of Gentlemen's Outfitters. He was manager of Mainwaring and Bracewell, in the precinct. He went every year. He loved his job. And he took it very seriously – liked to keep up with developments in the profession.'

'And it was a two day event? Did anyone travel with him? Was there anyone else from …' the WPC asked, looking at her notebook. 'Manning and—'

'Mainwaring,' Maureen said. 'And Bracewell. No, he tried to persuade one or two of the assistants to go with him. But they thought it would be too boring. He always ended up going alone.'

The WPC wanted to know if there was someone who could stay with her little boy while they drove her to the hospital, and Maureen said, confused, 'Oh, he's not little. He's six feet tall already, and still growing,' and the officers exchanged another look.

'How old is your son, Mrs Handle?'

'He's eighteen. He's starting University next week. So proud of him, we are, our Robbie.' Last week, Eric had said how strange it would be when Robert wasn't at home and it would just be the two of them again. Now it would just be her.

The sergeant asked whether she'd like to bring Robert downstairs, and they would break the news to him, but Maureen said no, she'd tell him herself, after she came back from seeing Eric.

'Don't you think it would be better to tell him now? You could even go together. It would probably help you both, Mrs Handle,' the female officer had said.

'No, I'll tell him when I come back. It'll be better. He won't be able to deal with being told by strangers. He's a sensitive boy, you see.'

'Won't he wonder where you've gone, though?' the sergeant asked, and the constable nodded. 'It's a good half hour drive each way. I really think it would be wiser to break the news to him now, before you go. And ...' he looked at the WPC again, 'he might feel bad afterwards that he was not able to support you.'

So, she had brought Robbie downstairs, and she had sat next to him, holding his hand, while the sergeant told him his father was dead.

Later, other details had trickled out. Witnesses had told them of a pair of youths wearing scruffy jeans and leather jackets, walking up and down the corridor and looking into the carriages, using foul language. Probably drunk or on drugs, a few people thought. One was short, with greasy, shoulder length ginger hair, and the other taller, with spiky jet-black hair and lots of cartilage piercings in his left ear. Nobody seemed to have seen where they got off, but they had been on the train at least from Clapham Junction. That was the only thing everyone seemed to agree on. There were twelve stations between Clapham and where the train had been stopped. If one of these youths was responsible, and it seemed likely, they could be living anywhere along the route, which covered three counties. It would be nigh on impossible to find them.

On their next visit the police had seemed more interested in whether Maureen knew of anyone who might have a grudge against Mr Handle.

'They didn't really seem interested, though,' she told Rob, sitting at the kitchen table, staring straight ahead, clutching a tissue. 'And there really wasn't anyone, anyway. It was as if they'd already decided one of these two lads must have done it. Everyone loved your dad. Nobody ever had a bad word to say about him. He'd do anything for anyone.' She laughed, without mirth. 'Yes, very obliging, was Eric. All things to all men. And women, it seems.'

Rob frowned. 'What? What are you getting at, Ma? What did he do?'

Maureen smiled, ruefully. 'I never even suspected. He kept the secret well. From me. From us. We thought he was a doting father – a loyal, faithful husband. When all the time he—'

'What, Ma? Are you saying he cheated? Dad?' Rob's brow was wrinkled. 'No. He wouldn't. Not Dad. He was far too ... principled for that. He was a good man. What gave you that idea? Did you find some letters? Photos? Did someone tell you? What?'

Maureen turned her head toward the window. 'Someone told me, at the funeral.'

'What are you talking about, Ma?' He grabbed her hand, and held it tight. 'Mummy?' The childhood endearment slipped out, unbidden. 'Who told you? How did they know?'

Maureen turned to face him. 'It was the guard. The man who found him.' She took a deep breath. 'He said her name, over and over, as he lay there, dying.' She wiped her eye, 'There's no other explanation except that he was having an affair. I couldn't forgive him for that.'

Then she told him the rest of it. The name. And how she'd come back to the house after the funeral and picked up every photograph of his father, framed and unframed, and put them in an old suitcase and, next day, hauled them up to the loft.

TWELVE

Well, Rob thought, back in his room, it certainly explained the way his mother avoided all talk of his dad, and it explained the missing photos.

They weren't all missing, though.

Where was it? He hadn't looked at it for many years. He scanned the bedroom. He had a feeling it was tucked inside a book, but which one?

He needed to see his father's face again. He'd forgotten it. If he concentrated hard, he could remember the individual features, the size of his nose, the way the crease at one corner of his mouth was slightly deeper than the other, the exact colour of his eyes. He could see his unruly dark brown hair, damped down with Brylcreem to keep it tidy for work, and the shape of his eyebrows, but he couldn't put them all together. If he could just find that photograph he could look into his father's face, and he knew he'd be able to tell if there was any truth in what his mother had divulged. Rob was far from convinced that his father's last words added up to unfaithfulness. It was hardly proof, he'd said to his mother. But it seemed that over the past twenty-something years this 'fact' had embedded itself in her mind and there was no shifting it. Maybe, he considered, it was easier to cope with losing a cheating husband than a faithful one.

He crouched down by his bookcase and started to scan the titles on the spines, hoping for a clue to where he'd put the photograph.

'What are you looking for, Robert?'

Rob nearly fell over backwards. He whipped his head round and looked at the bed.

'Paddytum! You're back!'

'Well, you didn't think I'd left for good, did you? I still have work to do.'

'But—where did you go? I was really worried. I thought I'd never see—I mean, hear you again.'

'Well, it took me rather by surprise as well. It seems I rather overextended myself yesterday. After that story session I was exhausted, and I just … well, I suppose I went to sleep. Or maybe it was more than that. I'm not entirely certain what happened, to tell you the truth.'

Rob went to sit on the bed and lifted the bear onto his lap. 'How do you feel now?'

'Chipper, my friend. Completely restored to my normal self. I suppose the enforced rest has recharged my batteries. Not that I have batteries, of course, but you get my drift.'

Rob scratched his head. 'Well, that's good, I suppose. But is it likely to happen again? I mean, are you likely to nod off every time you do that—voice control thingy you did yesterday.'

'What do you mean, every time? I don't believe I agreed to make it a regular event. But yes, if the necessity arises, we have to be prepared for an … absence … afterwards.

Rob stroked Paddytum's head. 'Well, I'm glad you're back.' He frowned. 'Anyway, there was something I wanted to ask you yesterday, you know, after the session. But you disappeared before I could.'

'Ask away, Robert.'

'How did you know? I mean, how did you know you'd be able to do that? To speak through me? Was it an experiment? I mean, you kept telling me to trust you; did you know for sure it would work?'

The silence that followed was so long, Rob feared Paddytum had gone again. When he spoke, Rob heard a tone he'd never heard before in Paddytum's voice. If he didn't know better, he'd swear it was guilt.

'I knew it would work, because I … took certain liberties. At times when you were unaware. Forgive me.'

'What do you mean, liberties? I'm not following.'

'I just had the idea one night, while you were asleep. To try something out. I was as surprised as you were yesterday that it worked when you were awake.'

Rob's eyes widened and his jaw dropped as he realised what Paddytum meant. He laughed. 'You made me talk in my sleep? Is that what you're saying?'

'Yes, Robert. That is the case.' His voice was full of remorse.

'Bloody hell! You little bugger!' Rob said, 'I'm not entirely sure I approve of you messing with my bodily functions while I'm dead to the world, but what a bloody little furry genius! How did you think of that?'

'I don't honestly know.' Rob could hear a smile in the voice. 'It's very difficult. I don't sleep, you see, so when *you're* sleeping ... I think I was bored.'

Rob threw his head back and roared with laughter. 'You were bored. Brilliant. I don't know whether to thump you for infringing on my human rights or hug you for saving the day yesterday.'

'I wouldn't blame you if you were angry. It was rather ... an imposition. I had no right. But I think, in the end ...' Rob heard an undertone of pride in his voice, 'it worked out rather well.'

'I can't argue with you there, mate. But listen; could you do me a favour? Just *warn* me in future. It freaked me out when you started moving my arms about. Thought I was having a seizure, or a heart attack.'

'I'm sorry,' the bear said. 'And I think it may have been the ... limb activity, rather than the speech, which sapped my energy.'

'Makes sense,' Rob said. 'Like you said, we'll have to go easy on it.' He rubbed his hands together. 'Right. So did you hear what Miss Jenkins—Rachel, said about having to wait to start the job? Or were you out of it by then?'

'No, I don't remember anything from when they all applauded me—us, until I woke up just now.'

'Okay. It seems I have to wait a week or so, for the CRB check – you know, the Criminal Records Bureau thing. And then she'll give me a call and I can start work when that's all gone through.'

'Good. I don't suppose there's anything to worry about there. You haven't done anything that's against the law, have you?'

Rob raised an eyebrow, surprised the bear even had to ask. 'Well, you've been with me since I was three. Surely you know I haven't?'

'Yes, of course,' Paddytum said quickly. 'Foolish of me.' He sounded embarrassed, and there was another note in his voice Rob could not identify. Worry? Fear? Surely not.

'Paddytum, there isn't anything else you want to confess, while we're at it, is there?'

'Well, as you're asking, there is one thing, Robert. I told you a lie. That first day.'

Rob smiled. 'Oh, it's all coming out now, isn't it? Go on, then.'

'I feel rather ashamed. I don't know what possessed me. It was when you asked about Sharp and those other toys. I couldn't resist.'

Rob waited.

'They can't really talk. I'm the only one.'

'What? And Sharp wasn't really—'

'Dead? No. He'd never been alive. You asked the question. I was only teasing.'

'So, you're telling me … I went out in the garden … and I buried a teddy bear …'

'Yes'

'In front of my mother.'

'Yes. I do apologise.'

Rob stared at him.

'I wasn't to know you were serious when you said you were going to bury the poor creature. When I saw you carrying it I thought you'd throw it in the dustbin.'

Rob pouted. 'Well, I feel really stupid now.'

'Robert?'

'I can't believe you lied to me. And I believed you. I'm such a doofus.'

'You have my word, I'll tell you nothing but the truth from now on.'

Rob did some weeding after lunch, and then remembered he still hadn't found the photograph he'd kept. He went to his room after he'd put the tools away, and sat on the floor by the bookcase. He pulled out a book, and started thumbing through it, hoping it wasn't too obvious what he was doing.

'Lost something?'

Rob sighed. He might have known he couldn't do this without the Furry Inquisition butting in. 'No, not really,' he said. 'Just looking for something to read. I thought I'd go and sit in the garden. It's such a lovely day.'

He picked out another book and fanned the pages with his thumb, looking for insertions. Nothing in that one. He tried the next, and then glanced over at his bed. If he carried on, Mr Nosey-Bear over there would know he wasn't just looking for reading matter. He'd have to leave it for another time. That was a joke. When? Much as he was glad Paddytum had returned, his constant presence might eventually start to feel intrusive and limiting.

'You know what, Robert,' Paddytum interrupted his thoughts. 'Those books must be ancient. You ought to join the library.'

Rob laughed. 'What?' He rubbed his nose as a cloud of dust rose from a volume he'd last read when he was about twelve. 'I'm going to be working there soon. Why would I want to join?'

'It's simple. Think about it – turning up there to join would impress your new boss. If you show you're interested in books, she'll know she made the right decision in picking you for the job. Also, if you start to spend some time there while you wait for your start date, it'll get you used to your new working environment, before you're thrown in at the deep end, so to speak. You can soak up the atmosphere, watch what they do, and so on.'

Rob stopped his perusal of the books. It might not be a bad idea. And he'd see Rachel again. His face was suddenly suffused with heat.

'No, I couldn't. I'd be too embarrassed.'

'Why? It's a Public Library, and you're a member of the public. I'm sure there isn't any rule saying that people who are about to be employed by the Library Service cannot avail themselves of its facilities. It's the best thing you could do to prepare yourself for this job. Look, until yesterday, you hadn't set foot in a library since your teens. I know they'll be training you, but unless you at least get a feel for the place and what goes on there, your first day will be as daunting as if you were about to start work as an airline pilot.'

'I suppose you're right.' Rob ran his finger along the top of the book in his hand, and wiped the dust off on his trouser leg. 'Won't they think I'm being a nuisance, though, hanging around there before I start?'

'Robert, my dear boy, why ever would they think that? For goodness' sake, stop apologising all the time, just for existing. They almost certainly would not give it a second's thought. In fact, I imagine they, or Miss Jenkins in particular, would be pleased to see you. You could even tell her why; she'd probably be impressed. Look, I'm not suggesting you take a sleeping bag along and camp out on the doorstep. But a visit or two, while you wait to start work, would be very sensible, and good preparation, and Miss Jenkins, if she is as discerning as I suspect, will recognise that and admire you for it. Besides, you do want to pick up some books, don't you?'

Rob laughed. 'Yes, when you put it like that, it makes perfect sense. On both counts. But there's another reason I'd be nervous about going back so soon.'

'I can guess what that is, Robert. Are you, shall we say, attracted to the young lady?'

'Oh dear, is it that obvious?' Rob touched his burning cheek.

'I've told you before; I can read you, young man, like a book. She is rather fetching. I'd be more surprised if you were blind to that. As strange as it may seem, that is even more reason to go. You can acclimatise yourself to Rachel. Desensitise yourself, if you like, before your first day working with her.'

Rob stroked his chin. 'Do you think that would happen? I'd have thought it would make it worse.'

'No. It is likely to do more good than harm, in my opinion.'

'Well,' Rob said. 'I probably will, then. But not today. And before you accuse me of chickening out, I'm not. I just feel it's too soon.'

'Fair enough. I won't argue. But try the same excuse tomorrow and I shall call you a coward.'

Rob laughed. 'All right, bossy-boots, but I won't. It's a good idea. You've convinced me.'

THIRTEEN

He rubbed his eyes as he stumbled to the bathroom next morning. He hadn't slept well last night, his head buzzing with his mother's revelation, still doubting the truth of it, until those thoughts were chased away by dread of his impending date with Frankie. He'd half-expected Paddytum to tell him he knew what he'd been up to in his 'absence'. Now it was apparent that the bear had no inkling of Rob's illicit Internet activity, he felt even more guilty, like a little boy who had stolen from the sweetie jar and was expecting someone to find the empty wrappers. He had no right to tell Paddytum off for lying to him while he was keeping his own guilty secret.

Being found out was inevitable. There would be no hiding it when the time came, and he already feared Paddytum's reaction; he'd left Rob in no doubt how he felt about chat-rooms. Well, what harm could it do? Surely he was old enough to make his own mistakes? And learn from them. Who was to say it was a mistake, anyway? At least he was doing something: combating his shyness and meeting a real woman. That was good, wasn't it? He almost wished he didn't have to wait so long. Yes, it would give him time to prepare, but he saw sleepless nights stretching out over the next two weeks. He'd be a nervous wreck. It's no good, he thought, I'll just have to tell him. He might even surprise me and tell me I did the right thing.

He changed his mind two minutes later.

'I've been thinking, Robert,' Paddytum announced as Rob dressed.

He held up two ties against the short-sleeved shirt he was wearing, decided against both, and undid his top button. 'Mmm?'

'While you're at the library, have a look at their listings of local clubs and societies.'

'Why would I want to do that?' he asked, maintaining an innocent tone. He was pretty sure he knew what was coming.

69

'You need a social life. I mean, a proper one, not a cyber-one. I am heartened to see that you have abandoned the dubious characters who lurk in your chat-room. The best way for you to make some friends – real, flesh and blood friends – is to get out into the world and meet them face to face.'

'But, Paddytum, those people on the net *are* flesh and blood. If I met them, I'm sure they'd be very normal. I mean, why wouldn't they be?'

'If they are, what are they doing up all night, every night, talking to strangers and probably pretending to be someone they're not, instead of getting out there and living? Isn't it somewhat shabby to hide in the shadows, shielded from any responsibility by the anonymity the World Wide Web provides? If they were leading full and satisfying lives, they'd be tucked up in bed at that time of night, too tired to tap away on a keyboard divulging their inner thoughts to someone they don't know from Adam. No, Robert, you must steer clear of it. Were you ever to meet any of these sad, desperate people, I'm certain you would be in for a disappointment.'

Shabby? Charming! There was no way he could tell him about Frankie now.

'Yeah, I suppose some of them must be like that, but what if the rest are just really shy and lonely? Like me. Don't you think you're being a bit intolerant?'

'Not really. What is wrong with the old-fashioned methods of meeting people? You should consider joining some kind of club, and getting involved in an activity or taking up a hobby. Perhaps you could enrol in an evening class. Learn a language, or an instrument.'

'I wouldn't know where to start. Besides, I'm too clumsy to play an instrument. I'd need to learn to read music for the piano, not to mention buy a piano so I could practice, and I'd get my fingers tangled up with a guitar.' He wrinkled his nose. 'Besides, I don't really fancy it.' He laughed. 'Imagine if I started squeaking away on the violin or squawking on a clarinet for hours every day. I reckon Ma would throw me out.'

'How about joining a choir? As I said yesterday, you have a fine set of pipes. You take after your father.'

'No way!' Rob said. 'I wouldn't have the confidence. Can you imagine me singing in public? I'd be a nervous wreck.' Rob shuddered, his throat tightening up at the very idea of it. He didn't know how his father had done it. He'd been a member of the local amateur operatic society – the Fleesham Savoyards. He'd admired the way his father could stand on a stage, reciting lines, no, not just reciting – *acting* – word perfect in front of all those people, *and* sing in a confident, unwavering voice. His father had once read out a review from the local paper after the first night of a Savoyards production in which he had played the lead role. The reviewer had said he was fit for the West End, and even that he outshone some performers who were household names.

When Rob was sixteen, his father tried to talk him into going along with him to a few rehearsals – maybe even to audition for the Men's Chorus. Rob recognised it as an attempt by his dad to bring him out of himself. 'We need more male voices to swell our ranks,' he had said. Secretly, Rob had been tempted. He'd always enjoyed singing, and despite himself, he had to admit that being in the Chorus wouldn't have been too challenging. There had been times since his father's death that he wished he'd gone with him at least once. Still, it was too late to regret that now.

Paddytum's voice interrupted his reverie, almost as if he'd been reading his mind. 'There's always the Savoyards. You could join the Chorus.'

'No. They'd make me audition, and the idea makes my blood run cold. I've been put on the spot already this week.' He thought back to the interview, and laughed. 'And before you get any ideas, Paddytum, please don't offer to help me through a singing audition, because that would be taking the ridiculous to new heights. What would I say? I can only sing when I have my lucky teddy?' He chuckled.

'No, I wouldn't have dreamed of suggesting that. Besides, you don't need me to sing for you. You're perfectly able to do it on your own. As for the audition, most amateur societies and choirs accept anyone with a pulse.'

He glared at the bear, and said nothing. How did he know that? It must be from that reality TV programme a few months ago, about the guy who formed a choir from the ranks of an inner city council estate.

'I'm just suggesting it's time you were proactive about getting yourself a social life, that's all. You can take my advice, or you can leave it.' Paddytum sounded rather put out.

'Sorry. I'm sure you're right. You have been so far. Okay, I promise I'll have a look, and see if there is anything I can join.' There won't be, he thought. And even if there is, I'll be too nervous to do anything about it.

He went downstairs. A manilla envelope was propped up against the cereal bowl his mother had put out for him. It was addressed to him, in neat handwriting. He poured himself a bowl of bran flakes, and opened the letter. He smiled. Good. Now he had the perfect excuse to go to the library.

FOURTEEN

Rachel finished arranging the kiddie chairs in their usual Story Time pattern and looked up to see a tall figure standing at the returns desk. 'Oh, hello,' she said as she went to stand behind the counter, 'I didn't expect to see you again so soon.' Rob stood with his hands dangling at his sides. No bag today. She grinned. 'You left Frederick at home today, did you?'

Rob laughed. 'I don't take him everywhere with me, you know.' He held out an envelope. 'I was coming this way today, so I decided to bring in my job acceptance in person.'

'Oh,' Rachel said, taking the envelope. 'Excellent. I've sent off your CRB form. Hopefully, it won't take too long, but you can never tell with these things.' She looked at Rob, who was looking down at the counter, and picking at his fingernails. 'At least you can enjoy your last few days of freedom,' she said, and then laughed. 'Sorry, that sounds as if you're about to be carted off to jail, doesn't it?'

'No, I know what you mean. It feels very different being out of work when you're about to start a job. Not like before, when I was just plain unemployed. It's like being on holiday, I suppose.' He cleared his throat. 'I do have an ulterior motive for coming in today, actually.'

Rachel looked up into his face. 'Oh? What's that?'

'Well, it may sound a bit silly, but I'd like to join the library.'

She gave him a stern look. 'I'm surprised you're not a member already,' she said. Rob blushed, and looked cowed. 'Don't worry. I'm only joking. I just thought, as you said you enjoyed reading so much …'

'To be honest,' he said, 'I seem to have fallen out of the habit, over the last few years. I'm afraid I've wasted my time doing other things instead. Less worthy things, I suppose.'

'Really,' Rachel said with a smirk. 'What would they be, then?' She was surprised at the flirtatious note in her own voice. It wasn't like her at all. Better be careful, she thought. Was it her imagination, or did he look more attractive than she remembered from two days ago. Not surprising, really. He'd been under stress, and he'd been wearing that suit with the air of someone who was ill at ease in formal clothing. The short-sleeved olive green shirt he was wearing today brought out the colour of his eyes.

'Nothing too awful,' he said. She hadn't noticed those dimples when he smiled before, either. But then, he hadn't really smiled a lot at the interview. 'Just wasting hours on the Internet, and playing computer games. That kind of thing. And far too much telly.'

'So, not so much a misspent youth as a misspent adulthood?'

'Something like that,' Rob said, with a chuckle. He sounded rather sexy when he laughed. Oh, get a grip, Rachel, she thought.

'Were you a library member before? We might still have your records on the computer.'

'Actually, I'd be surprised. I don't think it was computerised back when I used to come in every week with my four books. I still have my old library tickets somewhere, though, if that helps.'

Rachel laughed. 'Tickets? That's a blast from the past. Are they those beige cardboard ones, like little pockets? They used to take them off you and tuck the card from the book inside them, and file them away in a wooden box. Gosh, that's even before *my* time, and I've worked in libraries for—well, never mind how long, I'll be giving away my age.' And just why did that matter? Definitely need to watch myself. I'll be giving a girlish giggle in a minute, if I'm not careful, and batting my eyelashes at him.

Rob was watching her closely, with a rather comical expression on his face, and she felt her cheeks colouring. 'I can't imagine how time-consuming it must have been, filing all those little cards away, and having to rummage through them every time a customer returned their books.' She reached into a drawer under the counter, drew out a form, and took a pen from a pot by the cash register. 'Right. If you take this and sit over there at one of the tables, you can fill it in, and I'll get your membership set up today.' She handed him the pen and form. 'You can choose some books, too.'

Rob smiled as he scanned the form 'Great,' he said. 'How many? Is it still four?'

'Oh goodness, no. We trust you with up to twenty items these days. And not just books, either; it includes music CDs, audio

74

books, DVDs – though there's a small borrowing fee to pay for those and the music. Oh, and for the computer and console games … but perhaps you'd better keep away from those?'

'Yes, definitely.'

There was that sexy laugh again, and weren't his teeth nice? She'd always been a sucker for a slight overbite like his. She felt her cheeks get even hotter. What was up with her? She'd have to get over this before the guy started working here, or she could be in big trouble. She handed him a glossy printed A5 sheet. 'This tells you exactly what you can borrow, and about fines and suchlike. Mind you, when you're working here, you'll have no excuse for letting your books go overdue, will you?'

'No.' He studied the printed sheet, and grinned. 'And this can be my homework, can't it? Right, I'll go and fill the form in, then.'

'Good.' She rubbed her hands together. 'I'd better get ready for the kiddies. Oh, you might want to hide when they arrive, Rob.'

He looked puzzled. 'Oh? Why's that?'

'Well, we get a lot of the same children at today's session as come to the Tuesday one. If any of them see you and recognise you, they'll probably demand a repeat performance!'

'Good thinking. I'll go round to the reference section, just in case.' He started to walk off. 'Oh!' He turned on his heel and Rachel looked up. 'Do you happen to have lists of local clubs and that kind of thing? Pa—my mother said you might. I'm thinking of finding a hobby to take up. Another thing to stop me drifting back into my time-wasting ways.'

'Yes,' she said. She pointed round the corner. 'Of course.' You'll see some ring binders on the big table to the left of the racks in the Reference Library. Anything particular in mind?'

'No, not really. Just looking for inspiration at the moment.'

'Well,' Rachel said, 'There's quite a lot to choose from. Everything from sports, to photography, to creative writing and amateur dramatics.' She pulled a sheet of paper out of the laser printer under the counter and, as an afterthought, a second sheet. 'Here. Take these, to jot down phone numbers and email addresses. A few clubs and societies have their own websites, too. You'll be able to do your research at your leisure.'

His fingertips brushed hers as he took the paper, and she shivered.

'Excellent. That's a great idea. Thanks, er—Miss Jenkins.'

'Oh, please call me Rachel,' she said. 'We're all on first names around here. Miss Jenkins makes me sound like a grey-haired schoolmarm.' Or a librarian.

Rob disappeared around the corner to the reference section, and she found herself staring after him. She'd hardly given him a second thought since Tuesday, and now she felt just like a schoolgirl starting a crush. She frowned. This was not good news. Not good at all.

FIFTEEN

Rob sat in the park with his half-litre bottle of water on the bench beside him and his book open face down on his lap. Almost two weeks since the interview, he'd still had no word about a start date at the library, but yesterday when he returned with yet another batch of books (and took out eight more), Rachel told him it should be any day now.

'Honestly, if I've heard nothing by the end of the week, Rob, I'm inclined just to let you start on Monday. We'll just find you a pile of books to repair, or some odd jobs to do away from the public, and make a start on your training.'

He tipped his head back, letting the sun wash over his face. Whatever happened, he'd be an employed man next week, and he was determined to make the most of these last few days. The way he was using his time had the Paddytum seal of approval.

He'd fallen into a new routine. In addition to his nightly stroll after dinner, he now walked into town each morning, and then sat in the park to read for an hour or two before walking home, with an occasional detour to the supermarket armed with a shopping list compiled by his mother and him the night before. He'd been lucky with the weather, which had been glorious every day. He enjoyed the daily stroll so much he'd resolved to walk to work every day once he started. Unless the weather was really bad, a one-mile walk would set him up for the day, and the walk home again would help him unwind. His weight continued to fall, and his clothes were beginning to get uncomfortably loose again.

When he looked in the mirror, something he had only started to do recently, he had to look twice at the youthful face staring back at him. He'd avoided mirrors for years: most days he'd avoided shaving, simply because it meant looking at that face. He realised now that he was struggling not to think of himself – still – as a fat, ugly slob. And he hadn't just shed weight, but years as well. The heavy jowls and double chin were gone, and his dull, pasty complexion from all the years without exercise or sunshine had been replaced by a youthful glow.

'You know, you're not a such bad looking guy at all, Rob Handle,' he said, when he'd finished his shave one morning. 'If I do say so myself.'

Back in his room, Paddytum had said, 'You're looking pleased with yourself.'

Rob grinned. 'I was just thinking I look nearer thirty these days than forty. Where was this handsome devil hiding?'

'Whoa, steady now, Robert. Don't go getting over-confident.' But he'd sounded pleased, all the same.

Rob picked up his book, and resumed reading where he'd left off, but he found himself reading the same paragraph over and over. His mind wasn't on the story. Tonight would be his second *Conversational French For Beginners* class at the local college. He'd chosen it because it was a year round, join anytime, class, and he didn't have to wait until September to enrol. Last week he had found it in the Adult Education folder. He'd decided to grasp the nettle and go along that evening, before he had a chance to decide it would be better to stay home and watch *Celebrity Job Swap* instead. French had been one of his best subjects at school. He'd studied it to A level, and had achieved an A grade, so he wasn't, strictly speaking, a beginner, but after twenty-plus years he'd feared he might be rusty, especially on the spoken side. He needn't have worried. At the first lesson, it had all flooded back to him. When the tutor played them an excerpt from a recorded conversation he understood almost every word.

The tutor, a native French speaker whose name was Mademoiselle Lefèbvre, hadn't picked on him when it was time to answer the questions she fired at the class when the tape ended, but she warned him at the end of the lesson that next week she wouldn't give him such an easy ride, and would expect him to participate fully. He didn't relish that at all. Mam'selle was fearsome: half the class seemed to be in terror of her. She was an angular woman only an inch or so shorter than Rob, with a penchant for russet blusher, electric blue eye shadow, and lipstick the colour of calves' liver (by Chanel, no doubt) which overflowed onto her teeth. Last week, he had seen her reduce Joanne, an attractive woman of around his age, almost to tears, after she had pronounced three words in a row incorrectly and stumbled over most of the others. The woman was a termagant. He wasn't sure he was up to being bullied by an ageing Frenchwoman.

'Don't be a wimp, Robert,' Paddytum had said after Rob told him. 'It will be a trial by fire, and if you survive it, you will come out stronger the other side.'

'I came to the right place for sympathy then,' Rob said. But he knew Paddytum was right.

But what worried Rob even more was his fast approaching blind date next week. He still hadn't said a word about it to Paddytum. He itched to ask his advice, but didn't dare risk his contempt.

I could always just not bother with it, he thought. Frankie doesn't have *my* phone number. I needn't have any contact with her ever again. The only way she could possibly find him was through the chat-room, so if he just avoided it, he'd be fine. Perhaps he should just delete it from his bookmarks, just in case he wandered there by accident.

He could imagine Paddytum calling him a *recreant*, a *poltroon* and a *caitiff*, if the truth ever came out. Until he'd met the bear, he hadn't realised there were so many names for coward. Even the imagined insults made him feel angry and defensive, and he closed his book and squinted against the sunlight, replying, in his head, 'You're never satisfied, Paddytum. You didn't want me to get involved with people on the Internet in the first place, so why are you telling me off for blowing her out?'

'It's a matter of honour, Robert, a matter of honour. If you are going to back out of this arrangement, you should have the decency to tell her.'

'Fine,' he said out loud, drawing a troubled glance from a woman walking a miniature poodle. He shook his head. He couldn't escape from Paddytum. Now he was in his head even when he wasn't there. He'd have to go through with contacting Frankie, even if it was just to say he'd changed his mind. How could he get away with phoning her without Paddytum's knowledge? The bear could hear round corners and through walls, it seemed, so even if he rang from downstairs, Paddytum would know as soon as Rob made the call. He groaned. Then he remembered there was a payphone in the entrance to the college; he could ring her from there this evening.

Mam'selle was in a better mood this week, hovering on the edge of being pleasant. Rob looked at her over made-up face and thought, even if she is nasty to me, I can take it from someone who looks as if she's auditioning to be a clown. This week, the eye make up was a virulent sparkly lime and the lipstick a dark plum one shade lighter than black. Even more of it had strayed to her teeth this time, making her look as if she'd lost a few of them in a fight, and the problem increased with each utterance. Her mouth appeared emptier of dentition each time she said, 'You must pronounce your *vowels correctement, Mesdames, Messieurs.*' Rob was beginning to think this was her catchphrase. She had said it at least five times last week, and tonight it looked like she was going for the record.

She had just said it again, to Joanne. She obviously had issues with the poor girl; what was her problem? She was laying into her again now, and Rob feared she'd crumble into a tearful heap if it went on much longer.

Fair enough, Joanne spoke very quietly, hardly opening her mouth at all, and her accent wasn't good. *'Eeskavooz donnay-mwar un petee tassadatay?'* was the last phrase Joanne had come out with, provoking a *non, non, NON! Ça c'est terrible!* from Mam'selle. Rob caught Joanne's eye once Mam'selle had finished ranting, and gave her an encouraging smile, but her response to him was a stony-faced stare. Rob's heart sank, and he was whizzed back to his 'I'm a fat, ugly failure and nobody wants to know me' mindset. He looked down at his workbook.

But the voice in his head said, 'Now, stop it, Robert! You are not a failure. You are not ugly. You are not even fat any more. The woman is shy. She isn't rebuffing you. She's just too nervous to smile back.'

Are you *actually* talking to me? he thought. Sometimes the voice was so real that he wondered. Or has he conditioned me so well that I know what he'd say if he were here?

'*Rob-air, Rob-air,*' the Gallic Gorgon was calling, '*Attention!*' He looked up. She had her hands on her hips, and her lips, the colour of gangrenous seaweed, were pursed.

'*Pardon,* Mademoiselle?' he said. She repeated her question. And he answered it, hesitantly but correctly. At the edge of his vision he thought he saw Joanne watching him.

80

When the class broke for coffee, he helped himself to a cup from the counter and, taking a deep breath, strode to the table in the corner of the cafeteria where Joanne sat, alone, her eyes fixed on her own cup.

'Mind if I join you?' he asked. He saw her eyes flick to the side, before returning to her drink. Her shoulders went up a centimetre. A shrug? He couldn't be sure. Well, he had two options: stay and try to make conversation, or go and sit on his own. He looked at her. She continued to stare into her cup as if it were a crystal ball, perhaps hoping it would tell her the answers to the questions Mam'selle would ask in the next session. She looked terrified, poor girl. Oh well, in for a penny ... He pulled out the chair and sat down. He told himself that wasn't a flinch he just saw.

'Have you been doing this class long?' Rob asked. Joanne mumbled something. He decided it would be kinder not to ask her to repeat it.

'She's a bit scary, isn't she, that Mademoiselle?'

Joanne looked up, eyes the colour of dark chocolate meeting his for a nanosecond before dropping to his collar and then back to her cup. She nodded. 'Don't think she likes me.'

'Oh, I'm sure that's not true. She's probably like that with everyone. I'm Rob, by the way.' He held his hand out.

'I know,' she said, her hands not moving from the table.

This is going well, he thought. 'Are you going on holiday?' Oh, fine. Now I sound like a hairdresser. She looked up at him, her face blank. 'I mean, is that why you're learning French?'

She shook her head.

Blimey, this is hard work, Rob thought. What would Paddytum do? 'I just wanted to brush up on my schoolboy French,' he said.

No reply. Just a blank stare. Flogging a dead horse here, he thought. Might as well go back in the classroom and talk to the overhead projector; it'd be more responsive. He looked at his watch. Damn. Still five minutes of their break left. If he got up now, it would be rude, so he sat and drank his coffee in silence, and she did the same.

After the class had finished, he went straight to the payphone, and fished out the receipt with Frankie's phone number on it.

Other students filed out into the night, chatting, laughing and joking as they passed him. One or two of his classmates nodded to him as they passed.

He dialled the number, feeling strangely upbeat. Now he'd made the decision to call, perhaps he wouldn't cancel the date after all, and go through with it just to prove he could. As the ring tone commenced, Joanne crept past him, her eyes to the ground. The phone at the other end rang twice, three times, longer, until a voice told him *'the number you are calling is not responding.'* You don't say, he thought. It invited him to leave a message after the tone. He'd never been good with answering machines, even when he knew what to say to them, when he had something prepared in advance. This time he didn't, so he hung up the phone. He went outside, and as he did, saw an ancient-looking Jaguar pull into the car park, with a bald man behind the wheel. Joanne hurried over to the car and got in. Her dad? he wondered, a sugar daddy? She looked a bit old to be still living with her parents. He laughed to himself – a fine one to talk!

Back home, he chatted with his mother for a while, and then they settled down to watch a comedy show, but his mind had turned to Frankie again. What on earth was he going to do about this phone call? Not getting through tonight made him tempted, again, to forget the whole thing. He kissed his mother goodnight.

He was getting ready for bed when Paddytum piped up.

'All right, so what's the matter with you?'

'Eh?' Rob looked at the bear. 'Nothing. Why do you ask that?'

'Oh, it could be something to do with the frown lines embedded in your forehead. I can always tell when something is bothering you, Robert. You ought to know that by now.'

Rob sighed. What was the worst that could happen? The bear might even be able to help. He sat on the bed next to Paddytum.

'Well, I did something. And I don't think you're going to approve.'

'What, tonight? At the college?'

Rob scratched his head. 'No, a couple of weeks ago.' He took a deep breath. 'You know the night after the interview, when you sort of … weren't here?'

'Oh, you've been keeping secrets from me, have you?' Paddytum sounded amused. 'Well, I don't suppose I can complain, after the "Sharp burial" business. Go on then, spit it out.'

'That night, I went on the Internet. I was feeling a bit lost, because I thought you'd gone for good. I suppose I was feeling … lonely. Wanted to talk to somebody.'

'So you went into that dreadful chat-room.'

'Yes. Well, I don't think it *is* dreadful—'

'Perhaps we should agree to differ on that matter. Go on.'

'I sort of … arranged to meet somebody.'

There was a silence. Rob braced himself for the explosion. None came.

'Paddytum?'

'A woman, I assume?'

'Of course a woman.'

'Hmmm. So, who is this female? Where and when are you meeting her?' The bear paused. 'It is just *one* woman, is it? I mean, you're not going in for a *ménage-à-trois*?'

Rob snorted with laughter. 'Paddytum! Do you really imagine I'd do that? I doubt I could cope with more than one female at a time.'

'So, how did this happen?'

Rob raked his fingers through his hair. 'It's a girl I used to talk to a lot on there. Frankie.' Rob thought it wise not to mention the 'Foxy' part. 'I hadn't been online for a while and we just got talking and she said we should meet and I suppose I felt that I was carrying on the good work you started—'

'And now you're coming close to the date you arranged, you're having second thoughts.'

Rob looked at the bear. He was very good at this intuitive stuff, he thought. 'Well, we haven't *actually* arranged to *actually* meet yet, but I did say I'd ring her in two weeks, and now that's up.' He frowned. 'You're not angry with me?'

'Well, on the one hand, I am annoyed that you went back to the chat-room when you knew how I felt about it. But on the other, I admire you for being brave enough to agree to a meeting with a member of the opposite sex. As long as you arrange to meet her in a public place, I don't see much harm could come from it. There is one *caveat*, however.'

'Which is?' Rob asked, relieved that he wasn't about to be scolded after all.

'The problem with meeting people in person when you haven't seen what they're really like, is that they may fail to live up to your expectations of them. You could be in for a disappointment, and so could she, and then you'd be back to square one, feeling rejected and hopeless. It might even put you off trying, for good. This Frankie will almost certainly have a picture in her head of what you look like, what you sound like, and what sort of person you are. The reality is likely to shatter that illusion.'

Rob steepled his fingers under his chin. 'I see what you mean.'

'And don't forget, Robert. You were not exactly truthful with her. About anything.'

'No, you're right. She's likely to take one look at me and scarper.' He put his hand up to his cheek. 'So, do you think I should forget it?'

'Absolutely not! You must face the consequences of your actions. You can't carry on with this casual attitude. Be a man. You must go through with it.'

'Won't that do more harm than good?'

'Robert, don't forget, it may equally turn out well. You should not expect the worst, any more than you should expect the best. Keep an open mind, and be prepared for anything.'

Where did all this wisdom come from? This was a stuffed toy, which had spent all its life sitting on a bed in the room of a man who didn't get out much. He couldn't have learned it all from the television.

'Okay. So should I try ringing Frankie again?'

'Yes, most certainly. You made a promise; you have to keep it.'

'But she might not answer. She didn't tonight.'

'And that's up to her. At least you will have tried.'

'But what if she does answer the phone and doesn't like the sound of my voice? I mean, that could happen, couldn't it? Or I don't like the sound of hers? Do I just say I've changed my mind about meeting her? Or what if she's one of those bored housewives, like you said, and her husband answers, and asks what I want, and—'

'Stop!'

Rob flinched.

'You must stop over-thinking everything, and predicting disaster at every turn. I know it's become a habit, but it's the main reason you got yourself into your rut in the first place. Just let what happens happen.'

Rob rubbed his temples, noticing how heavy his limbs were. He needed sleep. He changed into his pyjamas and slipped under the duvet. At least telling Paddytum about Frankie was no longer a dark cloud over his head. He wished he'd told him earlier. Whoever or whatever he was, he really was batting in Rob's corner.

SIXTEEN

'Can you phone that Miss Jenkins at the library, son?'

His mother's cheery call as he opened the front door, on his return from his morning walk, made his stomach clench. This was it. The job was off. She'd changed her mind. Someone better had come along and she'd given them the post instead.

'Don't look so worried, she sounded cheerful enough, love,' his mother said, passing him the handset and a slip of paper on which she'd jotted down the number. 'Go on. It's probably good news.' She squeezed his arm.

Someone picked up the phone within a couple of rings, and identified herself as Marjorie Hackett. She sounded like the stern woman with the glasses. He'd seen her around on his library visits, usually peering at him over her bifocals, and her stony expression always put the fear of God into him. He asked to speak to Rachel and gave his name. He waited, willing the pounding in his chest to abate.

'Rob?'

'Yes. You asked me to call?'

'We had your CRB check back today, so you'll be okay to start on Monday, as planned, and we won't need to hide you away in the back room.'

'That's great.' Rob let out his breath. Monday – two days' time. Hordes of butterflies converged on his stomach.

'We'll see you, bright and early on Monday morning, then.'

'I'll be there. Oh. I meant to ask you. What's the dress code? I couldn't see anything about it in the job offer letter.'

'Well, we girls wear smart casual. I would think, for you, a shirt and tie, and a pair of smart trousers, would be fine. No jeans, obviously.'

'Obviously,' he said, 'Great. Well, see you on Monday, then. Boss.'

Rachel laughed, and said goodbye. Rob's mother came out of the kitchen as he put the phone down.

'Everything okay, love?' He told her, and she came over and gave him a hug. 'That's wonderful.' She looked him in the face. 'You're really looking forward to this job, aren't you? I can tell it's different from the others.'

'Yes. I have a feeling this time I'm going to stick at it.' He thought maybe he ought to tell her his other news. 'Ma?'

'Yes, love.'

'Um, I might be going on a date next Friday.'

Her mouth dropped open. 'A date? You mean, with a girl?' She put her hand up to her mouth, and giggled. 'Sorry, Robbie. Of course that's what you meant.' She wrinkled her brow. 'Not that it would matter if—oh, what am I saying? It's just such a surprise that's all, after all these—'

Rob was grinning. 'Yes,' he said. 'It's a girl—well, a woman I suppose.'

'Where did you meet her? Oh! Is it her? That Rachel? From the library?' She was beaming.

'No. Oh, no!' Rob felt his cheeks begin to flame. 'No, of course it isn't her. That would be unprofessional, wouldn't it? Anyway, Ma, she's way out of my league.'

His mother patted his arm. 'Oh Robbie, you must never think that, son.' She looked up at him. 'You are intelligent and kind, and now you're on the right track again, there's no reason why you shouldn't go out with anyone you want. I mean, look at you. Now you've lost weight, you look so much like—' She stopped, and looked away for a few seconds. 'So, who is this young lady, and where did you meet her?'

Rob looked at the carpet. 'I—um—haven't exactly—met her yet.'

His mother looked confused. 'Oh. Is it some kind of blind date?'

'Well, I suppose you could call it that. I met her in an Internet chat-room.'

Maureen's face fell. 'Oh, Robert!' Robert. Now he knew he was in trouble. 'Are you sure that's a good idea? Oh dear, it could be anyone – a criminal or something. What's her name, anyway? What does she do? How old is she? Where is she from? Is she—'

'Hold on, Mother. One question at a time. Her name's Frankie.'

Maureen made a face. 'Are you quite sure it's not a man? It might be one of those—those transvestuals.'

Rob didn't correct her. 'Well, yes, I suppose it might, but we'll be meeting in a public place, and I don't know how old she is or what she does, but I'm sure there'll be ample opportunity to find all that out on the night.'

Maureen was chewing her lower lip. She looked at him for a few moments. 'I suppose so. It's just that you hear such dreadful things on the news.'

'Yes, Ma, but that's usually school kids. I am forty-one, you know. I'm a big boy now.'

After lunch, Rob offered to go to the supermarket for her, and Maureen busied herself with the laundry. As she sorted the clothes, she pulled out a pair of Rob's trousers, and held them up, and then a polo shirt. She found herself starting a separate pile, of things that looked as if they wouldn't fit him any more.

He looked better than he had in years. The more she looked at him these days, the more he reminded her of Eric. Sometimes she felt a stab of anguish at the sight of him.

At forty-one, Robert had now outlived his father by over a year. Rob's fortieth birthday had been especially hard, because of its associations. Eric was exactly a week off his own fortieth when it happened.

For the special day, Maureen had planned a night out for them in London, just the two of them, with dinner and a musical. Eric had loved his musicals, especially his Gilbert and Sullivan operettas. She'd managed to get good seats for *The Mikado*, at the Coliseum Theatre, in a new production by the English National Opera company. He'd have loved that, especially as that man from Monty Python with the same first name as him was playing the lead. When her Eric read her a glowing review from his paper, she'd had to bite her tongue to avoid giving away the surprise. Not that she'd have known a good production from a bad one. She'd never been into G & S herself, or any musical theatre, although of course she'd been along to see him in some of his shows. He was very talented, she had to admit, if you liked that sort of thing. He always played a major role, and she'd been proud of him, but it really wasn't her cup of tea. But even though she hadn't looked forward to the actual show, she'd been looking forward to leading him off on a mystery tour, ending up at a swanky restaurant near the theatre, followed by the thrill of seeing the look on his face when they stood outside the Coliseum and he realised why they were there.

But it had never happened.

Instead of sitting in a fancy London restaurant that evening, she'd stood in the draughty Hall behind St Stephen's Church, up the road, talking to funeral guests.

She sighed. She wished that man had stayed away.

After the funeral, when she had finished greeting the mourners, she stood at the buffet table and was filling a small plate with food 'to keep her strength up' as everyone had told her she should, when a short, wiry man in his fifties approached her. There were so many people here she didn't know, most of them from the Savoyards. She recognised a handful of the perennial principals and stalwart chorus members, but most of the others were strangers to her. She just assumed this fellow was another of them.

'Hello,' she said, taking the hand he offered. 'Thank you for coming.'

'I hope you didn't mind me being here. I saw in the paper it was today.'

'Oh,' Maureen said, 'Are you not one of the actor-factor, then?'

'Actor-factor? No. What's that?'

'You're not one of Eric's amateur operatic people?'

He laughed. 'Oh no, love. Tone deaf, I am. No. I work for the railway. Ted Venner's the name. I'm the one—' He leaned in closer and lowered his voice. 'who found your poor husband. I just wanted to offer my condolences. Thought it was the right thing to do, seeing as I was the last person to, like, see him alive.' He took her hand in both of his. 'I'm very sorry.'

Maureen's eyes filled. It seemed normal, since she'd first heard the news, for her eyes to be wet, and she'd stopped even feeling embarrassed at it. She drew her hand away and reached under her sleeve for the ever-present damp handkerchief.

'Thank you so much for staying with him. I'm so glad he wasn't alone.' She wiped her eyes. 'There isn't much comfort in circumstances like these, so any comfort is worth having. It would have been so much worse if he had been found later ...'

'It was the least I could do, love. I only wish I could have done more. But I only know a little basic first aid, and he was bleeding so badly—I'm sorry; I don't want to upset you. I mean, upset you any more than you already are.'

'No, please. I'd rather know. It's so much worse when you have to imagine. Do you think he was in a lot of pain?'

'To be honest, love, he was more or less out of it when I found him. Drifting in and out, if you know what I mean. He was just repeating the same thing: Why? Why? he was saying, over and over.'

'Oh, my poor Eric.' Maureen sniffed.

'And he said your name a couple of times, too.'

'Really?' She dabbed at her cheek as fresh tears came. 'Oh, Mr Venner, you don't know how much that helps. That is so good to hear.'

'Yes. Only, I wondered ...'

Maureen blew her nose, and looked at the guard.

'I noticed, like, in the order of service – at the funeral, like. It said his name was George, but he was called Eric. Is it the same thing with your name?'

'I'm sorry, what do you—'

'Only, it said, his widow, Maureen. And the vicar talked about Maureen, too. Only it was a different name he was saying.' He stopped abruptly, looking at her face. 'Or maybe I got it wrong. I just assumed he was calling for his wife. But perhaps she's your daughter, is she?'

'Who? Who is my daughter? I don't have a daughter. Eric and I only have a son.'

'Oh dear. I must have got that wrong then. Not heard it right,' He looked embarrassed. 'I'm very sorry. Well ...' He cast his eyes about, as if looking for a means to escape. 'I'll let you get on. Let you attend to your guests.'

Maureen grabbed his arm. 'No, please. Tell me. What name was he saying?' The man looked mortified.

'Debbie,' he murmured. 'In between the whys, he kept asking for Debbie.'

*

Afterwards, she'd tried to find out if the woman had been a member of the Savoyards. Eric had kept all the programmes from every production in which he had been involved over the years. It amounted to twenty years worth, give or take. He had been with the Savoyards about a year when he started seeing her. A few weeks after they met he'd tried to persuade her to come along, too, but she protested that she couldn't sing a note. He said that didn't matter; she could help out with something behind the scenes. In the end, she'd ended up lending a hand with the costumes every year, but she'd never been interested much in the performance side, even as a spectator.

Debbie. The wound inflicted by the name had reopened when she told Rob the story.

The night after the funeral, Maureen had pulled an old, battered leather suitcase out from under the bed. It was where Eric kept all his show souvenirs. It was stuffed to the brim with programmes, photographs, cards, and little gifts given to him by other cast members on the last night of each run. Silly things – tokens – an eye-patch for *Pirates*, a tiny plastic gavel for *Trial by Jury*, a cheap plaster Geisha girl for *Mikado*.

She scoured the cast lists: the principals and then the members of the Chorus, and finally the lists of backstage crew – make-up, costumes, lighting, sound. She checked the acknowledgments at the back of the programmes – sponsors, well-wishers, even the printers who supplied the programme itself. She searched through twenty years of annual productions and found only one Deborah. And this woman couldn't be a candidate; Miss Robinson, the elderly accompanist who played at their rehearsals, must have been in her late sixties at the time of Eric's death. After Maureen finished ploughing through the programmes, she turned to the cards, sorted into bundles secured with rubber bands, She opened and read every one, even though her eyes blurred and her head throbbed. She read 'Good Luck' and 'Break a leg' and 'Nice working with you' and 'Here's to the next' and still she didn't find a single one signed Debbie, or Deborah, or Debs.

91

Eric certainly hadn't worked with a Debbie at his all-male workplace, so how else could he have met her except through the Savoyards? A fan, perhaps? Did am-dram people have groupies?

She wondered now, all these years later: what would she have done, had she found her? She had no idea. She had simply needed to know who this woman was who'd been so important to Eric that her name was the last to pass his lips at the moment he'd died. Eric – her love, the man who had vowed, and not only at the altar, to be faithful to her until death – had betrayed her. Not knowing the identity of the subject of his betrayal had prevented her from moving on, and because she hadn't, she had not been able to help Robbie.

She supposed she'd never know.

SEVENTEEN

Rob woke far too early on Monday morning, and lay in bed waiting for the alarm to go off. He'd toyed with the idea of getting up and having an early shower, but two hours before he needed to be at work should be more than enough time to do all he needed to do. What he didn't need was to be sitting at the kitchen table twiddling his thumbs, or pacing up and down the living room, waiting for it to be time to leave. Besides, if he got up now he might disturb his mum.

He hoped every morning wasn't going to be like this: waking too soon with a stomach full of butterflies. Butterflies? More like a swarm of bats or pterodactyls. He tried to calm himself down by itemising the clothes he'd bought on his shopping trip at the weekend. Thanks to a loan from his mother, to be paid back over the next month or so, he now had seven new short-sleeved shirts, two pairs of smart trousers, a pair of classy-looking tan brogues, a light summer jacket and a handful of ties. As an afterthought, he'd bought a pair of cream chino pants, and a bottle of cologne, with his forthcoming date with Frankie in mind. The thought of this – he still hadn't phoned her – whipped the pterodactyls into a new frenzy of fluttering, and he imagined he could feel them gnawing at his insides with their sharp little teeth. Great. Perhaps he was getting an ulcer.

Did he need all this worry in his life? Hadn't he been happier the way he was before, just waking up naturally, at nine-thirty every day, flicking the TV on and climbing back under the duvet, inevitably to fall asleep again to the lullaby of Jeremy Kyle shouting at his chavvy guests, and then waking briefly to hear what features were on *This Morning*, eventually going downstairs to pick up his sandwiches, and then back to watching telly till dinner time? And then the next day and the next day, the same thing all over again, except for weekends – when he had a lie-in, because everyone deserves a lie-in at the weekends, don't they?

He looked at Paddytum sitting next to his pillow. Hadn't he been better off before this thing started talking to him? No, of course not. Life was certainly uncomplicated before this bear had found a voice and started using it, but it hadn't been happy, not by a long chalk. What would he have become, if this mentor had not come into his life? Years and years stretched ahead of him, if he was lucky—or unlucky—if he didn't die of a heart attack or a stroke caused by obesity and lack of exercise.

Today was the first day of his life as New-Rob. Rob-with-a-future. And he should be grateful. He was grateful. If only he didn't feel so frightened.

He was startled out of his reverie by the first *bib-bib-bib-beep* of the alarm clock he'd only set a few times since leaving school. Never had an alarm function been so underused. He silenced it and slid out of bed, then padded along the landing to the bathroom. A shower might wash away the fear. And a good breakfast might still the gnawing teeth of the creatures in his solar plexus.

The bear didn't say a word to him as he dressed. As if he felt it would be too distracting this morning. You might at least wish me luck, though, Paddytum, he thought as he draped his new jacket over his arm and opened the bedroom door. You got me into this.

'Robert?'

Rob looked over his shoulder.

'Have a good day at work.'

'Thanks, mate.' Rob smiled and closed the door.

Despite walking as slowly as possible, he arrived at the library at twenty to nine, although Rachel had told him he needn't be there until nine o'clock, Breakfast had quelled his jitters for half an hour or so, but as he came closer to his destination, the activity in his stomach started up again. He paced up and down in front of the side entrance, chanting a mantra of calming phrases. You can do this, Rob. It's an easy job. You'll be fine. There's nothing to fear. It helped a little. He took deep breaths. The pacing was getting boring, and he wished for a second or two that he smoked.

A white Ford Fiesta sailed into the car park, and he froze, feeling he had no right to be here this early and that his presence would be challenged. He wanted to duck around the back of the library and hide until the other staff had gone in. A woman stepped out of the passenger seat of the car, and murmured

94

something to the driver, before waving him off. She bounded over to Rob, with a big smile. He'd noticed her on his library visits, but hadn't spoken to her. She looked a mumsy type, although Rob thought she must only be about his age, and was dressed in a crisp floral print dress topped with a mauve cardigan. Her face was round and dimpled, surrounded by a froth of brown curly hair.

'Hi,' she said, smiling and extending her hand. 'You're our new boy, aren't you? Rod, is it? Rachel said you'd be starting today. I'm Carole.'

Rob took her hand, which was soft but gripped his firmly. His anxiety level dropped a couple of notches at the warmth emanating from her. 'Rob. Nice to meet you.'

'You're early. That's good. Must be eager. That's what we like to see.'

'It's more a case of being too jittery to hang around at home.' Rob took a deep breath. 'I'm a bit nervous, to be honest.'

Carole patted his arm. 'Oh, there's absolutely no need, Rob. We're a very friendly little bunch. We don't bite.' She looked toward the car park, where another car had pulled into a space at the far end, and Rob followed her gaze. 'Except for that one, sometimes.' She cocked her head at the figure emerging from the car. 'But don't let Marge fool you. She's worked at this branch for twenty years and feels the need to fulfil the role of resident dragon-lady. Every library has one.'

Rob chuckled. 'Bark worse than her bite?'

'Well, she doesn't even bark, really,' Carole said. 'She just looks as though she might. She fixes the customers with that steely gaze over those glasses of hers, and they don't dare let their books go overdue. Morning Marjorie,' she called.

The new arrival was dressed in a pale blue blouse, with a bow at the neck, and a fawn tweed skirt, both procured, surely, from 'Librarians R Us', as was the gold neck-chain from which her glasses dangled. She hefted her large black bag – bearing more than a passing resemblance, Rob thought, to the one carried by Mary Poppins – into her arms, and nodded at him. 'Good morning.'

He nodded back. 'Hello. I'm Rob. Nice to meet you.'

She nodded again, and looked at her watch. Rob glanced at Carole, who winked at him. He had a feeling he'd found an ally.

'We have to wait for Rachel with the keys.' Carole crooked an elbow and studied her own watch, which had a green plastic strap and a picture of Shrek on the dial. 'She shouldn't be long now. I always get here early, because hubby drops me off on his way to work.'

'Well, at least it's a nice morning,' Rob said, looking at Marjorie, who countered his smile with a cold expression. She was going to be hard work.

'Yes,' Carole said. 'It's not much fun waiting out here when it's raining. No teddy-bear today then, Rob?' She grinned at him.

'Oh,' Marjorie said. 'You're the young man who entertained our toddlers a few weeks ago. Are you an actor?'

Rob felt his face colour. 'Did you see that, then?'

'We both did. It was brilliant,' Carole said. 'We stopped serving customers to watch you. But it didn't matter because they were all watching, too. Are you going to be doing that every week?'

Rob looked at his feet. He hoped he wasn't expected to. 'I don't think so. I'm really not very good at it. Actually, I surprised myself that day. I think it must have been adrenaline from the interview. '

'Well, you certainly impressed our Rachel. She didn't stop talking about it for days after.'

Rob felt a warm glow at the idea that he'd impressed his gorgeous new boss. 'Well, perhaps, from time to time. But I don't think I could do it regularly. It's a bit nerve-wracking. I'm not really a performer – more a stay-in-the-shadows sort of bloke.'

'Well, I can't say I approve of that kind of carry-on, myself. Not in the library,' Marjorie piped up. 'Libraries aren't supposed to be entertaining.' Carole grinned at Rob. 'Ah, here she is.'

Rob hadn't seen the blue Toyota Yaris pull in, and his heart started to pound as the slight figure walked towards them. Today, she wore her hair in a long plait, draped over one shoulder. He thought she looked like a mediaeval maiden, just waiting for her knight to sweep her onto his mount. Oh, to be that knight, he thought, and shook his head to rid it of the image.

'Rob,' she said. 'Good to see you.' She pulled out a bunch of keys from a tan, squashy leather shoulder bag. She unlocked the door, and stood aside for Carole and Marjorie to go in. 'Sorry I'm late on your first day. Usual Monday morning mad traffic. I see you've met the others.'

Rob followed her in, and stood awkwardly at the counter, his hands clasped in front of him.

'Right,' Rachel said. 'Ladies, I'll keep Rob with me this morning, and give him the Grand Tour. You can manage without me for a couple of hours, can't you?'

Both women nodded, and went off in the direction of the staff room. They were back within a minute, without their bags.

'Leave the returned books, girls,' Rachel said. 'Rob and I will work through them a bit later.' She turned to Rob. 'We'll let you get some hands-on experience today; then you can get started on your own tomorrow. Okay?'

Rob played with his hands. 'Sounds good to me,' he said, though the idea of being left to his own devices set off the flutters again.

'Great, now, first things first,' she said, rubbing her hands together. 'I'll show you where everything is. Oh, did you bring some lunch?'

Rob held up his carrier bag.

'Good. There's a café round the corner but we usually bring our own stuff in. We can drop that into the staff room first so you can pop it in the fridge.

Rob spent the next three hours trailing around the library in Rachel's wake, in a tour of all the back rooms. She explained things he knew he would forget within minutes of being told, instructed him on the Dewey Decimal Classification system, and the rules for the Public Access Internet. Rob felt as if his head had been in a blender by the time lunchtime came.

Rachel touched his arm. 'Don't worry, ' she said. 'I know there's a lot to remember. But don't be afraid to ask. Any of us. Carole's lovely, and Marge is, too, once you get to know her. I'm sure we'd far rather you asked us non-stop questions all day, than flounder on your own, not knowing what to do.'

At lunchtime, Rob took his plastic food container and mineral water out of the staff room fridge, and balanced his salad selection on his knee, while he chewed on a ham and tomato bap, reading about the mysteries of the Dewey system from the photocopied handout Rachel had given him, and wondering if he was supposed to memorise it all.

The door opened, and Rob jumped, toppling the Tupperware box off his knee. Thankfully, it just had one leaf of lollo rosso and a single cherry tomato remaining in it. Carole bent and picked up the tomato, which had been halted in its progress by her shoe, and held it up.

'You won't curry favour here by throwing salad at your colleagues, you know,' she said, laughing, and tossed the tomato into the bin by the sink. 'So, how's it going?'

'Fine,' he said. 'I think. There's so much to remember.'

'Oh, it seems like that, when you're new. You've never worked in a library before, have you?'

He shook his head, not sure if he should mention that he'd never worked anywhere to speak of. Had Rachel told Carole and Marge about his shameful employment history? He hoped not. But if she had, the two women were not, it appeared, holding it against him.

'Have you worked here long, Carole?'

'Yes and no. I mean, I've always been in library jobs, since I left school.' She unwrapped the cling film from a pile of crisp-breads, and placed a pot of cream cheese on the table, with a butter knife beside it. She pulled a can of diet cola out of her bag, and popped the tab. 'I was manager at another branch, and then I had a bit of a career break when I had my first child. I've only been here a year. It suits me now just to be one of the workers, rather than the boss.' She swigged her cola, and then started to pile cream cheese onto one of the crisp-breads. 'Oh!' She stopped. 'Nearly forgot. I was supposed to give you a message.'

Rob raised an eyebrow. 'Oh?'

'Yes, a lady phoned for you on Saturday afternoon.'

'A lady? For me?'

'Said she was a friend of yours.'

A friend of mine, but I don't have any— 'Did she tell you her name?' A sneaking suspicion crept into his mind.

'Well, that's the thing. She didn't. Said it wouldn't mean anything to you. She left a number though. There's a post-it note at the desk.' She took a bite of her crispbread, chewed for a while, and swallowed. 'Tell you what – it's lucky Rachel was standing next to me when she rang or I would have just put the phone down on her. I just kept saying there's no-one here called Rob, and then Rach reminded me.' She laughed.

Rob had a good idea of the identity of the mystery caller. What a cheek!

'Oh, well, I'm sorry about that. I'll ask her not to call again.'

She picked up her can and took another sip. 'Oh, don't you worry about that. Rachel's not too worried about personal calls as long as nobody takes the Mickey. So, have you just been on some sort of course, then?'

'I'm sorry?'

'Well, when I told this lady you hadn't started yet, she said you must still be away on your course.'

Well, that confirmed who it was. Rob ran a finger round the inside of his collar. It was getting hot in here. 'No. No, I think she must have got a bit mixed up.' He looked at his watch. 'Better get back to it,' he said, and left the staff room.

Outside in the corridor, he ran a palm over his face, and blew out his breath. That settled it. He had to ring Frankie as soon as possible. He didn't want her ringing here again.

He spent the rest of the day re-shelving returned fiction, first with Rachel watching him, and then on his own once she was satisfied he knew what he was doing.

'I'll leave you to it, then, Rob. As long as you can read the names on the spines and know your alphabet, it's not difficult. We'll do some non-fiction tomorrow, and you can see how the Dewey system works.'

'Thanks,' he said with a smile. 'I can hardly wait.' He immediately regretted it, wondering if he should save being cheeky till he'd been there longer. But Rachel laughed, and he let his breath out.

By the time he finished the task it was almost time to go home. The library didn't close until seven o'clock this evening, but Rob was only scheduled to work till five, and he couldn't say he was sorry. He was amazed at how exhausted he felt, but today had been good. Parts of it had even been fun, and his new colleagues were friendly and helpful. Well, Marge was helpful; perhaps friendly came later. He hadn't been asked anything by customers today, but after discreetly observing the others, he was sure he'd be able to deal with most queries without too much angst.

'I'll be off now, then,' he told Rachel.

She was leafing through a ring binder, and looked up. 'Oh. That's fine. Thanks for all your help today, Rob. See you tomorrow.'

He smiled. He didn't think he deserved any thanks. He hadn't made much of a contribution, unless following her round like an oversized duckling paddling after its mother counted. He waved to Carole, and pushed the door open.

'Oh, Rob.' He stopped and turned back. Rachel had followed him to the door.' Are you bringing Frederick in tomorrow?'

Oh no. Tuesday. Story Time. He'd forgotten. 'Um ... do you mind if we leave it until I'm a bit more ... established? I mean, I'd like to concentrate on learning the job a bit more, first.' He felt bad, saying no. He didn't want to risk annoying anyone so soon.

'No, that's perfectly fine. No problem at all. I just thought I'd ask in case *you* wanted to. You seemed to enjoy it so much the first time, and the children certainly did. In fact, a few of them, and their mums, keep asking when the "teddy man" is coming back.'

Rob raised a hand to his burning cheek. 'Oh. Maybe next week, then? Hopefully I'll feel a bit more at home by then.' He didn't relish the idea, but if he didn't do it, he'd feel as if he'd cheated to get the job. He'd have to talk to Paddytum.

EIGHTEEN

As soon as Rob arrived home, he took the phone handset up to his room. He told Paddytum about Frankie's call to the library. The number on the post-it note had indeed matched the one on the now tatty receipt lying on the bed in front of him. He dialled Frankie's number. What if she slammed the phone down? What if she didn't answer? He was over-thinking again, but he couldn't help it, whatever Paddytum said. It would be a hard habit to break.

The phone was answered on the second ring.

'Who is it?' Just three short words, but so aggressive Rob's heart began to hammer.

'Um, is that Frankie?'

'Who?' A pause. Then she spoke again. This time the voice was softer. 'Oh, hello! You must be Rob. I didn't think you'd bother ringing. Thought you were all talk. Like the others.'

Others. Rob didn't like the sound of that. Just as Paddytum had warned, the voice didn't fit at all with the picture in his head. He hadn't realised until now that he'd even had any expectations about what she'd sound like, but this raucous, rough-toned voice wasn't it.

'I've tried a couple of times,' he said. 'I didn't leave a message, though. I'm not good with voicemail. Have you met people from chat before, then?'

A harsh cackle assaulted Rob's right ear. 'Nah. I've given my number out, but most of them didn't call, so I didn't think you would, either. Seeing as you never came back online after we last chatted. Thought you'd chickened out.'

'No. No, I've just been busy lately.' He was rapidly going off the idea of meeting the person on the other end of this line. She sounded most unpleasant – like some of those women he'd seen on the Jeremy Kyle Show in the bad old days when it was the highlight of his morning. He pictured her with a fag dangling from her lips, squinting through the smoke. As if to confirm this, he heard a racking, fruity-sounding cough in the background.

'So, we still on for this meal, then?'

Rob panicked. He really wanted to say no and slam the phone down, but he thought she'd be able to find out his number now. He should have done that thing that withheld it from the person you were calling. What if she just rang straight back and gave him a mouthful of abuse? She might even start stalking him; she might start ringing him night and day and—'

'Robert!' It was Paddytum's voice. 'Calm down.'

Rob looked at his hand. It gripped the receiver so hard that his knuckles were white. He covered the mouthpiece with his other hand, and whispered, 'Paddytum, I can't. She sounds awful.'

'Then tell her you've changed your mind.'

From the other end of the line he heard Frankie asking if he was still there, and said, 'Sorry, just a minute. Someone's just come in.' He heard a long sucking in of breath. Either she was taking a mammoth drag of her ciggie, or she was about to have a go at him. But she just said, 'OK'. He covered the mouthpiece again.

'I can't. If I back out now she'll think it's because I didn't like the sound of her.' And she'll be right.

'Oh Robert, there you go again. Stop making assumptions about what other people are thinking. Either tell her you don't want to meet her, or make the arrangements. Either way, the world is not going to come to an end.

Rob took a deep breath. As much as he dreaded the thought of going anywhere at all with this rough sounding creature, he didn't want anyone, even someone he'd probably never speak to again, to think badly of him. There was only one option.

'Sorry about that. Yes, let's meet up.'

They arranged to meet at the *Cock and Bull* pub on Friday at 7.30.

'How will I recognise you, lover?'

Lover? 'Well, I'm tall. Thick dark wavy hair. I'll probably be wearing black trousers and a green shirt. How about you?'

'Medium height, long blond hair. I 'spect I'll wear my pink strappy sandals.' Fine, I always identify people by looking at their footwear, he thought. 'And a pink off-the-shoulder top.'

'Okay, I'll see you then.' He said goodbye and hung up.

'Done,' he said. 'I wish I didn't have such a bad feeling about this.'

'That's to be expected. It's not what I had in mind for you ...'
Rob wondered exactly what that was. 'But it may turn out to be just what you need to get a social life started. Just don't start getting ideas in your head about marching this woman down the aisle.'

Rob roared with laughter, feeling oddly light-hearted now the dreaded phone call was out of the way. In a way, it was a relief that she sounded slightly dodgy. This way he wouldn't feel as inadequate.

The next two days at the library went as well as the first one had, and by Thursday he felt as if he'd been working there for years. He was starting to do things on his own initiative, instead of having to ask the girls what he should do next, which he hated doing, especially if the askee was Marge. He still found her intimidating. Talking to Rachel was terrifying for an entirely different reason. When he did have a query, he tended to ask Carole, the only person there who didn't fill him with trepidation.

On Thursday, at lunch with Carole, Rob said, 'I don't think Marjorie approves of me.'

'Oh, don't you worry about Marge. It's not you, it's men in general, I think. Her experiences haven't left her with a good impression of the male population.'

'Oh?'

'No, her husband left her, in her twenties, apparently, when she was pregnant. But, from what she's said, she was glad to see the back of him.' she leaned forward, and whispered, 'Violent.'

'Oh dear. Poor lady.' He was surprised to hear Marge had been married. He'd assumed she was a confirmed spinster.

'Yes, and then the child, her son, gave her a dreadful time, growing up: expelled from school after school, then got into a really bad crowd – taking cars, burglary, drugs, you name it!' She pulled open a packet of cheese and onion crisps.

No wonder she looks so miserable, Rob thought. 'So, what happened to him? The son?'

'Oh, well he's completely different these days. Apparently his best mate died when they were about sixteen – an overdose, I think – and it was a wake up call for him. He cleaned up his act, got himself an apprenticeship, and trained as an electrician. To look at him now, you'd never think he'd been a little sod when he was a teenager. He did some work for Rachel not long back. Rewired her flat. Did an excellent job, too, she says.' Carole offered Rob a crisp, and he declined. 'Must make a good living from it, too. Judging by the amount of jewellery he wears. Bit of a poser, he is, to be honest. The sort that always has a blonde bimbo on his arm.'

'Marge must be proud of him,' Rob said, 'You know, after that transformation.'

'Hmm. I don't know. She always seems a bit wary of him. I think he inherited his dad's bad temper, and I have a feeling he thumped her once or twice in the bad old days. She always has a look of a cowed puppy who's been hit with a stick and thinks it might happen again, when he's about. If you know what I mean?'

Poor Marge, Rob thought. He'd have to make an extra effort to be nice to her.

On Friday, he asked Paddytum if he would be willing to do Story Time next week.

'I really only did that to help you out of a hole, Robert,' he said. 'If you hadn't been so clumsy as to kick the bag over, it wouldn't have been necessary, would it? She'd already offered you the job.'

'I suppose so.' Rob wondered what excuse he could come up with for not bringing Paddytum in. His stuffing needed replacing? His head had fallen off?

'Besides,' the bear continued, 'I'm not keen after what happened last time. It could happen again, and I might be "absent" for even longer next time. What if I don't come back at all?'

Rob pondered. 'Yes, it could be risky, I suppose.'

'And how do I know I could trust you to behave yourself if that were to happen, Robert? I feel there are still areas in which we could improve. You've come a long way, but I wouldn't want you slipping back into old habits.'

'Oh, I think there's very little chance of that happening. I love the job. I feel great. I feel … positive.'

'Good, I'm very pleased to hear it. So, how would you feel if I suggested that the next thing you should do is learn to drive?'

Rob's stomach did a backwards somersault. 'What? After last time?'

No response.

He waited. 'Paddytum? Are you there?'

'Uh-huh.'

What was up with him? Surely Paddytum couldn't have forgotten the driving lessons. 'I was rubbish, don't you remember? It was the biggest waste of money ever. I had one two-hour lesson a week and then spent the six days and twenty-two hours in between worrying about the next one. For eight weeks, I was on the verge of a nervous breakdown, until Ma agreed with me that I probably wasn't destined to be a driver. How could you possibly have forgotten that?'

'Well … it was a long time ago.' He sounded uncomfortable. 'It just slipped my mind. Remind me, how old were you, again?'

He doesn't know! Rob realised. He hasn't forgotten. Paddytum doesn't know I had driving lessons at all; I'd be willing to stake my life on it. If it had been a single lesson, Rob could have understood it but, because Maureen had paid up front for a course—non-refundable—he'd had to force his legs down the stairs, and out the front door, to meet the terrifying sight of frizzy-haired Mr Dowling leaning on the beige roof of the dual-control Austin Metro, ready to put him through all the torments of Hell, for two hours every Tuesday for eight weeks. Even now, the sight of a small beige hatchback was enough to turn his knees to jelly.

Rob was disconcerted. What on earth did this mean? Well, perhaps talking bears had a poor long-term memory. But that couldn't be right, either. His furry friend had no trouble recalling events from his early childhood.

'I was twenty.' He decided not to labour the point. 'Anyway, I couldn't go through that again, and I don't really need to drive, do I? I enjoy the walk to and from work, and, if the weather's bad, the library's on the bus route. I can manage the shopping a couple of times a week on public transport. Like Ma's always done.' He hated reminding himself of all the years he'd let his mother do that without offering to help. 'Besides, I couldn't afford to run a car.'

'Yes, but wouldn't it be good to be able to take your mother out to different places? Or your girlfriend …'

Rob shuddered, reminded of his fast-approaching date with Frankie. 'My dad didn't drive,' he said, defensively.

'Yes, I know.' The bear sounded sad. Rob thought about the implications. If his father had been a driver, would he still be alive? No, that was just silly. It didn't follow. Travelling by public transport hadn't killed his father.

'Well, I'm not having driving lessons, and that's that.' Rob smiled. It was the first time since his mentor had arrived that he'd said no to him.

Paddytum spoke, and wiped the smile off his face. 'So, about tomorrow night, and your *femme inconnue*.'

'My what? Oh, Frankie. I was trying not to think about that too much. Just gets me into a state. What about her?'

'Well, you are going to come clean about the lies you told her? With your new healthy lifestyle, you *might* just pass for someone in his early thirties …' Rob beamed at the compliment. 'But if the relationship comes to anything she'll soon find out you're not twenty-eight. You ought to at least tell her you were not, and never have been, a stockbroker. If you don't tell her sooner rather than later, you can put money on her finding out.'

'Well, you're right. But perhaps I should play it by ear? If it turns out to be one date, I'll have told her for nothing.'

Rob was not looking forward to it at all. It intruded on his thoughts several times a day. The only thing that stopped him calling it off was the idea that he'd need more courage to cancel than to go through with it.

NINETEEN

Rob walked up the hill to the *Cock and Bull*. He looked at his watch as he approached the pub. Ten minutes early. Should he go inside and wait there? He felt self-conscious and conspicuous standing at the door under the hanging basket of droopy looking dried up blooms; he was certain everyone who passed him knew he was a novice at this. If she didn't turn up – an outcome he both prayed for and dreaded – they'd all know he'd been stood up. He eyed the picnic tables on the pavement outside, If he got himself a drink he could sit down, and he'd be far more comfortable – and look more relaxed – when she turned up. *If* she turned up. He took a breath and walked into the pub. At the bar, he ordered a pint of Stella, the only beer he recognised from his short-lived pub-going days the year he'd done his A levels. He handed over a five-pound note and tried not to raise his eyebrows at the tiny amount of change the barman gave him. Blimey, he knew about inflation, but it was beer, not molten gold.

He sat with his pint, watching couples and singles walk past, and began to relax, enjoying the mild June evening. But his mellow mood lasted only until he remembered he wasn't just out for a quiet drink, and every time a female approached, his stomach tightened and he quickly looked down at his glass. At one point, he saw a flash of pink in his peripheral vision, but when he looked up, the person wearing it turned out to be about fifteen, and was with a group of other girls.

Maybe she *was* going to stand him up. He looked at his watch. It was still a few minutes early: far too soon to give up, down the rest of his pint, and go home. A group of young guys, college students by the look of them, piled out of the pub and went to sit at another picnic table. One of them started laughing, and the others joined in. He looked over, instantly convinced they were laughing at him, but not a single one was looking in his direction. Pull yourself together, Rob. Stop being paranoid.

He looked away. A woman was approaching. His heart sank. No! This couldn't be her. Could it?

The woman wobbling up the hill looked nearly as old as his mother, but was dressed about twenty years too young for her age. Rob glanced behind him. Could he escape around the side of the pub? No. She'd seen him now, and was making straight for him. She was wearing, as promised, an off-the-shoulder pink top, which clashed violently with skin one shade lighter than his mother's antique yew dressing table. Her top was so off-the-shoulder it was almost obscene. No bra, which was a big mistake, because she was in dire need of the support; her bosom ended at around waist level. Below the top was a tiny black leather skirt, and beneath the skirt were spindly legs encased in fishnet stockings, which didn't quite disguise the knobbliness of her knees. Her pink strappy sandals had heels so high he wondered if they came with free anti-vertigo medication. By the time she was level with him, he'd had a second or two to appraise her face, which was daubed with thick beige foundation ending abruptly at her jaw line, where the orange fake-tan took over. A triangular splodge of cerise blusher sat in the centre of each cheek. Her baby-pink lip gloss (to match the top and the shoes, no doubt) appeared to have been applied with a grease-gun, and the bright turquoise eye shadow surrounding each eye made her look rather like a dayglo panda. Fresh torrents of laughter assailed him from the lads' table, and this time he was pretty sure he knew the cause of their hilarity.

He stood. 'Frankie?' he said, praying it wasn't, and that this was some errant hooker who'd taken a wrong turn.

'My, you're a big one, aren't you?' the woman rasped, looking up at him, and twiddling a strand of brassy straw-like hair around one bony finger. She stretched up to give him a kiss on the cheek, and he narrowly avoided recoiling as his nostrils were assaulted by a smell rather like creosote mixed with acetone. He resisted the urge to wipe off the splodge of baby-pink grease he was sure was now dripping from his cheek. 'We going inside?' she said. 'It's a bit nippy out here.'

Well, it wouldn't be if you were a bit more covered up, he thought. But it might be a good idea to get out of the daylight, and away from the scrutiny of the kids at the other table. She was rather too well lit out here, and the murky interior lighting of the pub might tone it down a bit. 'Yes. I've booked a table.'

She draped a hand through the crook of his elbow, and Rob took in the baby-pink talons at the end of each finger. Baby-pink, that is, apart from the yellow-brown stains on two of them. 'By the way,' she said as they approached the eating section of the pub, 'my name isn't really Frankie. I just use that in chat rooms and forums and things like that.'

His reply was interrupted by the approach of a girl wearing a black skirt and white blouse, carrying two menus. 'Table for two?' She looked his companion up and down, and Rob cringed and wished he could ask for separate tables. There was only one table occupied, so he didn't bother to tell her he had a reservation.

'Yes please.' They followed her to a table near the entrance to the restaurant, and she waited for them to be seated, and handed them a menu each.

'Oh good,' the woman said, when the waitress had left. 'Nice and handy here, for when I go out for my fags.'

Great, Rob thought. 'So, what's your real name. Are you Frances? Or Francine?'

She emitted a bronchitic cackle. 'Neither. I call myself Frankie on the Internet because my surname is Franks. I'm Clementine.'

Rob laughed. And converted the laugh into a coughing fit when he realised she wasn't kidding. He looked at her Garfield-orange skin. 'Oh. It—it, er, suits you.' It really did. 'Well, I'm really called Robert. Rob.'

Another waitress came over to take their drink orders. He asked for another lager, and she ordered Pernod and cranberry. 'I always go for sophisticated drinks on special occasions,' she explained.

'So, what do you do?' he asked. He might as well go through the motions. At least he only need stay with this woman for an hour or two, and then he never need see her again. He couldn't wait to tell Paddytum how right he'd been. Why, oh why hadn't he listened to him?

'Oh, nothing special. I work up at the Toyota dealership. You know, just on reception, booking people in for services and MOTs and that. And you changed jobs, didn't you? How are you getting on at the library?'

'Oh, it's fine. I like it.'

'I would have thought it would be a bit boring after the last job you had. Is it just to tide you over until you find something else?'

'No, I'm quite enjoying it really,' he told her, truthfully. 'It's … a bit less … challenging, and less high-powered, but I think I might stick with it.'

She was rummaging in her tiny pink handbag. 'Well, I've never been much for reading books, myself. I don't have the attention span. Why read a story in a book when it'll probably be out as a movie in a year or two?' She drew out a packet of Benson and Hedges and a baby-pink (of course) lighter, and stood up. Mind if I nip out for a ciggie? It'll be ages till I can have another one.'

He said, 'Please do. Do you want me to order for you, if the waitress comes?'

She looked down at the open menu. 'Yeah, I'll have garlic mushrooms and then the salmon. Ta.' She tottered toward the pub entrance.

Rob sighed. Maybe he could use her smoking as an excuse not to see her again after this – plead some kind of allergy.

The waitress came over with their drinks, and he gave Clementine's order, and asked for soup followed by steak with a green salad for himself.

She came back two minutes later, trailing a miasma of cigarette smoke, and Rob wrinkled his nose as she sat.

'Hope you didn't speak to any strange women while I was gone,' she said.

He smiled sweetly. No, but I'm speaking to one now, he thought. Thankfully, the waitress reappeared with their starters. While he ate his soup, Clementine picked at her garlic mushrooms and chattered about her job, which seemed mainly to entail being annoyed by the demanding clients she had to deal with day after day. Rob interjected with the odd 'Oh dear,' and 'That's not very nice,' and 'No, really?' as she prattled on. She talked so much that she'd only managed to eat two of the five mushrooms on her plate before was up again, fag packet and lighter in hand.

'I never have much of an appetite,' she said. 'It's how I manage to stay so slender,' she said. Slender? More like scrawny, Rob thought. 'See you in a minute,' she said, and off she went, taking her Pernod and cranberry with her this time. She must survive on a diet of cigarettes, he thought.

When she returned from her smoke-break, she whinged and griped about her clientèle until the main course arrived. If she were to be believed, people who owned Toyotas were the most unreasonable on the planet, only slightly higher up the evolutionary chain than pond scum. She didn't fare any better with the salmon-en-croûte than she had with her starter, pushing the pastry aside and picking out a few flakes of salmon with her fork. One of these didn't quite make it all the way into her mouth and clung to her lip-gloss like a jewel. Most of her main course – including all of the selection of fresh garden vegetables – remained on her plate as she went outside for a third time.

Rob wiped his forehead. Only dessert and coffee to go now, he thought. Then it'll be over and I can forget the whole sorry business.

He was beginning to wonder if she'd left when she took much longer to reappear this time. The waitress handed them the dessert menu, but she declined, saying she had to watch her figure, but she wouldn't mind another drink, and Rob chose the fresh fruit salad. As soon as his bowl arrived, she picked up her glass and went for yet another cigarette. Rob had lost count by now. This time, she looked decidedly wonky when she teetered to the door.

Blimey, she's spent more time outside than in, he thought. He'd have been better off coming for a meal on his own. They hadn't exactly connected. She hadn't asked him anything about himself, and the only knowledge he'd gained about her was that she wore too much make-up, smoked like a steam engine, and had a dim view of Toyota drivers.

Finally, she sat in front of him again. 'I'm knackered,' she said.

I'm not surprised, he thought, with all that going backwards and forwards. At least she's getting lots of exercise. 'Had a busy day?' he asked.

'Yeah, sort of. Can't wait to get to bed.' And, to Rob's absolute horror, she winked at him and ran a baby-pink nail down the back of his hand. His blood froze in his veins.

No. Surely not. She can't be thinking what I think she's thinking. What have I done to encourage this? No problem. He'd

111

just say goodnight to her outside the pub, and go off to catch his bus.

'I won't bother with coffee,' he said, with a glance at his watch. 'I need to get off to the bus station. Don't want to miss my bus.'

'Where do you have to get to?' she slurred. Had that last Pernod been a double? Or had she been sneaking extra shots from the bar? Unbelievably, she was fingering the fag packet again. She'd only just come back from the last one.

'I live just past the Leisure Park.' He looked at his watch again. 'The last bus goes at half past.'

'No problem,' she said 'I'll give you a lift home. You're on my way.'

He groaned inwardly, wishing he'd told her he lived out in the country, and that it was at least a twenty-mile drive. He looked at her. 'Um … are you okay to drive?'

'Course I am,' she drawled. 'I've only had two drinks.'

'Well, I'll be fine getting the bus. Really.' Please, please God. Please don't let her insist.

'I insist,' she said. 'My car's only round the back. If you have to walk to the bus station and then wait for a bus, you won't be home for at least forty minutes. I know the buses round here. They go all round the houses. You'll be home in fifteen minutes if you go with me.' She grinned at him, dislodging the salmon flake on her lower lip. It fell into her cleavage. 'It's the least I can do after you've bought me this lovely dinner.'

Of which she'd only eaten about three mouthfuls. He didn't think he'd be able to get out of this one. Unless he ran off after he'd paid the bill. He took a handful of notes out of his wallet, enough to cover the meal plus a small tip, and followed her out to the pub car park, not at all surprised when she lit up another fag on the way.

She was still puffing on it when he got into the car, a Vauxhall – so much for brand loyalty. From the smell of the interior, she chain-smoked while driving, too. He tried not to breathe too deeply. He suspected the car was a carcinogen all on its own. She swerved out of the car park, and Rob winced as she missed hitting the wall by a centimetre. He sat in the passenger seat, with his hands in his lap, trying not to dig his nails into his palms as she weaved in and out of traffic, driving with one hand on the wheel and the other holding the cigarette to her mouth.

The car filled with fug, and his eyes shifted to the window-winder; he wondered if she'd mind him cracking the window open, but just then she ground her cigarette end into an ashtray which was already overflowing, and put her right hand back on the steering wheel.

Rob's relief didn't last. The next time she changed gear, her left hand drifted, not back to the wheel, but onto his lap.

He froze. Her hand settled on his thigh, the baby-pink talons digging in painfully as she gave it a squeeze. Help, he thought, suppressing a scream. The hand relaxed, and then began to creep. Higher. Toward his groin. Help me. He looked out of the window, trying to control his breathing. They were still at least ten minutes from home. Help me, please. He didn't think he could stand another second of this.

'Well, I've had a lovely time, Rob' she was saying. 'We must do this again sometime.'

No, we mustn't. 'Yes, it was very pleasant.'

She took her eyes off the road, to look at him. 'Really?' Her hand tightened on his thigh again, and he shrank into his seat.

'Mmm,' he said. No, not really. He wished she'd light up again. At least then she'd have to take her hand off him and put it back on the wheel.

Long minutes later, he directed her into his road, and she drew up outside his house. It had crossed his mind to get her to drop him off a few roads further on, but what if she waited for him to go inside? No, he had to face his fears. If she asked to see him again, he'd just have to say he'd call her. Or tell her the truth. He cringed at the thought.

'Well, thank you for a lovely evening, Clementine,' he said, putting out his hand to shake hers, but she was already getting out of the car. Why? he thought. Does she expect a goodnight kiss? He looked over at his house as he climbed out. All the lights were out except the one in the porch. His mother would be in bed by now. Thank goodness she wouldn't be looking out of the window.

He tried to dodge past Clementine on the way to his gate, but she reached up and hooked her arms around his neck, and lunged forward, planting her lips, now gloss-free – no doubt the cigarettes had sucked up all the grease – on his. He held his breath but, even so, he almost gagged at the aroma – an aniseedy, fruity top note, with a middle note of fish and garlic, and a base note of old ashtray. He pulled away just as a tobacco-laced tongue slithered between his lips, working hard to resist the urge to spit on the pavement. 'Well, it's been nice meeting you,' he said with as much politeness as he could muster. 'Thanks very much for the lift. I'll give a ring very soo—'

But she grabbed his hand and tugged him, striding up the path to his front door. 'Where are you go—'

She stopped on the doorstep still hanging on tight to his hand. It was beginning to get painful. 'Aren't you going to ask me in for a … nightcap?' She winked again, and his stomach turned. Oh no oh no oh no—

'Um, I haven't – we haven't – got any drink in the house, I'm afraid. My mother's a recovering alcoholic.' God forgive me, he thought.

'A coffee, then,' she said, snaking one arm up his chest. He backed away until he was pressed up against the door.

'I'd better not ask you in. You see—my mother—we might wake her up. And I've got to be up early for work, you see, and—'

She draped her hands on his shoulders again. 'Oh, we won't wake your mummy, Rob. Because I'll be *ever* so quiet.' She dropped her voice to a whisper. 'And *ever* so *good* …' Rob shuddered as she trickled a fingernail down his cheek. She must have mistaken his revulsion for desire, as she murmured, 'I have to be up early too. And I'll make sure you have a really good night's sleep. After.' She dropped the other hand to his chest, and slowly moved it toward his waistband.

He wriggled out of the way, and fumbled for his keys. 'No. I can't. Really. Honest, Clementine, I mean it.'

She pouted. 'Oh, you're such a spoilsport, Rob. Well, to be honest, I'm absolutely bursting for a wee. I don't think I'll last out till I get home. Can't I just come in for a minute?'

He supposed he couldn't really refuse. 'Oh … all right.' He opened the door and she stepped into the hall.

'And just a teensy-weensy cup of coffee? Please?'

It would be ungracious to refuse, after the lift. 'I suppose so. The loo's straight ahead, at the top of the stairs.' He closed the front door.

Her heels clattered on the parquet flooring as she staggered across the hall, and Rob put a finger up to his lips. She giggled and mirrored the action, then slipped off both her sandals. He watched her tiptoe up the stair carpet, and then went into the kitchen. He switched on the kettle, and heaped three teaspoonfuls of instant coffee into a mug, hesitating before adding a fourth. He filled a glass with water for himself, and sat at the kitchen table, watching the door. Five minutes later, with her freshly made coffee next to him, she still hadn't come back, and he hadn't heard the toilet flush. He hoped she wasn't ferreting around in the bathroom cabinet. She looked the sort who would. No, he mustn't be unkind. Perhaps she was just someone who took a long time in the bathroom. He sipped his water as the second hand on the kitchen wall clock swept one, and then two revolutions.

Where was she? Maybe she'd passed out on the bathroom floor. He went back into the hall and stood at the bottom of the stairs, looking up, and held his breath as he listened. He went up two steps to get a better look. The bathroom door stood open. Rob frowned as he ascended the stairs. He peeped inside the bathroom. Empty. He looked around. Nobody on the landing. His mother's door was closed, as was his own. He looked at his bedroom door again. Saw the little porcelain name plate his parents had bought in a gift shop on holiday when he was six. *Robert's Room*.

No, he thought, not taking his eyes off the door. No, surely she wouldn't. He looked inside the bathroom again, on the off chance he'd missed her the first time. Could she have slipped back downstairs without him noticing? No, he'd have spotted her from the kitchen, surely. Well, unless she'd climbed out of the bathroom window, and slid down the drainpipe, somehow managing deftly to re-latch the window as she left …

He glanced over at his mother's door, and shook his head, then slowly turned the handle of his own door and pushed it open.

'Hello, lover. I thought you'd never get here.'

115

And a second, more familiar voice. 'Robert, get this creature away from me NOW!'

'Pad—'

Clementine was in his bed. A single fishnet stocking lay coiled like a snake on the floor in front of him. Its companion dangled from one of the handles of his wardrobe. The rest of her clothing was in a heap by the side of the bed. She was on her side and facing him, propped up on one elbow. Her other arm was around Paddytum, his snout buried in her cleavage. Rob, in a burst of empathy, felt his breath cut off.

'Teddy and I thought we'd have to start without you,' she drawled, and moved the bear further down her body.

It was too much for Rob. With a flash of rage and revulsion, he snatched his poor stuffed toy out of her arms, and cuddled Paddytum to his chest, his hand over the bear's ear.

'Hey, calm down,' Clementine said, looking shocked. 'I was only playing. Come here, darling. We can have a little fun.'

Rob's jaw jangled for the first time since the day of the interview, and he had no time to prepare himself before his mouth opened and Paddytum's voice thundered across the room.

'Begone, foul hag!'

Clementine's mouth dropped open. She looked bewildered for a second, as if trying to decide whether Rob was being serious or not. 'What?' She stretched out a hand to touch Rob's arm.

'Leave my chamber, thou despicable harlot!'

Her hand paused mid-reach, her eyes wide.

'Desist, vile doxy! I fear I would be stricken with the pox from just one touch of your diseased flesh.'

In his head, Rob said, steady on, that's a bit strong, mate. And anyway, keep it down. Ma will be in here in a minute, wondering what all the racket's about. But underneath, he was cheering the bear on.

'Gather thy whore's rags, and hie from here. And never, ever return.'

Rob stifled a giggle, and looked across the landing at his mother's bedroom door, which remained closed.

Clementine was grabbing up her clothes from the floor. 'Don't you worry, mate, I'd wouldn't come back here now if you paid me.' She pulled her top over her head. It was back to front and inside out, but she didn't seem to notice. 'You're bleeding mad, you are. They warn people not to get involved with men off the net, and you're the reason why. You want locking up! Enticing me back here, and—'

'Shut thy disreputable maw, and leave!'

'Oh, I'm leaving,' she said, pulling her skirt on. She ran out of the room, leaving the fishnets where they were, and flew down the stairs. She gathered up her strappy sandals and, with one frightened look over her shoulder, up at Rob who stood on the landing clutching his bear, she opened the front door.

'Bloody nut-job!' she said as she left, leaving the front door standing open.

Rob padded downstairs, and watched Clementine's car speed off down the road, and then went back inside, closing the door as quietly as he could. On the landing, he listened outside his mother's room. If that hadn't woken her, it was a miracle. He waited a few seconds more, leaning toward the door, and straining to listen for movement behind it. Nothing. Maybe she had slept through it all. He let out his breath, and went back to his room.

TWENTY

Rob woke the following morning with a feeling that something momentous had happened the previous night. It wasn't until he turned his head and caught a whiff of Paddytum next to him that he remembered it all.

'Going to have to fumigate you, mate,' he said. 'Or we can just hope the smell wears off.'

The brief spell the bear had had in bed with the date-from-hell left him reeking of smoke and whatever that awful perfume was. He picked him up and breathed in. Ugh! He'd changed the sheets as soon as he'd returned to the room, putting the old ones, which still stank of Clementine, in the laundry basket outside the bathroom. How fortunate that it was Saturday and his mother would be at work, so he could wash them himself, or she'd wonder why he'd decided to change his bed in the middle of the night.

He and Paddytum had talked long into the night.

'You were a bit hard on her, mate,' he said.

'Huh!' Paddytum said. 'She deserved it. What a nerve, just coming in here like that and—I shudder at the memory.'

'We're lucky she didn't call the men in white coats,' Rob said, laughing. 'At least there's no danger of her wanting to see me again.'

'Perhaps now you'll agree with me that learning to drive would be a good idea, Robert. After all, you wouldn't have been in that position if she hadn't given you a lift home.'

'Yeah, but how was I to know what she'd do when she got here? Anyway, I didn't even invite her in. She sort of ... tricked me.'

'You're just too nice for your own good, Robert. You'll have to learn to be more assertive.'

The bear was right. He'd come a long way, but he was still too fearful, too concerned with other people's opinions of him, to stand up to them. Perhaps that would come in time.

He took his sheets and pillowcases out of the washing machine and pegged them out on the line, then went to sit in the sunshine with a mug of tea. How odd it felt to be sitting around at home after a week of getting up early and going out to work. He supposed, if it hadn't been for Paddytum, he'd still be asleep at this time on a Saturday.

His mother arrived home at lunchtime and came out onto the patio. She looked at the sheet and duvet cover on the line but didn't say anything.

'Sit down, Ma, I'll get you a cuppa. Would you like a sandwich?'

She took a seat. 'Ooh, thanks, Robbie. Just a glass of water, for the minute. It's too hot for tea.' She wiped her brow. 'How did last night go, son?'

He lowered his eyes, not even wanting to remember it, never mind talk about it.

'Okay. I suppose. She wasn't really my type, though.'

Maureen raised an eyebrow. 'I thought I heard talking last night. Did you bring her home?'

Rob stared at the table. He felt about fourteen, caught out behind the bike sheds by the teacher, having a fumble with one of the girls.

'She just popped in for a coffee. Didn't stay long, though. We kind of ... had a difference of opinion.' He wished his mug was big enough to hide his cheeks. They must surely be as red as they felt, which was two shades redder than a pillar-box.

'Perhaps not the best way to meet girls, then?' she said, putting her glass down on the white plastic patio table. 'The Internet?'

'Apparently not. You were right about that.' And so was Paddytum, he thought. I should introduce you. You'd get on like a house on fire.

Rob began his second week in full-time employment with the feeling he'd passed a milestone. He'd never lasted as long as this before – not even half as long, actually.

Another milestone, later in the week, was his acceptance by one of the library regulars.

He'd started to notice them last week, as he relaxed more and stopped being so worried about getting things wrong. One was a heavy-set woman in her forties, who always sat at the same table, on the left hand side of the reference section. She came in mid-morning, and sat tapping away on a shiny red laptop, occasionally turning her head to thumb through one of half-a-dozen dog-eared notebooks, or reaching out for the litre bottle of Evian water she unpacked from the same flowered holdall from which she took the laptop. He thought of her as 'Rosie', because of the pink cabbage-rose pattern on her bag. Once in a while she'd get up from her table and stroll to the window, where she would stand and stare into the distance for perhaps five minutes, before returning to her machine. Sometimes Rosie stayed a couple of hours, sometimes as late as two o'clock. Rob had a theory. He suspected that the duration of her stay was dependent on the endurance of her bladder. She always started to put things away after a few minutes of fidgeting on her chair. There was no public lavatory in the library: the nearest was five minutes walk away, so it was probably easier to go home than to pack up all her things, go to the loo, and then come back and set everything up again. He wondered if Rosie was doing a correspondence course or writing a novel. His money was on the latter.

Another regular was the one he thought of as Dame Maggie. She came in two or three afternoons a week, a tall woman around his mother's age. She carried herself with a regal bearing, and he imagined she'd been to one of those Swiss finishing schools in her youth, to learn deportment and proper etiquette. She dressed impeccably and her subtle make-up was flawless. When she exchanged pleasantries with Carole or Rachel, which she often did on her arrival or departure, Rob admired her crisp, clear, almost clipped diction, like the sort you heard in a thirties film. On her visits, she seated herself at the Public Access computers, and would either surf the net or appear to be typing emails, totally focused on her task. She never stayed long – Rob had never seen her log in again after her one-hour session had expired.

The third of the regulars, and Rob's favourite, was Archie. According to Marjorie, he'd been coming in every day, including Saturdays, for at least ten years. Nobody knew how old he was, but they suspected he was well into his eighties. He spent so long at the library during opening hours that he might have been a fifth – unpaid – staff member. Archie's first 'duty' on arrival was to read the *Daily Mail* from cover to cover, afterwards proclaiming 'what a load of cobblers' it was. He didn't bother reading any of the other papers, so Rob assumed he must have an even lower opinion of them. For the remainder of the day, he just generally hung around. Mainly, he lounged on one of the sofas in the middle of the library, reading fiction.

His taste was eclectic. In the morning he might read a chapter or three from Danielle Steel, and by two in the afternoon the volume in his hands would have changed to Anthony Trollope. He could be spotted in the company of Stephen King at lunchtime, and be putting the latest Sophie Kinsella back on the shelf at closing time. Rob wondered if he ever read an entire book. He certainly never took any home. Rob was beginning to wonder if Archie actually *read* any of the books he pulled from the stacks. More often than not, if you watched Archie, he was looking around, observing the people at the counter checking their books in or out, or staring – from a distance – at the screens of the Public Access computers.

'Where does he go at lunchtime?' Rob asked Carole, for Archie, on the dot of twelve midday, picked up his cloth shopping bag and marched out through the front door, returning at exactly one-thirty, stopping only to pick up another volume on the way back to his comfy seat.

'Home,' she said. 'He lives in one of those little houses in that terrace right opposite. 'Marge said he started coming in one winter, and she thought it must be because it was cheaper to sit here all day than to heat his own place.

On the Wednesday of Rob's second week, Archie approached him.

'You're the new manager, are you? How are you getting on, then, m'boy?' he asked. 'Whipping these young birds into shape, are you?'

Rob looked over at Marjorie. Young bird? He supposed Rachel and even Carole might seem like youngsters to Archie, but Marge? He laughed.

'I think it's more a case of them whipping me into shape,' he said. 'I'm very low down in the hierarchy,'

Archie reached up and patted him on the back. 'Good man. That's the way to play it. Always let the women believe they have the upper hand, my boy. You'll go far.'

Rob stared after him as went to the Crime section and picked out a Ruth Rendell.

Rob didn't think he could take much more of Mademoiselle Lefèbvre picking on Joanne. He'd endured it for three weeks in a row now, and the whole thing made him uncomfortable. What got him was that the other students didn't turn a hair at her obvious bullying. He'd looked around the classroom while it was going on, and their expressions varied from boredom to enjoyment.

'Madame,' Mam'selle was saying, jabbing a finger at Joanne's face, 'How do I 'ear what you say when you are speaking more quiet than *une souris*?'

Joanne studied her lap. 'Sorry,' she muttered. 'I find it difficult to speak loudly when I'm not sure I'm saying it right.'

'Madame, you *nevair* say it right. *Jamais!*' The French tutor shook her head, and sighed, moving on to another student. Blimey, she's really got it in for her, Rob thought. What is it? Personality clash? Why does Joanne put up with it? He felt a pang of sympathy for her. Empathy, even, because he realised he would almost certainly be the same. Perhaps that was why he felt so drawn to her. Perhaps, because he understood her shyness so well, it made him want to break through it, as if, somehow, helping her would boost his own confidence. He'd tried to catch her eye again, earlier in the lesson, but she looked away so quickly he wasn't even sure she'd noticed.

Maybe it was worth trying to chat to her again at coffee time. After all, nobody else seemed to be bothered with her. Actually, when he looked at his fellow students, he saw a pretty unfriendly bunch. During coffee last week, he'd noticed that the whole lot of them preferred to stand around the edges of the cafeteria or sit by themselves. He couldn't help wondering why any of them was doing a Conversational French class when none of them seemed to have mastered Conversational English yet. If Paddytum expected Rob to make any friends through this class, he was going to be disappointed.

Joanne hurried out of the classroom the minute Mam'selle told them to go for coffee, and Rob tucked in behind her in the queue at the coffee counter.

'Hello again,' he said.

She flicked him a glance over her shoulder, and flinched visibly. She grunted something that could have been a greeting, but he wasn't sure. He decided to be persistent.

'Are you enjoying the class?' Stupid question, he thought. She'd probably prefer slow disembowelment with a spoon.

She shrugged, still not facing him.

He knew when he was beaten. He took his coffee over to a table occupied by two matronly women, who shifted their chairs round to accommodate his and launched into cheery chatter. They were doing a 'Wine Appreciation' course and, by the rosy glow manifest on their cheeks, they'd already 'appreciated' the best part of a bottle between them. It was a pity he wasn't keen on wine, or he might consider switching classes in September.

After the break, Mam'selle played another of her tapes, and Rob listened intently, answering the first question to her satisfaction. She asked another question, and pointed to Joanne. Rob cringed as she mumbled a reply in mangled French.

'*Non, non, non!*' Mademoiselle Lefèbvre screeched. '*Imbécile!*'

'Oh, for goodness sake, give her a break!'

The whole class turned to stare at him. Bloody hell, had he said that? The voice had sounded deeper, more like— He looked down, half-expecting Paddytum to be sitting on his lap.

'*Pardon? Rob-air?* Did you say some*sing?*'

He stood up, amazed, and oddly empowered, by the anger coursing through his veins. 'Yes, I did. You, Mademoiselle, are nothing less than a bully!'

The colour drained from Mam'selle's face, leaving a russet-rouged blotch on each cheek, and emphasising the plum-coloured lips, surrounding a mouth which now hung open.

'Just what is your problem with this poor girl? She's paying you good money to come here every week and all she gets in return is insulted and humiliated.'

'I only try to 'elp *'air wiz 'air* French.'

'Well, perhaps you need someone to *'elp* you first, *wiz* your English, before you criticise *'air!* You make Pepé Le Pew sound

123

like Sir Patrick Stewart.' He heard a gasp from the other students, and a few sniggers, but he was on a roll now, and it felt so good.

'Well, I have *nevair*—'

'And I have *nevair* met such a nasty, cruel, tyrannical woman as you in my life. *Vous êtes une vraie salope!* You can take your French Conversation and ram it up your *derrière!*'

He turned on his heel and marched out of the classroom. He didn't once look behind him as he went toward the college entrance. He didn't dare.

Just as he reached the final stretch of corridor he heard running footsteps behind him.

'Wait! Hello? Excuse me?'

He swivelled round. Joanne stood there.

'I just wanted to say thank you,' she panted. 'Nobody's ever done anything like that for me before. I mean, stood up for me like that.'

He smiled. Now he'd stopped, he realised he was shaking all over. He held his arms out in front of him, and looked at his trembling hands. 'To be honest, I've never done anything like that before. I surprised myself.' He looked at her. Her bag hung from one shoulder. 'Have you, um, walked out too?'

'Yes, I didn't see how I could really stay after that.'

'No, I suppose not. Will you be going back next week?'

She shook her head. 'I don't want to. But then, I haven't wanted to for two terms. She's been like that with me since we started. Will you be back?'

'No way,' Rob said, grinning. 'Not after that. Anyway, it's not worth the money, is it? You'd probably learn more from watching French films and turning off the subtitles.' He looked at her face. It was the first time he'd seen her smiling. She looked nice. Very nice. 'Hey, do you fancy going for a quick drink?'

'With you?' The guarded look was back, her lovely smile swept away by it.

'No, with Mam'selle when she finishes. Of course with me,' he said, laughing. 'There's a pub next door. *The Slave of Duty*, I think it's called.' He'd spotted it from his bus stop.

She looked at her watch. 'I suppose we could.' The smile returned. 'Yes, why not!'

TWENTY-ONE

A few weeks later, Maureen watched her son going off to meet his new girlfriend, Joanne. She still marvelled at the change in him over the past few months. It wasn't just his new shape. No, it was his whole ... bearing, his attitude to life that had changed. It was nothing short of a miracle. What had happened? She'd seen the self-help books in his bookcase, but none of those looked as if they'd even been opened, never mind read. Perhaps all those nights she'd heard him talking to himself, it wasn't actually him but a self-help tape – one of those audio books.

Whatever was behind it, she was happy to see the results. Delighted to see her boy so settled in a job, and with the beginnings of a social life.

He hadn't brought the girlfriend home. He talked about her sometimes, without much enthusiasm or excitement. They were just friends, he told Maureen, so she wouldn't need to go out and buy a hat anytime soon. He said he'd invited Joanne round, but she'd refused so far.

'She's a bit shy, Ma.'

He'd had that other one round, though, the first one he'd gone out with. Something had gone on in his bedroom, she was sure of it. She been woken by the row, and she'd been tempted to open the door and see what was going on. Whatever the problem had been, the shouting had been quite scary. It didn't sound like Rob at all, and she even wondered for a moment if it was a man he'd brought back but, after it stopped, she looked out of the window and saw a tarty looking woman running out to her car, barefoot and carrying a pair of pink sandals.

And then, the following day she'd seen his sheets on the line. He helped her a lot around the house now, but he'd never washed his bed linen, either before that incident or since. Well, she hoped he'd been careful. You could catch all sorts, these days.

Rob sat in the *Slave* with Joanne, staring at the long case clock in the corner. She was a nice enough girl, but good grief, she was bloody hard work.

Following their escape from Mam'selle, he was glad when she suggested returning here next week. 'After all, we both have Thursday evenings free now, don't we?' It was an ego-boost for Rob that an attractive woman wanted to, chose to, spend time with him. But after that first week she had reverted to her former taciturnity, and Rob found it very trying and frustrating.

He tried to make conversation. Goodness knew, he tried hard. But it seemed Joanne outstripped him on the shyness front and his efforts were in vain.

He scraped around in his mind for something to tell her about his week at work since the last time he'd seen her, but that never took very long, and she never seemed interested anyway. On their second meeting, he'd considered telling her about The Clementine Experience, but worried in case she'd think him indiscreet, and might be concerned that he'd talk about her to other people as well. Besides, he couldn't really tell her that story without telling her all of it. Including the part about Paddytum. If he did that, she'd run screaming out of the pub and he'd never see her again.

He'd tried to entertain her with a story or two about the library customers, like Archie, or the woman who needed to change her Open Access Internet PIN on just about every visit because she'd forgotten it. But the whole time he talked, Joanne kept quiet, not contributing with encouraging remarks, or nodding or smiling. She looked bored. And, because she was bored, she was, Rob had to admit, boring.

She didn't talk about herself, either. She'd told him she had a boring job working in a data-processing office. She said she kept herself to herself, so there were no stories from her about work colleagues.

Yet, at the end of every date, she kissed him on the cheek, and said 'See you next week', and he always agreed. What did she get out of it? he wondered. What was *he* getting out of it, for that matter? Not witty repartee or stimulating conversation, that was for sure.

'Fancy going to see a film next week?' he asked.

'I don't really like the cinema,' she said. 'I just end up getting annoyed.'

'Annoyed? Why?'

'Well, there's always someone sitting right behind you, rattling their popcorn, or crunching sweets, or slurping their drink through their straw,' she said, pulling a face. 'Or talking non-stop. Or laughing.'

Rob grinned. 'They're allowed to laugh, though, surely? If it's a comedy.'

'Well, it gets on my nerves, and I end up sitting there all tensed up.'

That was that idea out of the window. He'd tried before to get her to go somewhere else, too. At the end of their third meeting, he'd asked her if she fancied going bowling next week.

'I don't like the idea of the shoes.'

'The shoes? You mean the bowling shoes?'

'Yes. Other people have worn them. Hundreds of other people. They might have verrucas, or athletes' foot, or goodness knows what else.'

'Oh. Well, you'd be wearing socks, wouldn't you?'

'And besides, I have wide feet. I'd be in agony by the end of it.'

'How about going for a meal, then,' he'd asked, with an internal shudder at the memory of Clementine.

'No, I'm self-conscious about eating in front of other people,' was her reply.

He was beginning to think it was time to call it a day and end the relationship, if that was how you could describe these weekly sessions of non-communication.

At a quarter past ten, as usual, she stood up, gave him the usual peck on the cheek and said. 'See you next week,' and he said, 'Yes, take care.' As always, she insisted he stay and finish his drink. That was strange, he thought. Every week after the first time, they bought three rounds – he bought the first two – he had his two pints of Stella, and she her two halves of Magners, but she always timed it so that she finished her drink at five minutes past ten. He could have set his watch by it. In fact, he noticed tonight that she sneaked a look at the clock frequently as it approached ten o'clock, and then drank up the rest of her cider quickly. Then, as usual, she went to the bar and bought him another Stella. This meant he always had the best part of a pint left to drink when she said goodbye. 'Don't worry,' she said, the first time, when he stood and offered to walk her to her bus stop, which she'd told him was on the other side of the college from his, 'Stay put. I'll be fine on my own.' Then he'd sit and finish his pint, feeling depressed at the thought of having to do this all over again next week. Perhaps he should start bringing a book. She probably wouldn't even notice.

That night, he confided in Paddytum. Up to now, the bear hadn't asked how things were going, other than asking if he'd had a nice time when he arrived home.

'It's like pulling teeth, trying to have a decent conversation with her. I thought I was shy, but she makes me look extraverted. And she's so negative!'

'If it's not working, you have to end it, Robert.'

'Yes, but she's the one who keeps asking to see me again. I don't want to hurt her feelings.'

'Then it would be kinder to finish it now, before she starts to become too dependent on you. You could perhaps suggest seeing her every now and again, just as friends. But this ordeal, week after week, is soul-destroying. You never know, she might feel the same way, and not want to hurt your feelings either.'

'But, what do I say? I'm no good at this stuff, mate. What if she starts crying? I couldn't cope with that.'

'If she's as negative as you say she is, she's probably half-expecting it.' The bear paused. 'Has she said anything about past relationships? Previous boyfriends?'

'She doesn't tell me about anything. She seems to expect me to do all the talking. Which would be fine if I had a lot to say. But I still find that sort of stuff hard, Paddytum. And it's even harder when you feel like the other person isn't really listening.' He sighed. 'You know, I think it's maybe that I don't want to give up on it yet, because she's ... you know ... my first girlfriend. And I'm afraid if I stop seeing her—'

'You're worried that you'll never have another relationship.'

'Yes, I suppose that's it.'

128

'I know it must feel like that, but, from what you've said, it's almost certainly the way she feels too. Does she seem bored, when you're together?'

'Yes. But it seems like she's bored all the time. Her job's boring, her home's boring, the programme she watched on the telly last night was boring ...'

'Oh dear. That's not good. I tell you, Robert, if you stay with her, her negativity will rub off on you, and you'll end up as depressed as she is.'

'That's half-true already, mate.' Rob said ruefully.

'Perhaps you need to talk to her about it. You won't know how she's feeling unless you ask her. And it's better that way than if you just let the friendship ... fizzle out, with neither of you feeling as if it enriched their lives.'

He looked at the bear. 'Where does all this wisdom of yours come from, Paddytum?'

'Oh, here and there,' he replied.

But, Rob thought, where exactly is 'there'? He'd hardly been out of this bedroom, except for the few occasions in his childhood when he'd taken his bear on an outing or to a party. And a handful of trips to the library on alternate Tuesdays.

On Paddytum's first return after the interview, the children had cheered when Rob went over to the circle of chairs, carrying his furry friend.

'It's Freddie!' a little girl had shouted.

'No, *little maid*,' Paddytum had proclaimed grandly, '*Never Freddie. My name is Frederick, and don't ever forget it.*'

Again, he had told a story which unfolded in Rob's head as Paddytum used his 'vocal equipment' just as he had before. Again, the bear had gone 'absent' straight after finishing it, and had not spoken until the following morning. It worried Rob that the storytelling had such an exhausting aftermath. So, the next time, at Paddytum's suggestion, he had asked Rachel to pick out a book or two.

'I can just read them out, in Frederick's voice. Because otherwise I might get stuck, if I can't think of a story to tell them.'

She thought it an excellent plan, and it had worked well. Paddytum had still taken control of Rob's voice, and he had been just as entertaining, performing the written words in the picture books using a different voice for each character. After the session, he still disappeared, but he recovered much sooner, and was back by the time Rob left the library in the evening.

'How does it feel, Paddytum,' he asked, when they reached home that day. 'I mean, when that happens. Do you get any warning?'

'It starts with an overwhelming tiredness. And then, the next thing I know is that I've woken up. It's not unpleasant, just a little … disconcerting. Reading the stories definitely dilutes the effect.'

The word was spreading among the mums and dads about the special Tuesday Story Time sessions with Frederick. Rachel told Rob that some of the kids who only used to come on Thursdays had started to come along on Tuesdays as well as – or even instead of – their Thursday session. One day, when there had been standing room only, she said, 'We'll have to start doing it on a first-come, first- served basis if this carries on. Or even ask the mums to sign up for it in advance, to save them a wasted journey.'

'Is it a problem?' Rob had asked. 'Perhaps I should stop doing it if it's making things difficult for you.' If he was honest, he wouldn't mind stopping. Although nothing had gone wrong, yet, he always felt that the next time would be the occasion when the bear would come out with something really outrageous, or go absent halfway through a session. It was like sitting on a time bomb.

'Oh no, you mustn't stop, Rob. They love it. And anything that brings children into the library has to be a good thing. I'm thinking of running a Fun Day, actually, in a few weeks time, to raise the library profile and get more people in. It would be really good if you could do Story Time at that – if you don't mind. It'll be on a Saturday, but you could have time off in lieu during the week.'

'That's fine,' Rob said. 'If you want me to.'

She looked at him. 'I know I've said it before, but you're really talented. Have you ever done any amateur dramatics? You're a natural.'

'I couldn't. I'd be far too nervous to get up on a stage in front of lots of people.'

She laughed. 'Do you really think adults would be scarier than toddlers? If anything, you've had a baptism of fire here. Treading the boards at some village hall or small theatre would be a doddle in comparison. Anyway, you wouldn't have to go for a big part to start with. You could dip your toes in with a walk-on, to build up your confidence a bit, and then gradually work up to a bigger role.'

He found it hard to meet her eyes. He couldn't explain that it wasn't actually him, doing the performing. He was an impostor.

'I'll think about it,' he said, with absolutely no intention of doing so. Just as he said to the occasional mother or father who came over and suggested he start working as a freelance children's entertainer. It would be wrong, anyway. It was one thing to make use of Paddytum's strange talent as part of his job, but it was something he didn't get paid extra for. He'd feel uncomfortable taking money for it. And it would be even more fraught with tension if there were the potential to ruin a child's birthday when something went awry. He didn't fancy facing the ire of a dissatisfied mother or father. He'd watched enough episodes of 'The People's Court' and 'Judge Judy' to know you could get sued for lesser things.

'Well, there are lots of amateur groups around, if you look in the folder. Oh, that reminds me.' She went behind the counter and took out a roll of thick paper. 'Could you pop this up on the notice board for me, Rob?'

He took it. 'Sure.' He went to the entrance and rearranged the flyers and posters on the board to make room for it. Archie came over to watch. When Rob stood back, he leaned forward to inspect the poster.

'The Mick-adoo. What's that, then, Boss?' He still thought Rob was the manager.

'*The Mikado*, Archie. It's a musical. Well, an opera, really, I suppose. It's Japanese.'

'Japanese, eh? Here in Fleesham?' Archie shook his head slowly. ' I don't know that there'd be much call for that kind of nonsense. Nobody'll understand a word of it, will they?' He scratched his chin. 'Unless they have subtitles.'

'No subtitles, mate. It's at the theatre. The Cornmarket.'

'I've never trusted the Japs, Boss. They don't cook their fish, y'know. And some of it's poisonous. Kill you with a single mouthful. Make jolly good cameras, though. And cars.'

'It's in English, Archie.'

Archie's eyes widened. 'Well, that's clever. Good of them to go to the trouble of learning our language. Must have taken them ages.'

'No, Archie, the people performing it are local. Fleesham people.'

'Oh, I think you've got that wrong, Boss. No Japanese around here. Lived here all my life, I have. Never seen a single Jap. Now, the Chinese is a different matter altogether. We've a few of them, on account of them being needed to run the takeaways. Indians, too. You sure you're not getting them confused?'

'The people in this are all English, Archie.'

'Well, why the blazes did you say it's Japanese then? You want to make your mind up, lad.' He walked off, shaking his head and muttering about false advertising.

Rob gave up.

TWENTY-TWO

One Monday afternoon in August, Rob was re-shelving books near the computers, when he noticed Dame Maggie peering at her screen and scratching her head. He was confident enough now to approach customers and ask if they needed help, and he enjoyed the sense of satisfaction when he was able to provide it.

'You all right there?' he asked.

Dame Maggie glanced over at him, and scratched her head as she looked at the screen. 'This silly computer keeps telling me I'm spelling something wrong, and I'm dashed if I can find the correct spelling.' With her perfect, precise diction, she reminded Rob of his secondary school Drama teacher. As always, she was dressed in classy, tailored clothes. He went over to her and she looked up at him. 'You wouldn't be an absolute darling and fetch me a dictionary, so I can check, would you?'

Rob smiled. 'Well, I could, but actually, you can check yourself, without either of us moving. Are you connected to the Internet?' He looked at the library card on the table beside her: *Mrs D Pickering.*

'I am. You see, I'm in the middle of writing an email, and the blasted thing keeps putting that red squiggly line under one of my words.'

'We can look it up. See?' He went round to her right, and sat in the empty seat next to hers. He wriggled the mouse, clicked on the browser, and then clicked the 'Dictionary' link in the corner. A small box popped up in the top right of the screen.

'Oh,' she said with a smile that showed off perfect teeth behind her pink lipstick. 'All the time I've been coming here and using this machine, and I didn't even know that was there. You see, I have a cousin in the north who's mad keen on gardening, a bit of an expert, really, and I wanted to ask her whether I should buy these plants.' She pointed to the email she was typing. 'Look. It doesn't like it if I spell it this way.'

He looked where she was pointing. *Bizzie-Lizzies* – underlined with a red squiggle.

'I've tried it with a *Y* as well. *Bee, eye, zed, zed, why*,' she spelled out. '*Bizzy*.'

'Perhaps you have to spell it the normal way,' Rob said. '*Bee, you, ess, why*. Busy.'

She put her hand up to her mouth, and laughed. 'Oh dear. Do you think it's as simple as that?'

'Well, we can check it with the online dictionary.' He moved the cursor to the little box, and typed in Busy Lizzie, and pressed the left mouse button. The definition appeared.

Busy Lizzie – Impatiens wallerana Hook, also known as Busy Lizzy, Balsam or simply Impatiens ...

'Oh I say,' Mrs Pickering said, laughing. 'How silly. I never thought to try the most obvious spelling. I just had a mental blank. You must think I'm a fool.'

'No, not at all,' he said. 'I would probably have tried the other spelling first, too.'

'You're too kind, young man. You'd never believe someone who taught English for thirty-five years could make such a silly mistake, would you?' She smiled up at him, and studied his face. Her expression changed and she sat staring at him as if puzzled.

'Can I help you with anything else?'

'No, no,' she said, still examining his face. 'I'm sorry. It's just that you look extraordinarily like someone I used to know. A very dear friend.' Her face clouded with a sudden sadness. 'You could be his double. But of course, you couldn't, because he would be a lot older than you are, were he alive.' Her eyes strayed to the laminated ID badge clipped to Rob's pocket, and her mouth opened. 'Oh my goodness. R Handle! Oh, I am sorry, my dear, but ... are you, by any chance, Eric's son?'

'Yes,' Rob said. 'Eric was my dad. I'm Robert.'

'Robert! Of course. He used to talk about you a great deal. Oh, your father was such a wonderful man. What a tragedy it was.' She looked at Rob with kind eyes. 'How old were you, when you lost him?'

'Eighteen,' Rob said. 'I'd not long left school.'

'Oh, how dreadful. You poor boy. And your poor mother, too.'

'How did you know him? Was it through work or something?'

'No, no. I'd known Eric ever since school. We were in the same class at Fleesham Grammar. And then we joined the Savoyards together after we left school. You know, the Gilbert and Sullivan Society?' Rob nodded. 'We had such great times. Such a loss, such a dreadful loss. He was probably my dearest friend, you know. And so talented, such a performer. He could have turned professional, we all thought so.' She turned her head and gazed into the distance. Rob had to strain to hear her next words, spoken softly. 'His cocoa was a triumph.'

His cocoa? How on earth would she know that? As far as Rob remembered, his dad never drank the stuff, never mind making it for random women. He looked at the woman's library card again. Oh! Mrs *D* Pickering. No, surely not. He looked at her again. Why not? She was an attractive woman, charming and well turned out. She would have been a stunner twenty-odd years ago. But she didn't look someone who would ever have been called Debbie. Deborah, perhaps, but never Debbie, in a million years.

'So, Robert, have you followed in your father's footsteps? Do you sing?'

He laughed. 'Not if I can help it,' he said. 'It'd frighten the horses.'

'Oh, I don't believe that for a minute. I think he brought you along to some of our performances, you and your mother ... Do you remember?'

'I didn't go to many. I suppose once I reached my teens I must have thought it was a bit ... uncool. From what I can remember, I did enjoy the shows, though. Good, um, tunes.'

'Oh, they are indeed, Robert. And Gilbert's lyrics so witty – years ahead of their time, in many ways.'

'So ... are you still a member? Of the Savoyards?'

She shook her head. 'Oh no, I stopped a long time ago. And they're called *FLOATS* nowadays, you know? Fleesham Light Opera and Amateur Theatrical Society. What a mouthful! Savoyards is a lot easier. Do you know, your dad used to call us—'

'Saveloys.' Rob said, with a laugh. 'I remember that.'

Mrs Pickering chuckled. 'Yes, he used to say it was because we were a bunch of silly sausages prancing about on stage singing Victorian operetta. I believe they changed the name because someone decided most people didn't know what Savoyards meant.' Her hand went to her throat. 'Yes, I had to call it a day, ten years or so back; the poor old voice is too wavery and croaky now, so I leave it to the younger people to carry on the tradition. Like your young lady boss, there.' She pointed over to the counter, where Rachel was chatting to a customer.

'Rachel?' Rob said. 'Oh. Is she a member?'

Mrs Pickering raised her eyebrows. 'She's not just a member dear.' She leaned closer to him, and lowered her voice. 'She's their star player.'

'Really?' Rob looked over at Rachel.

'Yes, dear. A soprano, like I am—was. But my dear, her voice—' She looked over at Rachel, and then back to Rob. 'You must go and see her perform next week, dear. I swear, you've never heard anything so beautiful.'

'Next week?'

'Yes—look. Haven't you seen the posters?'

Rob looked to where she was pointing. Rachel hadn't mentioned that she was in it when she'd given him the poster to put up.

'Oh. *The Mikado*. It's on next week then, is it?' Perhaps he should ask Joanne if she'd like to go and see it with him. He was seeing her tonight. On second thoughts, he imagined she'd turn it down flat. And besides, he thought with a flutter of nervousness, tonight was the night he'd planned to tell her he didn't want to carry on with their Thursday meetings. He would be wary of asking his Mum if she'd like to go with him, in case it brought back too many painful memories. Still, there was nothing to stop him going on his own, was there? He was sure Rachel would be pleased one of her staff was supporting her. He could ask Carole to go with him. He turned to Mrs Pickering.

'Would there still be tickets available?'

'Well, yes, I should think so, especially midweek. The weekend shows tend to fill up quickly,' she said. 'Wait, though. Would you like to go? I have a spare ticket for the last night. I'm an honorary member now, so they send me a couple of complimentaries each year. My poor husband usually gets dragged along with me, but the poor soul has seen so many Gilbert and Sullivan operettas now, he probably knows the librettos off by heart. It would be lovely to let him off the hook and take along someone new for a change. Especially the son of such a dear friend.' She touched his arm. 'Please do say you'd like to. It would give me such pleasure.'

Rob thought. He hadn't been to the theatre in years, and after what she had said about Rachel's singing, he was intrigued.

'Yes,' he said with a smile. 'Yes, I think I would like that. Thank you very much.'

TWENTY-THREE

He arrived at the *Slave* before Joanne, as usual, got a pint of Stella from the bar, and settled down to wait for her. Nervous about his plans for tonight, he'd managed to drink half of it by the time she entered the pub and sat next to him. He felt despondent now at the sight of her glum face, and he knew this was the right decision, but he dreaded having to carry it out.

'Magners?' he asked. If she asked for something different, he decided it would be a sign that he should give her another chance.

'Yes please.'

He stood at the bar, thinking, if she asks me about my day, like I always start by asking about hers, I'll put it off until next time. He took her Magners over and placed it in front of her.

'Ta.'

He waited. Nothing. He sighed. 'So, how was your day?'

She shrugged. 'Bit boring.'

What a surprise. It was enough to make you lose the will the live.

'Jo?'

'Mmm?' She took a sip, not even looking at him.

He swallowed. 'I just wondered, um, do you want to keep doing this? I mean, meeting me here every week.'

She frowned and turned to him. 'Yeah. Why?'

'Only, you never seem as if you, um, get a lot out of it. You don't seem to, um, enjoy my company much.'

He saw her hand clench around her cider glass. 'I do, Rob! I look forward to seeing you on Thursday evenings.' She gulped at the drink. 'I look forward to it all week.' Another swallow. 'Why? Don't you?'

Oh dear. 'Um, yes, of course I do.' No, don't lie. You absolutely don't. Tell her. 'It's just that you never seem all that, how can I put it?' He scratched his chin. 'Happy.'

She smiled. Now, why couldn't she do that more often? She was classically pretty, with her alabaster skin, black, wavy hair, and those chocolate-brown eyes, but she spoiled it by always looking, well, grumpy. 'No, I'm very happy. I don't know where you got the idea I'm not.'

Because you always look like you've just been given a week to live.

'Oh, well, that's all right then. Another Magners?'

Great. That went well, he thought as the barman pulled him another pint.

At ten o'clock she looked at the pub clock, downed her drink and stood up and got him another pint, and at a quarter past, she kissed him on the cheek and said, see you next week, then, and left.

He imagined the telling off he'd get from Paddytum, when he arrived home and he told him he'd failed.

You'll be seeing this woman for ever, every Thursday night the same. You're out of one rut and straight into another. I'm ashamed of you, Robert.

It just wouldn't do. He stood up, looking at his almost full pint, shrugged, and dashed outside in time to see Joanne entering the campus next door, and hurrying towards the main building. She slowed her pace to take something out of her bag. It looked like a roll of Extra-Strong Mints. She unpeeled the wrapper and popped one in her mouth.

He followed, in a fast walk, but was surprised, when she reached the college building that, instead of carrying on round the side to the back gate, she went in through the main entrance. Strange, Rob thought. Perhaps she needs the loo.

He stood at the door. He'd wait for her to come back out, so he could tell her he didn't want to carry on seeing her.

He looked at his watch. Almost ten-thirty. The adult education lot would be pouring through these doors any minute now. Where was Joanne? She'd miss her bus if she wasn't careful. Actually, he'd miss his, too, if he didn't get to his bus stop soon.

Just then, he saw an old Jag pull into the car park. Now, he'd seen that car before, and the man behind the wheel. As the double doors behind him opened, and a dozen or so people filed past, he remembered. The last time he'd seen the car was right here, picking Joanne up after their French Class. But why was he here, when Jo always caught the bus?

Out of the corner of his eye he saw a woman hurry through the throng of departing students and run down the steps. It was her. She had the French Workbook they'd used in their class tucked under her arm. He watched as she reached the Jag, got into the passenger seat, and fastened her seatbelt. He scratched his head as the car disappeared through the college gates.

What the hell was going on?

TWENTY-FOUR

The following Tuesday, Rob was surprised to see Mrs Pickering standing at the returns counter as he came out of the staff room carrying Paddytum. She gave him a little wave and he went over.

'Hello there,' he said. 'We don't usually see you so early in the day. Can I help?'

'Well, Robert,' she said, it was actually you I came in to see. I'm visiting someone nearby and I thought I might as well drop your *Mikado* ticket in.' She took a small envelope out of her handbag and handed it to him. 'Just in case we can't meet up before the show, for any reason, on Saturday. I've scribbled my telephone number on the back.' She reached out and ruffled the fur on the top of Paddytum's head. 'What a handsome chap! What's his name? Does he belong to the library?'

Rob grinned sheepishly. 'No, Frederick's mine. It's okay, though, he's here in an official capacity. On library business, you might say.'

Mrs Pickering laughed. 'Frederick! Oh, how lovely! It suits him perfectly. I expect you named him after your father, did you?' She continued, before Rob could ask what she meant. 'What is he here for?'

Rob scratched at his temple, still perplexed at Mrs Pickering's remark, but he didn't have time to quiz her now – the toddlers were swarming into the Children's Library. 'Well, we do this sort of ... act, for the kids. Read a story out, and Frederick does all the voices. Well, I do them, but I pretend it's him.' He felt himself colouring at the lie.

'Oh, what fun!' she squealed. 'I'd love to see that. Would it be all right if I watch? I'll do it very discreetly, of course. From a distance.'

Rob looked over to where Rachel was already seated on the beanbag, with a book on her lap. She raised her eyebrows at him as if to tell him to get a move on. 'I don't see why not.'

'NO!' Paddytum's voice stopped him in his tracks.

'What?' he muttered.

'I can't do it. Not in front of that woman. I refuse.'

'Don't be silly, Paddytum,' Rob said, out of the corner of his mouth. 'It's not like you to be shy.' He continued into the Children's Library and sat next to Rachel. She opened the book, and Rob waited for the jaw-tingle.

Nothing happened. Oh, great. That was all he needed: a bear suffering from artistic temperament.

'Are you ready, Frederick?' Rachel asked, with a quizzical glare at Rob.

Come on, Paddytum, he thought, don't mess me about. Not when that nice lady's watching. Mrs Pickering was sitting at a table in the main library, looking over at them and smiling. Archie, he saw, was making his way over to join her. Rob cleared his throat. The tingle just wasn't happening. Rob cursed the bear's stubbornness.

'What's wrong?' Rachel mouthed at Rob.

He cleared his throat again, and followed it up with a coughing fit. There was only one way out of this if Paddytum insisted on playing silly buggers. 'Sorry,' he gasped, getting to his feet, with his hand clutching his neck. 'Got a tickle. In my throat. Need a drink of water.'

'Oh, okay.' She turned to the children. 'Poor old Frederick needs to get rid of his tickly cough. Tell you what, we'll just read the first one without him, shall we, while Mr Handle takes him off to get a glass of water?' Rob hurried out of the Children's Library.

'He is coming back, isn't he?' one of the toddlers asked his mother loudly as Rob passed.

Mrs Pickering stood as Rob reached her. So did Archie.

'Oh, what a shame,' she said, touching his arm. 'Those bothersome tickles are a nuisance, aren't they? I remember how dreadful it was to be caught out by one during a show.' Rob nodded, still holding his neck and clearing his throat. Archie was also nodding as if in agreement with Mrs Pickering. 'Listen, I ought to get on, Robert. My friend will be expecting me, so I'd better not stay, after all. Perhaps I'll catch your performance next week.' She squeezed his arm. 'See you on Saturday night. I'll meet you in the Cornmarket foyer.' She waved, and headed for the door.

'Bye, dear,' Archie said, waving after her, as Rob continued to the staff room.

'What the bloody hell was *that* all about?' Rob asked Paddytum, as soon as he'd closed the door.

'Aren't you going to get a drink? For your tickle?'

'I don't bloody *have* a bloody *tickle*! What I have is a temperamental teddy bear!'

'Well, I'm fine now, Robert. You don't have to shout at me.'

'What? You want to go and do Story Time, now?'

'Yes, I told you, I'm fine. Tell you what, I'll do an extra one on Thursday if you like, I'll even do a solo. Do own of my own stories. To make up for it.'

Rob sighed. 'All right. But that was really embarrassing. We'll discuss this later.' He left the staff room and went back to his audience of toddlers.

'Sorry about that,' he murmured to Rachel as he sat down again.

Two days later, Rachel waved off the last of the Thursday toddlers after the second Story Time of the week. She rearranged the beanbag, inspecting the grubby yellow cover. Time it had another wash, she thought. Rob was on his way back to the staff room with his teddy bear. She'd been delighted on Tuesday, when Rob had offered his services for a second session. Today he'd performed one of his off-the-cuff, made up stories, and the kids, some of whom hadn't ever witnessed the Frederick experience before, had loved it.

She marvelled at the brilliance of the tales Rob told during these solo sessions. He really ought to write them down, she told him. But he'd shaken his head, and said he couldn't even remember them afterwards. In a way, this didn't surprise her. She'd watched him during these sessions. When she didn't have to turn pages, it was easy to observe him, and it fascinated her. When Rob did a session with just Frederick and no books, he went into a sort of trance. She'd noticed the look of surprise that flickered across his eyes at some of the things he was saying, as if he wasn't expecting them. He was always a little strange afterwards, too. Dazed, almost disorientated, as if he weren't sure, for a minute or two, what was going on or where he was.

143

The children loved Rob and his bear, with the books and without them. It wasn't Rob they loved, though, was it? She sometimes needed to remind herself that the bear wasn't the one doing the talking. The voice which issued from Rob's mouth was so different from his usual quiet-bordering-on-apologetic one, it was as if he were a different person altogether. The children's eyes hardly strayed from the bear during Story Time, and she thought they fully believed it was Frederick talking. She suspected even the parents half-believed it, when Rob was in full flow.

Rob came back out of the staff room, and smiled at her as he took a returned-books trolley and pushed it to the end of the Fiction shelves. She smiled back, and watched him as he worked.

He was almost unrecognisable as the painfully shy, overweight, sad man who had turned up for interview. He'd picked up the job quickly, and was able to help the customers with just about any query. He was doing all the same things now as Marjorie and Carole, with as much competence as if he'd done it for years, but for a much lower salary. Last week she had phoned her own boss, the County Librarian, and asked if there was any possibility of a promotion for Rob. The answer was a firm no. Only if Marjorie or Carole left. And even if that happened, they would have to advertise the post, and Rob would have to apply, just like anyone else. It was 'policy'. But it was unlikely to happen any time soon. Carole hadn't long been back from her career break, and Rachel sometimes thought the only way Marjorie would leave was feet first. Not that she wanted to lose either of them; she was fond of her staff. She'd liked her boss's other suggestion even less. If she wanted her Mr Handle to be promoted, she should encourage him to look at the job vacancies posted on the Library Service Intranet, and apply for a job at another branch. This suggestion provoked a response that surprised even her. She'd become used to having Rob around, and she didn't think she could imagine her library without him.

She'd told her boss, 'He doesn't drive. And I don't think any other branch would be easy for him to get to on public transport.' It was probably true, but was it fair to hold him back from a possible promotion? She sighed. Was she being selfish?

She'd only just begun to admit to herself how she felt about Rob. She hid it well; at least, she hoped she did. But she found herself seeking him out often during the day, as if her eyes needed to be nourished by the sight of him. When he looked over and caught her eye, his sudden smile back made her heart flip, and she'd have to look away quickly, and ration herself until the next guilty glance. Like a secret crush, it was exciting, but it was painful, too. Perhaps a transfer *was* the solution. She couldn't get involved with a member of her own staff but, if Rob were safely tucked away at another branch, it would be fine.

He was such a contrast to Paul, who'd been the last in a long line of the same type: good-looking, arrogant, and ultimately, cheating rats. She'd been with him for three years; had moved to Fleesham to be with him. And she'd been happy. Until the day she'd come home one afternoon with a migraine which had plagued her all morning. Sadly, she was unable to have the lie-down she'd craved during her drive home. The bed would have been a little too crowded, occupied as it was by Paul and the woman next door.

Rob would never do anything like that to her.

But it was no use. He had a girlfriend. Joanne, wasn't it? She'd heard Carole ask about her just a few days ago. Rob's face had turned crimson, and he'd hurried away, muttering about having some CDs to sort, but the stab of jealousy which shot through her had made her feel quite ill.

At least she had rehearsals to take her mind off it. She frowned. Except they didn't, really. Even when she was in the middle of a scene with Ko-Ko or Nanki-Poo, she caught herself thinking of Rob – especially with Nanki-Poo, and especially when they were going over 'the kissing song'. At the end, when she and James, her Nanki-Poo, went into a clinch, and feigned a passionate snog, she had to try hard not to picture James as Rob, even though James was younger and shorter.

She heaved a sigh. This was ridiculous. She needed to pull herself together. She was a thirty-six year old woman, not a thirteen-year-old schoolgirl.

Hang on, though. Maybe there was a solution, after all. She'd been looking at it the wrong way round. She went behind the counter and logged in to the Intranet, and clicked on Vacancies.

She didn't want Rob to get a transfer, but there was no reason she shouldn't look for one herself. She was mobile, and wouldn't mind driving a few extra miles. And, if she carried on like this, she'd start to make silly mistakes, and end up losing her job through sheer incompetence.

Carole peeked over her shoulder.

'Rachel!' she cried. 'You're not thinking of leaving us, are you?'

Her eyes automatically strayed over to Rob. He was staring at her, and the look in his eyes made her heart turn over. She closed the page.

'Just keeping an eye on what's going on in other branches,' she said, stealing another glance at Rob, who'd gone back to rummaging through his returns trolley. She must have imagined his shocked expression.

Rob breathed slowly and deeply. Rachel going? No! How would he carry on working here if she went? He loved the job, but a large part of how much he enjoyed it was how he felt when he was near Rachel. He tried not to look at her too often, in case she noticed. He'd be punching above his weight – he had no illusions about that. But he liked to imagine that, whenever their eyes met across the racks of books, he saw an echo in her eyes of the way he felt. It was all complete nonsense, of course. She looked away really quickly, every time. She must find him repulsive, however well she hid it. She was a nice person, that was all.

But when she was near, and he could smell the strawberry scent in her hair, he longed to reach out and touch her, take the band off her ponytail and run his hands through that glossy sheet of chestnut brown, and take her in his arms and—Stop it. Just. Stop. It! he thought. This is doing my head in.

If she really were leaving, he'd just have to live with it. Yes, he'd stay on here; he'd have to. He'd never find another job as nice as this one, and there was no way he wanted to slip back into the meaningless existence in which he'd been mired before. But he'd feel like his world had come crashing down. Again.

If it happened, he still had the bear to get him through it. Paddytum wouldn't allow him to give up. He'd have to talk it over with him when he came back. He was in a post-Story 'absence' at the moment, and would be gone, most likely, until tomorrow morning.

146

He was used to the bear's absences now, and he'd even started thinking of the longer ones as his nights off. As much as he loved having Paddytum around, he valued his short periods of privacy. It was a novelty to be able to watch a DVD, knowing his viewing would be uninterrupted. Sometimes, he even went online, though he hadn't dared revisit the chat-room in case Clementine was there. As it was, he half-expected her to appear, like a harpy, in the library one day, and announce to Rachel, Marge and Carole, and assorted customers, that he was a complete nutter and that they should immediately have him thrown out.

He looked over at Rachel again, and dropped his eyes straight away, because she was looking at him. Funny, that was happening more and more these days. Was something wrong? He dared a glance back at her, and she was looking at the monitor again, and her expression wasn't happy. Was she planning to give him the sack? His month's trial had been up ages ago, but that didn't make him immune from ever being fired. The days of having a job for life were long gone, they said. Rachel had said over and over again that she was pleased at how well he'd picked things up, and he couldn't think of anything he'd done wrong. Had she been asked to get rid of someone and it was a case of 'last-in, first-out'?

He knew what Paddytum would say to him about putting two and two together and making five hundred. 'You always do this, Robert. It's not all about you, you know. Rachel might be worried about any number of things, none of them anything to do with you.'

'Excuse me?'

Crouched behind his trolley, sorting books, Rob hadn't seen the man approach. Shortish, stocky, bald, middle-aged. He stood rigidly, looking down at Rob, his hands clenching and unclenching at his sides.

'Hello. Can I help?'

'Your name Rob?'

Rob stood. 'Yes.'

'So, you're the bastard who's been messing with my wife.'

TWENTY-FIVE

Rob gaped at the man, aware that Rachel, Marjorie and Carole had all stopped what they were doing, and were staring, too. As was Archie, who sat stock-still, peeping over the pages of his Wilbur Smith.

'I beg your pardon?'

'You heard me, you philanderer. She told me all about it. I got the whole sick story out of her last night. Planning on seeing her again tonight, were you?'

What day was it? Thursday. Oh shit. Oh bloody hell.

'Do you mean …' Rob swallowed hard. 'Joanne?'

'So you admit it, then?' The man had his fists clenched, and Rob wondered if he might punch him. He might need to stand on something to do it, though; he was at least half a foot shorter than him.

'Well, I know Joanne, of course. But believe me, mate, I had no idea she was married.'

'So *you* say! Are you denying that you lured her away from her French class and into your arms?'

'No! It's not like that. And she's never been in my arms.' Rob looked over at Rachel. Her eyes were narrowed, and her arms folded. This couldn't be happening.

'Not for want of trying, I'll bet. If I hadn't phoned the college yesterday and spoken to that Madam Le Froufrou, or whatever her name is …'

'Lefèbvre,' Rob said quietly.

'I don't give a shit what her name is,' the man shouted, his face crimson, 'The thing is, she told me my Joanne left her class weeks ago and that some big bloke stopped coming at the same time. It took a while to get the truth out of Joanne, but she's told me all about how you talked her into meeting you instead. Is this a regular thing with you? Do you prey on innocent married women at all these evening classes? You're a complete—'

'I didn't! I'm not like that.'

'Please!'

148

Rob turned. Rachel stood behind him.

'Robert, could you and this gentleman please take this into my office?'

The man turned to her. 'Oh, don't worry, Miss. I've finished. I only came in to tell … Casanova, here, that if he ever goes within a mile of my missus again, he'd better watch his back.'

And with that, he stalked out.

Rob stared after him, and then turned to Rachel.

'It's not how it looked,' he said.

'Rob,' she said, a chill in her voice, 'Your private life is none of my business. But please try to keep it private.' She walked away, and disappeared into her office.

Rob kept a low profile for the rest of the day. He didn't think he could ever look Rachel in the eyes again. Well, he guessed tonight's date with Joanne was off. Every cloud has a silver lining, he thought.

That evening, while his mother was preparing dinner, Rob made a start on the pile of ironing that had built up over the past few days, more to take his mind off what had happened at work than anything else.

As usual, he left his mother's garments well alone. He had no idea how to iron a dress or a skirt. He thought blouses must work on the same principal as his shirts, but his mother's were all made of materials that looked like they'd burn too easily if he didn't have the iron at the correct temperature, and some of them had ties or flounces at the neck. Best to let her do those herself.

He'd set the ironing board up in front of the TV, and was half-watching the news. His mother came in, and fingered the blue shirt he'd just hung on the back of a chair.

'Robbie, isn't this too big for you now? It looks as if you could fit two of you in it.'

Rob unconsciously dropped a hand to his waist. 'I think most of them are, now. I could do with going shopping for new ones again,' he said.

'Well, you must almost be at the stage now where you don't need to go any lower.'

'As long as I don't start putting it back on again.' He stood the iron on its base, and looked at the shirts he'd finished. 'If I get rid of the ones that don't fit me, it'll be a deterrent.'

Maureen ran her hand over the pile again. 'Were you thinking of giving them to charity? Some of these here, you've only had a month or two. Look,' she pulled up the sleeve of a lilac shirt Rob had bought on his last shopping trip. 'This looks nearly brand new. Perhaps you should sell them on one of those websites. What's it called? E something? Joan from work was telling me her daughter Alison sold some baby and toddler clothes the other week. Made quite a bit of money.'

'Ebay? Yes, I was considering that myself. But I don't know if I can be bothered with the hassle of it all. For a start I'd have to buy a digital camera, so I could take pictures of them all, and then upload them, and write out descriptions, and so on. Then after you've sold them there's all the palaver of packaging them and queuing in the post office to send them to the people who'd bought them, and all that rigmarole.'

'How about a car boot sale, then? At least you'd get some money, that way.'

'Mother, there's a fundamental flaw in that little plan,' he said, with a grin. 'It's tricky to do a car boot sale when you don't have a car. The clue's in the name.'

Maureen punched him lightly on the arm, but she laughed, too.

'No, I'll just bag them all up, and take them to the Save the Children shop, or Oxfam or Cancer Research, or whatever. That way, I get to go round feeling smug for a few days, because I've done A Good Thing.' He laughed. He wondered if his mother was right, though. It would be good to recoup some of the money he'd spent on these clothes. It wasn't as if he had expensive hobbies or went out boozing or clubbing every night, but if he were just to sell some of the *better* stuff on Ebay, he could perhaps put the money towards a little holiday for him and his mum. They hadn't been anywhere since his dad died. And digital cameras weren't as expensive these days as they used to be.

Some of his older stuff wasn't even good enough for a charity shop, but there were a few things that he'd consider too good just to give away. Anyway, he thought, it was about time he had a good clear out. He'd do it tonight, after his walk, and take advantage of Paddytum's absence. He'd only interfere anyway.

He unplugged the iron. 'Ma, it's not such a bad idea, you know. I'll sort out all my stuff, and I'll put the newish shirts and trousers and that to one side so I can put them on Ebay sometime. The rest can go to charity. Except for what's only fit for the dump. I'll be able to drop off the charity shop stuff over a few lunchtimes. There are a few near work. I'll just take a bag along with me every day till they're gone.'

'Will you be sorting out them tonight, then? I thought you'd be seeing Joanne?' his mother said, her head on one side.

'That's over,' he said. His mother opened her mouth to say something, and then closed it again when she saw the look on his face. 'I might as well do it while I'm in the mood. I'll ditch all those old books, too. I'm not likely to read any of them again. And some of my DVDs and CDs. I could sell most of those. And all those old toys. It's time they went.'

'Well, if you're doing it tonight, I could drop them off at a charity shop for you tomorrow.'

'Oh? How come?'

'Joan's invited Barbara and me for lunch to celebrate her sixtieth. We're going to that restaurant that used to be an old coaching inn ... What's it called?'

'*The Turnpike Inn*?'

'That's the one. Anyway, because it's not on any bus routes, Barbara's offered to pick me up. I'll check with her first, but I'm sure she won't mind putting a couple of bags of things in the boot of her car and coming home via a charity shop or two.'

'Well, that would save me having to take them on the bus. You sure she won't mind?'

'Barbara's a sweetheart. And she's always giving things to charity herself, so I think she'd approve of the reason for the detour.'

While he strolled round the block on his usual circuit of the neighbourhood, Rob kept his eyes open for empty cardboard boxes. Sometimes people left them by their bins. He found two – a large one which had once contained a small hi-fi system, and a smaller one which had held packs of nappies. He carried them up to his room, grabbing a roll of black bin bags from the kitchen, too.

He peered at Paddytum, sitting on his bed. 'Mate?' he said. 'You back yet?'

No reply.

He set the boxes and three bags in a row on the carpet, and rubbed his hands, eager to start.

'Ebay. Charity. Rubbish. Right!' He turned the TV on so he wouldn't have to work in silence. The bags would do for the clothes and soft toys. The larger box would do for books, DVDs and CDs to go to the charity shop, He'd put potential Ebay items in the smaller one; he could keep it in the bottom of his wardrobe until he'd bought a camera.

First, he opened the wardrobe and pulled out all his shirts and trousers, and piled them, still on their hangers, onto his bed. The one thing he left hanging, right at the very back, was his father's dark blue suit. He'd rescued it a few days after his father's funeral, when his mother wasn't looking, from the pile of his father's possessions she had left in the hall, ready for the Salvation Army to collect. At the same time, he'd salvaged his dad's black leather overnight bag, which he hid at the back of the wardrobe's top shelf. He had no idea why he'd felt the need to take them. He'd opened the bag once, and the only thing in it was a spare pair of his father's reading glasses. The suit would probably fit him now. Perhaps he'd try it on one day.

He turned to the pile on his bed, and started to pick up the garments, one by one. He put some straight back on the metal rail, or took others off the hangers, folded them, and laid them carefully in one of the black bags. It took less time than he thought it would, and he was pleased to see a much neater, emptier wardrobe when he'd finished.

Next, he turned his attention to the chest of drawers. He pulled out the top drawer and laid it on the bed. Socks and underpants by the dozen. He had no doubt he'd be able to feed the rubbish bag from this one. First to go in was a bundle of about twenty odd socks. 'Just where do their partners go to?' he said. 'Do washing machines need one sock from each pair for fuel?' He sorted the remaining pairs of socks, ditching half of them. Finally, around twenty-five pairs of XL and XXL underpants joined the socks.

He took out the last pair from the drawer, uncovering a small white envelope. Ah, there it was! Not in a book after all. He opened it and pulled out the photograph. His father was sitting on a wooden bench in a garden or a park. Rob chewed his lower lip and tried to remember where this was taken. He had a feeling it was the day they went to Longleat Safari Park, when he was about fourteen or fifteen. He gazed at the face. God, he looked like him, didn't he? He could see now why his mother stared at him sometimes with that sad look on her face. His dad's hair, like his own, was wild and wavy. Before he went to work each morning he'd had to tame it with Brylcreem. His dad had the same wide mouth, straight nose, and thick, dark eyebrows as he did, but his eyes had been bluer. Rob's eyes were more like Maureen's.

He brought the photo closer to his face, and, as he did, a slip of yellowing paper fluttered to the bed. It was the announcement he'd clipped from the Births, Marriages and Deaths section of the local paper, twenty-three years ago, just before the funeral.

George Handle (Eric). Cruelly taken
on 27 March 1986. Beloved husband of Maureen
and devoted father to Robert.
Sadly missed. Funeral will be held at …

He never thought of his dad as a George, though he had known from a young age that it was his real first name.

He tucked the photo and the clipping back into the envelope and went back to his sorting. The second and third drawers were T-shirts, jeans and jumpers. He ditched all of these except a couple of T-shirts and jumpers which would do for gardening, and one pair of jeans, which would be loose at the waist but nothing a belt wouldn't solve.

Next, he turned to his books. Most of these could go, he decided. They were all in excellent condition; he had been brought up to treat books with respect. He wondered if any might turn out to be rare, or collectors' items. He slid out one of his Rev W Audry Railway stories. These might be worth a try on Ebay. From what he'd seen at the library, Thomas the Tank Engine and his friends James and Percy and Gordon, were still popular. He hadn't noticed any of the kids borrowing Enid Blyton's Famous Five books, but they might still be worth something. He lifted them off the shelves and arranged them carefully in the smaller of the two boxes, and put all the others in the large box. This left a handful of books he thought he might read again, or didn't want to give away because they'd been special presents, with a dedication written on the flyleaf. Finally there was the small pile of self-help books. He added them to the charity box. He stood back and looked at the bookcase. His remaining books looked a little lonely, taking up just a single shelf. He'd now be able to move his stack of DVDs and CDs from the windowsill to one of the empty shelves. He turned to these next, deciding to keep most of the CDs. He sorted the DVDs into two piles. He'd hang on to his comedy ones. He realised that he'd never watched any of the films twice since buying them, so he put the whole lot in the Ebay box.

All that was left to sort was the pile of toys. Had he left them till last for some deep psychological reason? Without a doubt, some were too tattered and stained to give to a charity shop – they would immediately be dumped in the nearest skip. He knew if he didn't deal with them now, he'd weaken and leave them where they were. He took the three tattiest toys: a blue rabbit with one ear, a dog with a missing eye, and a bear with one fat and one thin leg, and put them in the rubbish bag. Action Man, in perfect condition apart from his nakedness, went into the charity bag, along with Panda.

When his final plushie had been assigned to a bag, he looked at his watch. Good grief, he hadn't realised how late it was, and he had to be up for work in a few hours. He yawned, and then pushed the boxes and bags into the corner of his room. He'd take the charity ones downstairs in the morning and leave them in the porch, ready for his mum to put them in her friend's car. He climbed into bed and hooked his arm over the still-silent Paddytum, and said, 'That's that, little buddy. You're the only one left now. Hope you're pleased with me.'

'Morning, mate,' he said, stretching.
No reply. He sat up and looked at the bear.
'Hello?'

Strange. Paddytum still wasn't 'back'. Oh well, perhaps he was having a longer rest than usual. Two sessions in one week must have taken its toll. Rob had no time to worry about it now. He had work to do. After he'd washed and shaved, he shifted the bag with the items he planned to list on Ebay, along with the smaller of the two boxes, into the bottom of his wardrobe, and then carried the larger box downstairs, leaving it by the front door. He'd bring the bag of clothes and toys down after breakfast. The bag of rubbish could wait till he got home.

'Oh, by the way, I'm going out tomorrow night,' he said, as he took his cereal bowl to the sink to wash it.

'With Joanne? I thought that was over.'

'It is. I'm going on my own.' He put the bowl on the draining board, and wished there were something else to wash up so he wouldn't have to turn round. Perhaps she wouldn't notice if he washed the cereal bowl again. 'To the theatre.'

He didn't want to tell her it was a Gilbert and Sullivan production he was going to see. He especially didn't want to bring up the subject of Mrs Pickering and how she was an old friend of his father's in case she turned out to be Debbie. He decided to tell the truth but bend it a little. He turned round.

'It's *The Mikado*. Rachel is a member of *FLOATS*,' he said with as much nonchalance as he could muster, 'and I thought it would be nice to go along and support her.'

'Oh. Fancy that. Well, it'll bring back some memories, I expect. Was that one of the ones you saw with your dad?'

'I really can't remember. There was one about ghosts, I think. I liked that one. And another one, set in Venice. I don't think I've seen the Mikado? Have you?'

She stared into the distance. 'Yes, it was one of your dad's favourites. He played, what was his name? Ko-Ko? He was very funny, as I remember. And everyone said he was very good in the part. But then, he always got picked for the comedy roles.'

Ko-Ko, Rob thought. Of course. *Cocoa*. He smiled.

His mother came out of her reverie and looked at Rob, and then at the kitchen clock. 'You'd better get a wriggle on, son. You'll be late.'

He gave her a kiss, and left.

Halfway to the library, the idea that he'd forgotten something important started to niggle at him. Three-quarters of the way there, he stopped. Damn! The bag of clothes for the charity shop was still on his bed. His mum would only take the box when her friend arrived this afternoon. He couldn't turn back now, but he didn't really want that bag hanging about over the weekend. He'd have to ring Ma from the library – not a request he wanted to make after the bad vibes Rachel was giving off yesterday afternoon.

Rachel looked up from the desk, unsmiling. His heart was heavy as he asked if he could make a quick call.

She shrugged. 'Feel free,' she said, when he asked, and walked off.

His mother answered straight away. 'Ma, there's a box of stuff for the charity shop by the front door. I forgot to tell you.'

'Yes, love. I saw it. I'll put it in Barbara's car when she gets here, don't worry.'

'Thanks, but there's another bag of stuff on my bed. Would you mind taking that too? I meant to go back up and get it before I left, but we got talking and I forgot.'

'On your bed? No problem. See you later.' He said goodbye, and hung up.

Carole chuckled. 'Sounds like someone's been having a clear out. I hope you don't mind me saying, Rob, but I'm not surprised. You must have dropped a few sizes in the time you've been here.'

Rob blushed. 'Is it that obvious? Well, I feel so much better for it, and my wardrobe now has a new lease of life. You wouldn't believe how much stuff I chucked out.'

'Oh, it does us all good to de-clutter, once in a while,' she said. 'By the way, what was all that business yesterday, with the bald guy?'

He rubbed a hand over his face, and groaned. 'Carole, to tell you the truth, I don't even know myself. That girl, Joanne, his wife, well … it was all a huge misunderstanding.' He started to tell her about the French class, and how he'd been seeing Joanne on Thursday evenings. 'I never knew she was married, honest.'

'Hmm,' she said, when he'd finished. 'The Lothario thing didn't really sound like the Rob we've come to know and love. It sounds a little to me as if you were the fall guy.' She lowered her voice. 'Look, I'll make sure I go for lunch with Rach today, if you like, and tell her your side of it. Make sure she knows you're the innocent party in all this. Unless you want to tell her yourself?'

'I don't think I could. I'd be really grateful. Would you mind? I hate the idea of her thinking I'm like that, when I'm not.'

Carole grinned. 'I can imagine. I'm thinking you have a soft spot for our little Rachel, don't you?'

Oh no. Was it that obvious? Rob looked down at his feet, wishing he didn't blush so easily.

'Don't worry,' Carole said, patting him on the shoulder, 'Your secret's safe with me.'

He didn't see Rachel much during the morning. She spent most of it in her office, and Rob was thankful that he didn't have to face her. After lunch, Carole, emerged from the staff room first, and gave Rob a thumbs up as she passed. Rachel followed, and Rob was relieved to see a smile on her face. She joined him behind the counter.

'Rob, do you fancy doing a special job for me this afternoon?' she asked.

I'd do anything for you, Rachel, he thought. Special or not. Shine your shoes, carry your shopping, feed you peeled grapes while fanning you with ostrich feathers ... 'Sure,' he said. 'Whatever you want.'

'Well, the Crime section, and the Fantasy and SF sections are becoming a little overcrowded, and some of the books are beginning to look ... tired. We haven't weeded for ages. Would you take a spare trolley over, and go through them all? Look at the date stamps. You might want to make a note of this.' Rob peeled a sheet of paper off the memo pad beside the phone, and picked up a ballpoint pen, and scribbled as she continued. 'Anything that hasn't been borrowed for over two years, take it out. And also, anything that looks tatty, have a look at the date stamps. If it's something that looks popular, we'll replace it with a new one. Then, when you've finished, we'll put a couple of trolley-loads in the entrance and sell them all off for twenty pence a copy.'

'Great,' he said. 'Can I be cheeky, and ask for first refusal on the Science Fiction?' He could use this as an opportunity to re-stock his bookcase. 'If you don't mind, that is.'

'Course you can, Rob. Do that section first, if you like.'

Carole was walking past with a pile of returned computer games. 'You want to watch him, Rach. He'll make off with half the stock. Want me to spy on him, boss? Make sure he doesn't cheat?'

Rachel laughed. 'Don't be mean, Carole. I'm sure our Rob is above reproach.' She draped an arm loosely around his shoulders, and he had to control his breathing to keep from passing out on the spot. The warm glow being back in Rachel's good books gave him, lasted until it was time to go home.

'Oh Rob, look at all those,' Carole said, when she saw the two piles of books Rob had amassed for himself. She winked. 'I hope they're all legit. Here, you'll need something to carry them in.' She rummaged under the counter, and pulled out two of the used supermarket carrier bags which a few faithful users donated regularly, for the use of customers who didn't bring in their own bags.

He left carrying his bags of books, and didn't notice the woman waiting outside the library until she spoke, behind him.

'Rob.'

He turned. Joanne. And he'd been in such a good mood. Well, he had nothing to say to her. He stalked off toward the pavement.

'I don't blame you for not wanting to talk to me. I know Dennis came to see you.'

Rob swung round, and dropped the bags beside him. 'He called me a philanderer and a Casanova! In front of my boss and all my colleagues. Why did you tell him I made you leave the French class? You know it wasn't like that! I could have lost my job because of him. And you.'

'I'm really sorry, Rob,' she said, her eyes fixed on his shoes. 'I couldn't think of anything else to tell him. When he found out I'd stopped going, he was livid.' She raised her eyes to his, and lowered them again, this time focusing on his knees. 'It was his idea, you see. He paid for me to go to that class. He said if I learned to speak French I could get a better job.'

'Yes, but why not just tell him you didn't get on with it? You used me, Jo. I thought you wanted to see me every week because you liked my company.' Though, actually, she'd had a strange way of showing it.

'I know. It wasn't very … nice. After you stood up for me, too.' She twiddled with a tassel on her bag. 'I don't know what else to say.'

He looked at her, this downtrodden soul, and softened. It must have taken a lot of courage to come and apologise. 'It's okay. But you should learn to stand up for yourself, Jo. You'll end up …' What? Like him? 'Never mind. Perhaps you should get hold of some self-help books,' He should have hung onto the ones he had: he could have passed them on to her. 'Work on your confidence, and then you won't need to lie to that husband of yours, eh?' He touched her on the shoulder, picked up his bags, and left.

He let himself into the house. His mother was in the living room, sitting with her feet up on the footstool, looking elegant in a smart lilac suit. For a change, she was wearing make up.

'You look nice, Ma. How was your meal?'

'Lovely, thank you, dear. I'll have to go there again some time. The food was delicious and the service was excellent. We went out and sat in their garden after the meal. Beautiful roses, they've got.'

'You don't get out enough, Ma. I'll take you there for your birthday, if you like.'

'Oh, that would be wonderful. Do you want a cup of tea?' She went to stand up, but Rob put his hand out. 'You stay there and rest. I'll make it.' He put his carrier bags on the coffee table and headed for the kitchen.

'What are those, love?' his mother called.

He filled the kettle and switched it on, then went back to the living room. 'Just some withdrawn books.' He laughed. 'Cost me the grand total of two pounds forty.'

'Good idea. You can start filling your bookcase again. By the way, I found your bag of stuff.'

'Great. Did your friend mind carting them around in her car?'

'No, she was fine. We took them to the RSPCA shop in the end, because it was the easiest one for parking.'

Rob made the tea, and then sat and chatted for a while with his mother about her afternoon out. He climbed the stairs to his room, carrying the two bags of books. He wondered if Paddytum was 'back' yet, realising, with a pang of guilt, that he'd hardly spared him a thought since he left this morning.

He saw, as soon as he looked at his bed, that Paddytum wasn't there. He wasn't just 'absent'. He was physically not there. He'd gone.

TWENTY-SIX

Rob's gaze darted around the room. The rubbish bag still stood under the window where he'd left it. He rushed to the wardrobe and flung both doors open. The other bag and the box were where he'd left them, too. He opened the bag, even though he knew the bear couldn't possibly be in there. He went back to the bed and pulled it out from the wall. There wasn't a big enough gap for the bear to have fallen into it, but he looked anyway. He knew, just knew, that the only explanation for his bear's disappearance was the one he couldn't face.

He ran downstairs. Outside the living room door, he stood with his hands on the doorframe. He had to compose himself. If he appeared as frantic as he felt, his mother would be rattled. It was just a stuffed toy, for goodness sake. He took two long, slow, deep breaths, and went in.

'Ma, where's my teddy?' He felt stupid just asking, and a giggle threatened to rise up and escape from his throat.

His mother was sipping at her tea, and leafing through a magazine. 'Your teddy? Which teddy?'

'Frederick. He was on my bed.'

She flinched. 'Frederick? I didn't know you had one called Fred—'

'I mean Paddytum. Where is he?'

'Paddytum? He was in the bag with all the others. Oh!' She put her hand to her mouth. 'The bag had fallen over. Some of the toys were spilled out on the bed. I just gathered them all up and put them back in. And you did say you were getting rid of all your toys. I didn't think—'

Rob sank onto the armchair. 'He wasn't supposed to go. I was … keeping him.' He felt like a little boy of three again.

His mother stood and came over to him, and put her hand on his shoulder. Rob stared at the carpet. He couldn't look at her, didn't want her to see how upset he was at the loss of something made of fur fabric and stuffing.

'I'm sorry, son. You've had that bear a very long time. I ought to have realised you wouldn't want to let him go.' She kneaded his shoulder with her hand. 'Oh, I feel awful now.' Rob dared not speak. 'Perhaps we can get him back. The shop was about to close when we got there. They won't have put him out on display yet.'

A glimmer of hope. He looked up. Caught hold of his mother's hand. 'Sorry, Ma. It's not your fault. And I shouldn't be making such a fuss. But he was *special*.' Just *how* special the bear was, Rob couldn't possibly explain without giving her serious doubts about his sanity. 'Do you think he'll still be there? If I go first thing tomorrow?'

'Well, as I said, we only got there a few minutes before four, when they shut. They took the bag straight out the back. And they locked the door after us as soon we left, and turned the sign round.' She ruffled his hair. 'I don't think you're silly at all. That bear must hold lots of memories for you, Robbie. I can quite understand why you'd be upset. Look, you'll have to go down there first thing. Do you want me to come with you? They should remember me from today.' She frowned. 'Unless it's a different woman tomorrow morning, of course. Those places are run by volunteers.'

'No, it's okay, Ma. You've got work in the morning, haven't you? I'll go on my own. Any idea what time they open?'

'Not really, son. I think most charity shops open a bit later than the normal shops. If you get there about nine, you might have to hang about for a while, but you'll at least get in there before they have a chance to put him out on display, won't you?'

For the rest of the evening, Rob was subdued. He watched television with his mother, but couldn't really concentrate. Occasionally he glanced over at Maureen and caught her looking at him, concerned.

He wondered when Paddytum had woken up. Had he come round to discover he was in a black plastic bin bag, in the boot of a strange car? Or had he woken to find himself in a musty back room, surrounded by people's cast-offs? What if he never saw him again? He hadn't even had a chance to say goodbye. He hadn't been able to thank him for everything he'd done, for turning his life around, for putting him on the road to a future. He wanted to cry.

Rob tossed and turned all night, thoughts rolling around his head. He went over and over all the possible scenarios. That the volunteers in the charity shop had taken one look at his bear and thrown him straight in the rubbish; that one of them had taken a fancy to him and decided to take him home, or worse still, give him to a grandchild who was bound to treat him badly, pulling him about so he lost all his stuffing; not treating him with the respect he deserved.

Stop this, Robert, he almost heard Paddytum's scolding, telling him off for predicting the worst outcome to every situation, and that made him feel sad all over again.

Eventually, he got up, switched on his bedside lamp, and picked up one of his new books. He settled back against the pillows, trying to read to take his mind off it. It was no use. His mind kept drifting back to Paddytum, lying somewhere, confused, angry, and abandoned. He dropped the book onto the floor, and closed his eyes again, not bothering to switch off the light.

At around four, he heard the dawn chorus begin, and a little later the rattle and hum of the milk float.

When he next opened his eyes, the sun was streaming through the gap in his curtains. Oh no! What time was it? He grabbed his alarm clock and brought it close to his face. Ten twenty-five! Bloody hell, he'd overslept! Shit! Why hadn't his mother woken him? Then he remembered it was Saturday and she'd have left early.

He shot out of bed and pulled on the clothes he'd been wearing last night – no time to wash, no time for breakfast. He ran out down the path and in the direction of town. The bus would be quicker but he had no idea how long he'd have to wait. As he ran, pictures ran through his head, of Paddytum being bought and taken away from him, never to be seen again. Sweat trickled down his sides and the small of his back, cooling as he ran. He kept an eye out for a bus, a taxi, anything at all that would get him there quicker. He ran past a bicycle propped against railings outside Patel's Sub-Post Office and considered hijacking it. Then, as he glanced behind him to see if anyone would notice he saw, with relief, a bus approaching. Thank goodness, the stop was within easy reach and he slowed to a fast walk, then jabbed his arm out to stop the bus. He panted 'Town centre, mate,' to the driver, thrusting a pound coin into his hand, and tore off the ticket, waving away the twenty pence change. He perched on a seat near the front, trying to catch his breath, and hoping he wasn't too late.

The bus took only fifteen minutes to reach the shopping centre but, to Rob, it seemed hours. Each time the bus stopped to let more passengers on, Rob jiggled his leg impatiently. Anyone observing him would have thought him a terrorist, shifting impatiently in his seat, occasionally biting his knuckles, sweat pouring down his temples. At the stop before the shopping centre, an elderly man got on, and took an interminably long time to find his bus pass, with much muttering and tutting. Rob wanted to strangle him or, at least, jump up and pay his fare.

At the entrance to the shopping centre, Rob leapt off the bus before it had come to a complete halt, and raced round the corner, to the old part of town where the RSPCA shop stood. Finally, he stood in front of the old shop, panting. It looked as if it might once have been a ladies' boutique, or a gents' outfitters not much different from the one where his father had worked.

Rob pushed the door open, and a bell tinkled above his head. He wiped his sweating brow with the sleeve of his jacket, and looked around the shop. An elderly woman wearing an overall with an embroidered RSPCA logo approached him. She looked him up and down, taking in his dishevelled appearance, and glanced up past his head. Rob turned and following her gaze to a CCTV camera above the door, next to the bell. He had no time to wonder why a charity shop would have surveillance equipment, before she asked him if she could help him.

'I'm looking for a teddy bear,' he said.

The woman's wary expression softened. 'Oh, yes, we have plenty of those. In fact, I believe my colleague was putting out a new batch not long ago. Someone donated quite a few just yesterday. We'd been getting low, so that was handy, wasn't it, Mavis?'

Another grey-headed woman stood behind the cash register, unclipping gilt brooches from a purple velvet-covered pad, and rearranging them. 'It was, Rita. They go quickly, do teddies. Everybody loves a teddy.' She beamed at Rob, and he managed a half-smile back.

He looked at the other woman. 'Could you show me where they are, please?'

He followed her to a section near the back, where jigsaw puzzles and boxed games were piled high. Around the corner from those was a soft-toy menagerie. Rob scanned the pile quickly. Rabbits and dogs in unlikely colours sat side by side; a giraffe with its neck at a painful-looking angle, a furry dinosaur, and about ten teddy bears, six of which had been his. And there was Pandy. Pand*a*. His heart soared. It plummeted again as he moved his eyes back and forth over the stack of furries. No Paddytum.

'Are there any more?' he asked the woman called Rita.

'No, dear, we put all of them out. Like I said, we were running low on stock and—'

'There's one in particular. It *must* be here.' The woman narrowed her eyes at him. 'I'd better explain.' He took a deep breath. 'Most of these ones here—' He waved his hand over the furry pile, 'are ones my mum brought in, yesterday, but there was one that wasn't supposed to be in the bag she brought in. He got in there sort of by accident when the bag fell over and she put him in with the others but she wasn't meant to bring him.' He realised he was gabbling and stopped. 'Anyway, I need to get him back.'

Rita put her hands on her hips. 'Well, dear. You'll have to buy him back. We can't just hand him over to you, you know. We only have your word for it that he was yours.'

For goodness sake, Rob thought. I'm talking teddy bears here, not priceless paintings. 'Yes, of *course* I'd pay for him. After all it was our—my, mistake. But I can't see him here. Are you sure there isn't another one out the back, in your store room or warehouse or whatever it is?'

'Well, the only thing left back there is one of those Action Man things. Mavis left him because he wasn't wearing any clothes. It wouldn't be very nice to have a naked man on display.'

'Look, it's really important that I find him. I've had him since I was three. He's ... got sentimental value.' Rob was afraid he'd break down in front of this old lady if he had to explain any more. She looked up at him, studying his face.

'You do seem rather worked up about him. Perhaps Mavis knows where he is. Mavis?'

The woman at the counter had finished arranging her jewellery, and was now folding used supermarket bags. 'Yes, dear?'

'This young man is looking for his teddy bear which was brought along by mistake. You haven't sold one today, have you?' Rob fixed his eyes on Mavis, willing her to say no.

'Well, yes. I did sell a rather nice teddy not ten minutes ago, just before this gentleman came in.' Rob felt the blood drain from his face, and a cold sweat adding to the dampness of his already soggy clothes.

'What? What did it look like?' He tried to keep the panic out of his voice, and failed. He sensed Rita drawing away from him.

Mavis put a finger to her chin. 'Now, let me see ... It was about ... so big.' She held her hands apart like a fisherman who'd made a modest catch, 'and it had a rather grumpy expression. It was in very good condition, I thought, but not really what you'd call an *attractive* bear. I wouldn't have bought it, myself. I suppose the lady just took a fancy to it.'

'What lady?'

Mavis jumped. Rob hadn't realised he'd shouted. Rita shot a warning look at Mavis, and, as one, they looked up at the CCTV above the door.

'Don't you take that tone with my colleague, young man,' Rita said, drawing herself up to her full height of at least four feet eleven. 'Your actions are being recorded on our security camera, and we can call the police, you know. I'm the Manager, here, and I will *not* tolerate abuse of my staff.'

Hardly abuse, Rob thought. And what the hell did they need CCTV for, in a *charity* shop? Were they worried that a gang of international criminals was going to make off with one of their second-hand *souvenir of Margate* egg-cups, threadbare quilted potholders or knitted tea-cosies?

'I'm very sorry,' Rob said, hoping he sounded contrite, and trying to calm himself. 'It's really important I get my bear back. It probably sounds completely stupid and pathetic, but he means a great deal to me.'

The women looked at each other. Mavis shrugged. 'She was wearing a red—'

'Mavis, shhh.' Rita lowered her voice to a whisper. 'I'm not at all sure we should tell him. It's a breach of confidentiality.'

Confidentiality? Rob thought. You're a bloody charity shop, not MI5! We're talking teddy bears here, not State secrets. 'Well, if you could just give me a clue … you wouldn't really be telling me her identity, would you?'

Mavis seemed the more sympathetic of the two, so he targeted her with what he hoped was a pleading, desperate expression. He wanted to stop short of getting down on his knees and actually begging. But he would if he had to.

Mavis looked at Rita. Rita shrugged. 'On your own head be it, Mave. I'm washing my hands of any responsibility if you decide to divulge information regarding our clientèle.'

Mavis appeared to be struggling with her conscience. 'At least tell me if she put him in a bag,' Rob pleaded. 'If she didn't, and it was only a little while ago, I might be able to spot her and catch her up.'

Mavis shot a guilty glance at Rita.' The younger one just carried it in her arms. I think they were mother and daughter, and it was for the daughter's little girl.'

Rita frowned. 'Oh, you've said too much now, Mavis.' She turned to Rob. 'Now, young man, if you don't intend to make a purchase, I'd like you to leave the premises.'

'Okay,' Rob said. He smiled weakly at Mavis. 'Thanks for your help.'

Rita turned on her heel and headed toward the back of the shop. Rob pulled on the door, setting the bell tinkling overhead.

'Excuse me?' he looked round to see Mavis standing next to him. 'The older lady was wearing a short red jacket, and her daughter had blonde hair, you know, done in that sort of spiky style they all wear. She was wearing a leather jacket with a fur collar, and white trousers.' She turned her head towards the back of the shop, briefly, before continuing in a whisper. 'They said something about going for lunch at the new Italian place in the Square. You know, the one with all the tables outside. They asked

167

if I knew if it was any good, and I told them I'd heard it was popular.'

'Mavis,' Rob said. 'I could kiss you.' Mavis backed away, looking nervous. 'It's all right; I'm not going to. Thank you. Thank you so much.'

'Well, don't tell anyone I told you.' She had another quick look towards the back. 'She's a bit high-handed. Has ideas above her station, that Rita. Just because they made her Manageress. I hope you find your teddy bear, dear.'

Rob headed back to the shopping centre, so he could cut through it to the Square. He had to hurry. He hoped Mavis was right about where the women had gone. It occurred to him that she'd just made it up to get rid of him. Or perhaps the women had changed their minds about eating, and were speeding off somewhere in a car. Paddytum might, even now, be in the hands of a strange toddler, his ears being pulled, and his eyes being poked with lollipops. Rob tried to push all these thoughts, and worse, away as he wove through the crowds of Saturday shoppers.

Finally, he reached the Square. It was bordered on one side by a row of small shops, one selling pottery and gifts, a patisserie, and a boutique which specialised in clothes for ladies of a certain age and income. The other three sides comprised eating-places – all with tables outside – a French bistro, an American burger bar, and the *Trattoria Napolitana*. The green, white and red banners enclosing the *al fresco* area outside the *Trattoria* looked bright and new. This must be the place Mavis had meant.

He walked up closer to the *Trattoria*, and scanned the tables. Very few were occupied, and none by a pair of women. The clock on the small brick-built monument in the middle of the Square said twenty past eleven. It was early yet for lunch, and they probably hadn't been coming straight here. Oh dear, Rob thought. Perhaps they weren't coming here at all, and all this would have been a complete waste of time. Should he go in search of the women, or stay here and wait? He wouldn't know where to even begin to look, in a big shopping centre. He crossed the road to stand outside the patisserie. His stomach clenched at the sight of the exquisite cakes and cream-laden pastries in the window, reminding him he'd had no breakfast. He couldn't possibly eat, though, not now.

He'd been standing there about five minutes, watching the back doors of the shopping centre, when a pair of women emerged. His heart leapt. One wore a light cotton scarlet jacket, and the tall young woman with her sported a black leather jacket with a brown furry collar, and had spiked blonde hair. He groaned; neither woman was holding Paddytum. But the older one carried a large, bulging white paper bag with cord handles, bearing the name of a women's clothing store. His heart began to pound.

He waited where he was while the pair took seats at a table at the edge of the *Trattoria*'s seating area, and, as they each perused a large menu, he ambled casually over to look at the chalkboard a couple of tables away from them. The bag was on the ground, just yards from his feet. He slid his eyes from the list of pizzas and pasta dishes, to the left and down. Something beige and furry was just visible inside the bag. His heart stopped, and then started to hammer again. He froze to the spot. He was close enough to grab the bag by its handles and run off. For just a second, Rob thought he could do it. Until his mind took over with a picture of himself being manhandled by a couple of very large police officers and carted off to the station as a common thief. No, that wouldn't work. And how would he explain why he'd stolen a bag of women's clothing? He'd have to think of something else.

He approached the two women and cleared his throat. The older lady looked up.

'We're not quite ready to order yet. Oh, unless you want to take our drink order? What would you like, Julie?'

'Oh, I'm not a waiter,' Rob said. He looked down, surreptitiously, into the bag on the ground. Now he could see Paddytum. 'I think ... I think you might have bought something of mine ... from a charity shop, not long ago.' He pointed into the bag, 'That's my teddy bear.'

The woman looked at her daughter, and raised her eyebrows, before looking back at Rob. The daughter glared at him.

'Well, actually, I think you'll find it's *our* teddy bear now,' the older woman said in tones of crushed ice. 'Or, I should say, it's my granddaughter's teddy bear.'

'Yes, it's for my little girl,' Julie chipped in. 'She'll be over the moon when she sees it. Sorry, chum. If you didn't want it to be sold, you shouldn't have given it away to charity.'

Rob pulled up a seat from the adjoining table, causing the two women to look at each other again, in disbelief.'

'You see, the thing is. I didn't,' Rob said. 'My mum did. By mistake.'

'So,' Julie said, 'you expect us to just hand over this bear you say is yours, do you?'

'Oh no!' said Rob. 'No, not at all. I'll give you what you paid for it.' The women looked unimpressed. 'More. I'll give you more than you paid. Double.' They stared at him. 'I'll give you enough to buy a brand new one. Look. He's old. I mean, I've had him since I was three. That makes him ... thirty-eight years old. Wouldn't your little girl prefer a new one?' Rob pulled out his wallet, and started looking through it. He only had a ten pound note. Damn.

'Hang on a minute. If he's so old, does that make him collectible?' Julie said, her eyes narrowed to slits. 'Here, Mum. I bet that's why he wants it. He's probably an antique dealer or something.'

'No. No, I just work in a library. An ordinary lending library. I wouldn't know an antique if it came up and bit me. Honestly.' He thought he might cry if they wouldn't believe him. 'Look. He's just an ordinary teddy my mum bought for me in an ordinary toy shop when I was three. He hasn't even got a label. Have a look if you don't believe me.' He looked around the square. Next to the boutique was a bank, and outside the bank was a cash-point, an ATM. He pointed. 'Name your price. I'll go to the machine and draw out as much money as you want for him.'

The older woman stood. 'Now, wait a minute. I know exactly what's going on here. You must take us for fools!' She turned to her daughter. 'We need to be very careful, Julie.' She reached into the bag and lifted Paddytum out by one arm, and held him at arms length. 'I've heard about people like you. If you're willing to pay so much money for a scruffy old thing that only cost us a pound, there must be more to it than meets the eye.' She held Paddytum as far away from her as she could. 'He's stuffed full of illegal drugs, isn't he?'

170

'No! Really, he's not. It's like I told you. He's not stuffed full of anything … except stuffing! I'm not a drug dealer, or an antique dealer. I'm just an ordinary bloke who wants his old teddy bear back.'

She thrust the bear at Rob. 'Take him.' Rob took the ten-pound note out of his wallet, and tried to give it to the woman, but she batted his hand away. 'No, I don't want your dirty money!'

'But—'

'Just go.' She turned to Julie again. 'I think we had a lucky escape, darling. We could have been arrested for possession.'

'No, I'm telling the truth. I'm not like that. Please take this. I'm just so grateful to have him back.' He hugged Paddytum to his chest.'

Julie stood and plucked the ten pounds out of Rob's hand. 'Well, he may not be a drug runner, Mum, but I think he's got a screw loose.' She gave Rob a withering look. 'You'd better go, you nutter, and take your stupid bear with you. I didn't much like the look of it anyway. It looks dead grumpy. It'd probably give our Kayleigh nightmares.'

Rob didn't need telling twice. He stood up, still holding Paddytum close, and fast-walked away, just in case they decided to change their minds and call the police, demanding to have Paddytum cut open in a search for crack and heroin.

As he reached the door of the shopping centre, he heard the voice he'd feared he'd never hear again. 'Well, Robert. You took your time.'

TWENTY-SEVEN

Rob made his way through the underpass leading to the big park on the outskirts of the town centre, clutching the bear to his chest, and ignoring the stares of passers-by. He wished he'd brought along his backpack, to put Paddytum in, but he'd left in such a rush that such thoughts had been beyond him. Besides, he now realised he had only half-believed his rescue mission would be successful. He badly needed a shower, but couldn't face getting on a bus just yet. After the stresses of the last hour, he needed to sit down and catch his breath. What if those women did decide to call the police? He'd be easy enough to find: a tall, sweating man carrying a stuffed bear and looking frazzled.

Let them, he thought. At least he had Paddytum back now. What was the worst that could happen? If they cut him open they'd soon find they were wrong, and he could always sew him up again. He glanced over his shoulder as he walked. Nobody seemed to be in pursuit.

The park was full of people – singles, couples and groups, sitting and lying on the grass, soaking up the August sunshine. A young family sat on a large picnic blanket, unpacking a cool-box and laying out clingfilm-wrapped sandwiches and bowls of salad, reminding him he was starving. In the distance was a kiosk, with a board outside advertising ice cream and cans of drink, and he was suddenly seized by a raging thirst, due, probably, to the amount of fluid he'd lost in sweat. He put a hand in his trouser pocket, and pulled out a twenty pence piece and a few coppers. Well, that wouldn't get him very much. It looked as if he'd have to walk home, after all. But he really needed a sit down first.

He took a seat on a bench by the boating lake, and watched a couple of girls paddling across it in a pedalo. The sight of the cool-looking water made him thirstier still, so he closed his eyes. The bear hadn't said a word since they'd left the shopping centre, which was fine with Rob. He wasn't in the mood for his recriminations. There'd be time enough later to discuss his adventure.

A few minutes later, the bear spoke. 'Rob, wake up. Look who's here.'

He opened his eyes and looked up. Standing by the bench, grinning down at him, was the last person in the world he wanted to see, at the same time as being the only person in the world he wanted to see. He blinked.

'Rachel. Fancy seeing you here!'

'I was just about to say the same to you,' she said. If she thought it strange that he was sitting on a park bench in broad daylight on a Saturday afternoon, cuddling his teddy bear, she gave no sign of it. 'Mind if I join you?'

He shifted along the bench, allowing her to sit, and watched her as she slid the strap of her large fabric bag off her shoulder, and set it down on the bench beside her. Her long hair, with the colour and gloss of freshly exposed conkers, flowed loose onto her shoulders. She wore a calf-length dark blue cotton skirt, the wide suede belt emphasising her tiny waist. The cerulean blue of her fitted T-shirt accentuated the blue of her eyes, her pupils large, like those of a child, despite the bright sunlight. What a time for her to turn up, when he must look dishevelled and sweaty. He hoped he wasn't too smelly. He wished he could disappear, and he wished he could stay here with her forever.

She rested her back against the bench with a sigh.

'Gorgeous, isn't it?' she said. *You* are, he thought. She reached into her bag and pulled out a small plastic bottle of water, uncapped it, and took a swig, then offered the bottle to Rob. Oh, you angel. He took it and tipped it back, resisting the impulse to drink the whole bottle in one chug.

'Hey, you're thirsty,' she said, watching him. He held the half-empty bottle out to her. 'No, keep it. I've got another in my bag. I can just refill it in the Green Room.' Rob raised his eyebrows in a question. 'I'm on my way to the Cornmarket. We have our matinée today at two. I thought I'd cut through here and make the most of the lovely weather, since I'll be spending the rest of today stuck in a dressing room. That is, when I'm not out on stage.' She looked at her watch, and sighed again. 'Why ever the Society decided to have our G & S show in the middle of summer I'll never know. Still, I can sit here for another half hour or so.'

'How's the show going?' Rob asked. 'I'm coming along to see it tonight.'

She sat up and turned to face him, a look of delight and surprise on her face. 'Really? That's great.' She added, quietly, 'Are you bringing your mother?'

'No. I am going with a lady, though ...' Surely he had imagined the flicker of disappointment which crossed Rachel's face. 'Just a friend ... I met at the library. A Mrs Pickering.'

'Deirdre?'

Deirdre! Not Debbie.

'Oh, I didn't know that was her first name,' Rob said. 'Do you know her, then?'

'I've met Deirdre a few times, yes. Apart from at the library, I mean. Smashing lady. She's one of the Society's most ardent supporters. Did she tell you she used to be their star soprano?'

Rob smiled. 'Actually, that's what she says you are.'

Rachel returned his smile shyly. 'Well, I don't know about that. How come she invited you? Are you a Gilbert and Sullivan fan? You never said.'

'Oh, Robert! This is going well. Don't mess it up,' Paddytum said. 'Did you see her face when you said you were taking a woman? She has her heart set on you, my boy, take it from me.'

Rob took another sip of water, ignoring him. As glad as he was to have him back, he wished the bear knew when to keep quiet. 'She used to know my dad. Years back. They were at school together, and then in the Savoyards. That's what it was called before it was *FLOATS*. But I expect you knew that.'

'Oh.' Her eyes widened, and she put a palm to her forehead. 'Oh! How silly of me. Of course! *Handle*. I didn't make the connection. Was he called Eric?'

'Yes. Why? Have you heard of him?'

'Heard of him? He's a legend.'

'Why?' he asked, over the strange noise, like a gasp, he heard in his head.

'He died very young, didn't he? Maybe that's why. Oh, I'm sorry, Rob, that was insensitive of me.'

'No, it's fine. Do they remember him, then?'

'They remember him all right. There's this shield, you see. The Eric Handle Memorial Shield.'

Rob heard another gasp from the bear. What was bothering him? Perhaps it was the heat. 'What's that, then?'

'It's presented every year to a *FLOATS* member. For outstanding service. Sometimes it's awarded for a particularly good performance, sometimes just for promoting the company, selling tickets, working hard on the scenery and so on.' She picked at her fingernails. 'I won it last year.'

'I never even knew about it. Wonder if my mum does.'

'Well, I'd be surprised if they didn't tell her. You'll have to ask her.' She turned to look at him, her enormous blue eyes gazing straight into his. 'There's a little photograph album that goes with the shield. With pictures of him from some of the shows he was in.' She studied his face. 'I can't believe I didn't make the connection, Rob. You're the image of your dad.'

He tried to tear his eyes away but couldn't. God, she was stunning, up close in the sunlight. Suddenly he couldn't think of a single thing to say. All his words had dried up and it was as if his tongue was stuck to the bottom of his mouth with superglue.

'What are you waiting for, Robert?' Paddytum said. 'Now's your chance.'

What does the stupid bear expect me to do? Rob thought, with irritation. His answer came with the sudden tingle in his jaw, and Rob thought, Oh bloody hell no not here not in public not now with her with Rachel you can't Paddytum you can't, please.

But his diaphragm drew down, sucking in a lungful of air. A really deep breath. The amount of breath you'd only need if you were about to—No, not that, you can't do this to me.

And his mouth opened and the air rushed out past his vocal cords, and Rob heard a voice, and it was his voice, only he'd never, ever heard it like this before.

> *'Oh, is there not one maiden breast,*
> *Which does not feel the moral beauty.*
> *Of making worldly interest,*
> *Supporting it to scenes of duty.'*

He tried to stop singing, and he tried to look away, but he could do neither. Rachel appeared, also, to be transfixed. He was vaguely aware that a woman walking her Labrador behind them had stopped, and two boys, who had been having a kick-about with a football, stood watching, yet the voice carried on. And then, to his horror his hand, the one nearest to Rachel, lifted off Paddytum, reached out, and took hold of Rachel's. She didn't pull away. She simply carried on gazing into his eyes.

'Who would not give up willingly
all matrimonial ambition
To rescue such a one as I
from his unfortunate position,
From his unfortunate position?'

He stopped, and looked at his hand, holding Rachel's. Should he let go? She didn't seem to mind. In fact, she clasped his hand tighter.

'Wow!' she said. She blinked at him. 'Wow! Where did that come from?'

'I have no idea,' Rob said. 'Sorry.'

She was still making no move to let go of his hand. The boys started to kick their ball about again, and the woman moved on, with her dog, but twice looked back at them, smiling.

'God, Rob, why would you apologise for that? It gave me shivers! Talk about hiding your light under a bushel. First the teddy bear act, and now this.' He watched in bemused wonder as she reached up with her free hand and wiped a tear, which had trickled from the corner of her eye. 'That was Frederic's song, wasn't it?'

'It was?' He looked down at Paddytum.

When he looked up, Rachel was grinning. 'No, not that Frederick. The one from *Pirates*.'

'Pirates?'

'*Of Penzance*. Don't you know what you were singing?' She shook her head. 'Rob, you're a funny one,' she said, giving his hand another squeeze and then letting it go. 'You absolutely *have* to audition for *FLOATS*. Your voice is amazing. You're a much better tenor even than James.'

'A tenor? Is that what I am? I have no idea. I don't sing.'

Rachel took one look at his wide-eyed, bemused expression and threw her head back and laughed.

'You're too funny, Rob. You just delivered a note perfect rendition of that song, in one of the most wonderful tenor voices I've ever heard, and you say you don't sing.'

Her laughter was infectious. He couldn't help it; he was suddenly in fits of laughter too.

They were both wiping away tears when Rachel stopped, and looked at her watch again. She took a deep breath, and said, 'Look, I've got to go or I'll be late. When you see me tonight, you'll see just why I have to be there ages before the performance.' She stood and picked up her bag. 'Rob, come up to the bar after the show. We're having a last night party, and I'd love to introduce you to some of the gang.'

'Are you sure that'll be all right?'

'Absolutely. Deirdre usually comes along to it, in any case. Just tell her I invited you.'

And then, she was gone.

What on earth had just happened? He'd ask Paddytum, but he suspected he'd disappeared again; he must have expended all his effort and energy in making him sing. He rubbed his jaw, curious that there was no trace of the tingle, which normally lingered for at least twenty minutes after Paddytum's interventions.

'Shouldn't we go home, Robert?' Rob jumped. He looked around. There was nobody nearby, but he kept his voice low, all the same.

'What … why are you still here? I mean, why didn't you—'

'Actually, I'd prefer to discuss what happened yesterday, if you don't mind.'

'Oh dear,' he said, shamefaced. 'I'm sorry about that. But I didn't know the blooming bag was going to fall over, did I?' He rubbed the bear's head. 'Was it really awful for you? I mean, when did you wake up?'

'Probably when the bag fell over. And then your mother came in, and it all happened so quickly after that. I was very afraid, Robert.'

'It's a shame my mum can't hear you, like I can.'

'I know. I tried calling out to Min, but I couldn't make her hear me at all.' Min? Rob thought. Who's Min? 'The next thing I knew, I was in that car, in the dark, headed goodness knew where.

177

And last night, Robert, stuck in that store room among all those musty clothes …'

'I'm very sorry. But you're back now, and that's all that matters. I was worried sick, if it's any consolation. Come on.' He stood up. 'Let's go home.' Something was still bothering him, though. 'I still don't get why you didn't pass out or whatever it is you normally do. After making me sing like that.'

'Oh, that's easy. I *didn't* make you.'

'But … but my jaw tingled. And then you made me take a breath. I felt you do it.'

'Yes, and that was *all* I did. I was trying to get you to say something to Rachel. I had no idea you were going to burst into song. You did that all on your own.'

Rob sat down again on the bench. 'But I don't even know that song. I've never heard it before in my life.'

'Well, apparently you have. And you sang it very nicely, too, I must say. It even surprised me. Rachel is absolutely correct. You're an exceptionally fine tenor.'

Rob rubbed at one temple. He felt the beginnings of a headache, probably from dehydration. 'No. It must have been you; I had my hand on your—' And then he remembered he hadn't, not all the way through. 'Oh my God!' He covered his face with his hands. 'Was that me … grabbing her hand? I mean, on purpose, all by myself? Whatever must she think of me?'

'Well, yes. I must say I wondered what you were doing. But she didn't seem to object, did she?'

No, she didn't, Rob thought. But she was just being nice. 'How did I know that song, then, if you say you didn't help me? It's not even from any of the Gilbert and Sullivan things I've seen, as far as I can remember.'

The silence was so long Rob thought Paddytum wasn't going to answer, but then he said, 'Your father sang those songs often in your presence. He even used to sing them to you as lullabies when you were a tiny baby. The one you just sang was your very favourite. As it was … his.'

'Oh. So it's been lurking in my – what – my subconscious, or whatever?'

'I suppose so,' Paddytum said. 'Now, let's get home. I hope you don't mind me saying, but you're a little pungent.'

178

'Thanks a bunch, mate.'

Rob didn't wonder until later how the bear he'd been given on his third birthday would know what songs his dad had sung him when he was a baby.

TWENTY-EIGHT

Rob arrived at the Cornmarket theatre at 7.30pm, dressed in his new olive-green peachskin shirt and cream chinos. His mother had told him the shirt looked smart and really suited his colouring. The chinos were loose at the waist but were still a better fit than any of his other trousers. 'You'll soon disappear if you turn sideways, Robbie,' his mother had told him. 'You're not overdoing this diet, are you?'

Deirdre Pickering stood in the foyer of the theatre, chatting with the Mayor and his Lady Mayoress, but she broke away from them with a wave when she spotted him. She looked glamorous in a purple crushed silk evening dress, and Rob wondered if he should have worn a suit, but when he surveyed the foyer, most of the other people gathered there, and lining the curving staircase up to the bar, had opted for smart casual.

'Robert. There you are. You have your ticket?'

'Yes, thanks.' He patted his back pocket. 'Oh. Would you like a drink, Mrs Pickering?' he asked, taking his wallet out.

'Deirdre, please.' She glanced at the tiny gold bracelet watch on her wrist. 'Not for me, thank you, dear. It's getting close to curtain-up, and I do hate to hurry a drink. But perhaps we could pre-order some for the interval?'

As they made their way over to the long counter, where front-of-house staff were taking orders and payment for interval refreshments, he said,' I wouldn't mind a chat with you, actually. In the interval.' She looked at him, enquiringly. 'About my dad. I mean, if you don't mind?'

'Of course I don't mind, dear. I'd love to tell you anything you'd like to ask me.' But she looked puzzled. They ordered a gin and tonic and a Budweiser, and Rob paid, then they headed for the auditorium. All afternoon Rob's head had been buzzing. He'd tried having a nap after his shower, to try and get rid of his headache, but in the end he'd ended up getting up again and going for a long walk. The incident in the park, or rather, what the bear said afterwards, had made him wonder. Some things about

Paddytum didn't add up. Or rather, they added up to a conclusion Rob didn't want to face. He didn't believe in that sort of thing, did he? But then, he wouldn't have believed in a talking teddy bear either, a few months ago.

They took their seats: good ones, three rows from the front, and dead centre, with an excellent view of the stage. As the lights dimmed and the chatter faded, Rob was transported back to the first time he'd come to this theatre to see his father performing. He felt an echo of the thrill, the magic he'd felt then. He shivered in anticipation.

He stared at the undulating folds of the burgundy velvet curtain and lost himself in the long overture and then, as it ended, the curtain rose, revealing an assortment of men of all ages, shapes and sizes, in Japanese dress.

Within minutes, Rob was immersed in the story. The 'wand'ring minstrel', Nanki-Poo, who must surely be the James Rachel had mentioned, made his entrance, and sang his aria in a competent but not outstanding voice. The man playing Pooh-Bah was pomposity personified, and had the audience in gales of laughter. A hush fell over the auditorium as the Lord High Executioner, Ko-Ko, made his grand entrance.

This was the part his father had played, which Deirdre had described as a 'triumph'. The middle-aged man playing the role now had chosen to portray him as a Cockney wide-boy, and did so with panache. What had his father's interpretation been like? He remembered him in the two shows he'd seen, and he could suddenly imagine exactly how his father would have played it. He heard in his head exactly how his dad would have spoken Ko-Ko's dialogue – almost as if he heard it every day.

After Ko-Ko had described the contents of his 'little list', about thirty schoolgirls, some of them a good few years past school-leaving age, flocked on stage like giggling geese, and there was Rachel in their midst, looking like a Japanese doll in a kimono the palest of pale pinks, carrying a fan the size of a peacock's tail. When the 'Three Little Maids' sang, Rachel's voice rang out across the auditorium, outshining her two companions. He looked at Deirdre, and she beamed at him.

Near the end of the first act, a single line of dialogue from Ko-Ko jolted Rob out of his immersion in the story:

181

'Am I never to be permitted to soliloquise?'

He knew exactly when and where he'd heard it before, and it was another step towards confirmation of his growing suspicions.

The curtain came down after the first act finale, and Rob followed Deirdre to the bar. They found their drinks on the counter which ran the entire length of one wall, and Deirdre said, 'Let's take these downstairs, where we're less likely to be disturbed.'

They found a quiet corner by the box office with a sofa and a table.

'So, Robert,' she said. 'Was there anything in particular you wanted to know?' She tapped her chin. 'I wonder what it is you think I can tell you that you couldn't ask your mother.'

'The thing is, Mrs Pick—Deirdre,' he said, 'It's tricky, with my ma. She doesn't talk about Dad.' He sighed. 'Or, if she does, she always changes the subject quickly.'

'Oh dear,' Deirdre said. 'That's a great shame. How frustrating. Is it just that she finds it upsetting? Because of … how he died?'

He looked at her, wondering if he should just come out with it. Would it be disloyal?

'She doesn't talk about him because she found out something that … upset her … after he died.' He stopped, and swallowed. 'The thing is, she thinks he was having an affair.'

'Eric?' Deirdre gaped at him, her eyes wide. 'Never in a million years! He adored your mother. He was always talking about his Min.'

Rob froze. 'Min?'

Deirdre studied his face. 'Did you never hear him call her that?' She took a sip of her gin and tonic. 'Perhaps not. When he first started seeing her, he called her Mini because she was so petite, so tiny next to him. Mini-Maureen. Or Mini-Mo. And then he shortened it to Min.' She sipped again. 'Where did she get the idea that Eric was being unfaithful?'

Rob repeated the story his mother had told him about the guard's words at the funeral.

Deirdre's brow wrinkled in thought as she stared at the low table in front of them. 'Debbie … I can't recall anyone in the Savoyards with that name when your father was there. Oh, wait. Miss Robinson, our accompanist. *Her* name was Deborah, but she was as old as the hills. And besides, nobody would have dared shorten her name.' She looked at Rob. 'Perhaps she was a work colleague? I honestly can't believe it of him, though. He was so devoted to his family.'

'No, he only had male colleagues. And clients, come to that.'

'Mmm, I suppose so.' Deirdre played with the cocktail stick in her glass. 'Well, perhaps, if he was losing consciousness when he said this name, he was just ... rambling. They say one's life flashes before one, when one is ... dying.' She looked up. 'It could even have been a childhood playmate. Couldn't that explain it?'

'Yes, I wondered if it was something like that. But my mum has it fixed in her mind now. She doesn't even have any photographs of Dad up anywhere in the house.'

Deirdre shook her head. 'Oh dear, that is dreadfully sad. For you both.' She took another sip, reminding Rob he hadn't even touched his beer. He picked up his glass and swigged it. Deirdre continued. 'Well, I suppose I can understand it – such a shock to hear something like that, on top of the dreadful blow she ... you both ... had just received.'

'I suppose so.' Rob said, and took another mouthful. 'There was something else I wanted to ask.'

Deirdre nodded.

'You said the other day, at the library, about my bear being called Frederick, after him. My dad.' He gave her a long look. 'Only, his name – his first name – was George. And his middle name was Eric, not Frederick.'

Deirdre smiled. 'Yes, but Eric wasn't the name his parents gave him.' Rob gave her a quizzical look. 'I don't suppose you've ever seen his birth certificate? Or your parents' marriage certificate?' He shook his head. 'I don't think he ever changed it legally.'

'His name was Frederick?'

'His middle name. He hated it. It all started with a rather trivial incident at school. Very silly really.'

'Why? What happened?'

Deirdre leaned back in her seat. 'Well, it was during a music lesson, in the second form. We used to sit next to each other in Music. I suppose that was when we started to be friends. We were studying Handel's Messiah; the music teacher had brought in an

LP. I don't suppose you remember those.' Rob nodded, and she carried on. 'He played some excerpts, and then told us a little about the composer.' She paused. 'And it caused enormous merriment when the class realised that your father's name was ...'

Rob's eyes widened in realisation. 'Oh no! It wasn't, was it?'

She nodded. 'George Frederick Handle. I mean, honestly, what must his parents have been thinking?'

Rob had only a vague memory of his grandparents, but he suspected the closest they'd ever come to classical music was Mantovani's Greatest Hits. 'Perhaps they didn't even realise ... So, that was why he dropped the Frederick? Because of a bit of teasing at school?' He shook his head.

'I know. It did seem something of an over-reaction, but your father ... well; he was always a sensitive soul. Artistic temperament, I suppose ...' She tailed off, and gazed into the distance.

Rob studied her face. She may not be the mysterious Debbie, he thought, but I wonder if there was something there. At least, on her side.

Deirdre sighed, and continued. 'Any other boy would probably have laughed it off and forgotten about it in a day or two but he announced, the next day, that he wanted us all to call him Eric from now on. The teachers weren't in on it, and they still called him George, of course. But before long, everyone was calling him Eric, and Eric he remained. By the time we left school, most people had forgotten he'd ever had any other name. Why he chose it, I have no idea.' She drained her glass.

'I wonder why my mum's never mentioned it.'

'Well, she's only ever really known him as Eric, don't forget. I mean, she'll have known what his given names were; he'd have had to sign the register as George Frederick when they married. Perhaps she didn't think it was important, and if she hasn't been talking about him ...'

Rob remembered his mother's face yesterday, when he came down and asked where his bear was. Where Frederick was.

'I found it ironic, later, that he dropped the name Frederick,' Deirdre said. She looked at her watch. 'Oh good, I think we still have a minute or two. Because it was also the name of the character he most yearned to play, and couldn't.'

184

Paddytum, in the park, this afternoon. *It was your very favourite song. As it was his.*

'He could never play Frederic from *The Pirates of Penzance*—'

'Because his voice was too low. He was a baritone who longed to be a tenor. And especially that role. He always had to make do with Major-General Stanley.' She looked at Rob. 'Do you know *Pirates?*'

'Not really, no.'

'The Major General's a great part. With one of the best G & S "Patter" songs. Are you familiar with that term?'

'Are they those tongue-twister-y ones? Like—' His eyes lit up, and he sang softly, '*I am the very model of a modern Major-General, I've something something something something animal and mineral*—'

Deirdre laughed and gave a little clap. 'Exactly! Very good, Robert. Your dad was the master of all those, so he was always first choice for the comic baritone roles. But deep down he longed to be the dashing young tenor lead, like Nanki-Poo, or Richard Dauntless from *Ruddigore*. or Marco from *The Gondoliers*, or—'

'—Frederic from *Pirates.*'

'Him especially,' she said, looking up as a voice on the PA system announced the final call for the second act. Rob realised he hadn't heard the previous announcement. He finished his drink, and he and Deirdre returned to their seats.

Rob could hardly concentrate on the performance during the first few songs, his head was buzzing with what he'd learned. Even seeing Rachel again, her pink kimono now swapped for a jewelled white one, for Yum-Yum's wedding day, didn't help to take his mind off things completely.

His mentor, it seemed, had been giving him subtle clues all along. Another line of Ko-Ko dialogue, towards the end, '*I prefer to be a disembodied spirit.*' made him shake his head, sadly.

But why hadn't he recognised the voice? And what was he supposed to do now he knew the truth?

TWENTY-NINE

Rachel looked out into the audience as she and James stepped forward from the rest of the company into thunderous applause. She quickly found Rob, having located him earlier, a few rows back in the front centre stalls, just after she'd finished her aria, her big solo. She'd scanned the auditorium quickly and her eyes had gone straight to him. He had smiled back at her. Or perhaps he had been smiling anyway, like the rest of the crowd.

The company took two curtain calls – the norm for the last night, and then a little girl from one of the local primary schools ran from the wings, dressed in a pretty dress bought, no doubt, just for the occasion, and presented her with a bouquet of pink and white roses, before the curtain fell for the last time, and she left the stage. She wove her way through the beaming faces of her fellow performers, elated at another successful production, everyone calling out 'well done' and 'see you at the party', back to the dressing room she shared with Pitti-Sing and Peep-Bo, in real life called Karen and Alison. No 'Star' dressing rooms for the Principals in a provincial amateur production. The men's and women's choruses fared even worse, crowded together in four large rooms, bumping elbows and bottoms as they changed in and out of their costumes, and fighting for space around the small mirrors to apply and remove their make-up. But she'd served her time as a chorus member, both here and in Swansea, and she appreciated the extra space.

She peeled off her false eyelashes, wiped away the thick black eye-liner, and rubbed cream into the ivory base, before wiping that off, too, finally dressing in her normal clothes and hanging up her kimono for the last time. Or at least until the next time they decided it was time to do The Mikado. She opened up her own make up bag, and applied a little blusher, mascara and lipstick, ready for the party. She hoped Rob would be there. He had intruded on her thoughts frequently since this afternoon.

Once upstairs, she looked around the bar, her heart sinking. There was Deirdre Pickering, standing with a crowd of local dignitaries, talking animatedly, as much with her hands as with her mouth, ever the actress. But no sign of Rob. She was tempted to go and ask Deirdre if he'd gone home, but decided, instead, to go and join Peter Simmonds, who'd played Pooh-Bah, and Maria Jones-Matthews, a secondary school head teacher and their majestic and very scary Katisha.

'Another one over and done with,' Peter said, in his broad Mancunian accent. 'Looking forward to a nice long rest before the next one, Rach?'

Rachel laughed. 'Yes. But I'm fully prepared for the post-production blues, aren't you? I always feel down in the dumps for at least a week afterwards. It's like a bereavement, isn't it? Or the break-up of a relationship,' She took a glass of white wine off a tray which passed under her nose.

'Oh, me too,' Maria said. 'It's probably because we all fall just a little in love with the current show while we're doing it, and all the songs, and even each other, I suppose.'

'Did you fall in love with me, Maria?' Peter asked, giving Maria a broad wink.

'Behave yourself, Pete,' she replied, shaking a finger at him, the nail still bearing Katisha's black and red varnish. 'I'm a respectable, happily married woman, and I never dally with cast members.' She looked over Rachel's shoulder. 'Ooh, who is that rather handsome chap hovering next to Deirdre Pickering? He keeps looking over here. Is he a friend of yours, Pete?'

Rachel swung round, her heart suddenly in overdrive. She put her glass down on a table and went over to Rob.

'Hello! Oh, I'm so glad you came.' She turned to Deirdre. 'Do you mind if I borrow Rob, Deirdre? I'd like to introduce him to a few of the others.'

'Feel free, dear,' Deirdre said. 'I expect he'd rather hang around with you youngsters than with an old lady like me, anyway.' She waggled her fingers at Rob. 'Off you go. And thank you so much for your company tonight. It made a nice change from having Graham sitting next to me looking bored.'

'And thank you so much for inviting me,' Rob said. 'I loved it. It was fantastic.' He looked down at Rachel. 'And you were amazing,' he said, blushing. 'Your voice is just … brilliant.'

'Hey, you're not so bad yourself,' she said. 'Deirdre, did you know Rob can sing? I mean, really sing. And he's a tenor.'

'Oh, I don't know about that.' Rob said, looking anxious.

Rachel laughed. 'Don't worry, Rob, I'm not going to ask you to prove it,' She flashed him a grin. 'Yet.' She linked her arm through his, and led him over to the other group saying quietly, on the way, 'And I'm not going to tell anyone how I know, either.'

Rob smiled sheepishly. 'I'm very relieved to hear that.'

'Pete, Maria, this is Rob. He works with me. His father used to be a member of the Society.'

'Nice to meet you, mate,' Peter said. 'So, is our Rachel planning to rope you into our ranks then? Are you planning to follow in your dad's footsteps?'

'Yes please,' Maria said. 'We're crying out for men. Always.'

'I'm not really a performer,' Rob said.

Rachel winked at him. 'He says that. But he is really. He just doesn't realise it yet.'

'So, were you two in the show?' Rob asked.

Rachel looked at the smudges of black eyeliner around Peter's eyes, and suppressed a giggle. 'Yes, Maria was Katisha.'

'Oh. The scary lady! You were excellent. I didn't recognise you without your make up.'

'I should hope not,' Maria said. 'My grandson was in last night, and he told me I looked just like Darth Maul from Star Wars.' They all laughed.

'Pete was one of the main parts, too, Rob. Can you guess which one?' Rachel asked, grinning at Peter.

Rob studied his face. 'Well, I know you weren't Ko-Ko. I don't really know the names of the others. You're too tall to be the minstrel one. And you're too young to be that pompous bloke who was the Lord-High-Everything-Else.'

'Oh, but that's exactly who he was,' Maria said. 'He was our wonderful Pooh-Bah, weren't you, darling?'

Rob stared at him. 'No! Really?' He looked uncertain. 'He was my favourite. Apart from Rachel, of course. But you don't look old enough. And you sound completely different.'

'Ah' said Peter, laughing. 'Well, Rob. That would be down to Melissa, our stage make up artist, who did an excellent job turning me into a wrinkly old codger. And the grey wig.' He wiggled his fingers at Rachel. '*How-de-do, little girls, how-de-do!*' His face contorted in the Pooh-Bah sneer, transforming it completely. 'And my voice was different on account of the fact I was doing this thing they call acting.'

'Oh, Peter!' Maria said, slapping Pete's hand. 'Don't be so mean. He was very good, wasn't he, Rob? Even members of his family said they didn't recognise him in his make up. And he does that voice very well indeed.'

Rachel was looking at Rob, worried in case Peter had offended him. But he didn't look upset at all. The opposite, in fact. He looked as if he'd had some kind of revelation. 'Of course,' she heard him say, very quietly, 'His voice was different because he was acting.' She wondered if Rob was all right.

Maria spoke. 'So, was your father a performer, Rob? How long ago was he a member? I've been with *FLOATS* a few years. I might remember him.'

Rachel shot Maria a warning look. 'Yes, I think you might. Rob's dad was Eric Handle.'

Maria's mouth dropped open, and Peter looked impressed, too. 'What, *the* Eric Handle?'

'You're Eric's son?' Maria asked. Rob nodded. Maria sipped her gin and tonic and looked at Rob over the rim of the glass. 'How old were you when … when it happened?'

'Eighteen,' Rob said quietly, looking away. He suddenly looked as if he wanted to flee. The atmosphere had changed from jollity to gravity, and Rachel tried desperately to think of a way to change the subject. The others looked uncomfortable, too.

Rob broke the silence, with a brightness that sounded forced. 'Well, it was lovely to meet you all. I'd best be getting off home now. My mother's on her own.'

Oh dear, thought Rachel. She felt almost like crying. If he left now, she'd feel terrible. Guilty … and well, disappointed. She put her hand on Rob's sleeve. 'Could I have a quick word, before you go? About the Fun Day.' She turned to Maria and Peter. 'Work stuff, you know.'

Rob looked down at her quizzically. 'Yes, sure.' He smiled at the others, and followed her out of the bar.

'Let's find somewhere less crowded.' she said, and led the way downstairs to the theatre restaurant, which was in semi-darkness, as it was closed after a show. There was a small sofa just inside, and she sat, patting the seat beside her. Rob hesitated, and then perched next to her, his hands tensed on his knees. He looked as if he was ready to jump up and run.

Rachel gazed at his troubled face, and felt a rush of tenderness. He looked so lost it was all she could do not to throw her arms around him and hug him close. But this feeling was more than compassion, and the strength of it surprised her.

'Are you all right, Rob?' She put her hand over his. 'Is it because we were talking about your father?'

Rob tore his eyes away from hers, and looked straight ahead. 'No. No, it's fine. I'm okay. Really.' His lips were lifted in a smile, but it looked as if this was a struggle. With dismay, she saw that his eyes were moist.

'Were you very close to him?' She tightened her hold on his hand. 'Oh, I'm sorry. If you'd rather not talk about him ...'

He turned his face to hers. 'No, honestly, it's fine. Yes, we were pretty close. It's difficult, though. It makes me feel disloyal if I talk about him with strangers.' Rachel frowned. 'No, I don't mean you, Rachel. I suppose it's because of how he died.'

'Oh?' She wasn't sure what to say. She'd assumed it was some kind of illness. Cancer, or something like that. 'Was it sudden? An accident?'

Rob looked away again, and didn't answer, but she felt the hand under hers tighten as he clasped his knee tighter.

'Rob?'

He looked straight ahead, his eyes glistening. 'He was murdered.'

Involuntarily, she took her hand away, to cover her mouth.

'Oh my God,' she said. 'Rob, I had no idea. I'm so sorry.' She dropped her hand to his again. 'And you were only eighteen?' He nodded. 'How awful for you. And your poor mother.'

'It's why I didn't go to University. Why I hid myself away.'

'Because you were frightened? That the same thing might happen to you?'

He gasped, and turned to her. 'I never thought of it like that, Rachel. I think you could be right. I don't think I've ever admitted it to anyone, not even to myself. I think it must have become a sort of phobia. Because if someone could get stabbed, someone as

190

good, as harmless as my dad, just doing something as innocuous as travelling on a train, it might happen to me, too.'

'He was stabbed? Oh, Rob, how awful.'

'Doesn't that sound selfish, though? I mean, my poor mother didn't have anyone to support her. I let her cope with it all on her own. I didn't even go to the inquest.'

She looked at him; saw his torment and his shame. 'You were just a kid.'

'I was eighteen. An adult. I was meant to be the man of the house. I should have been stronger.' A tear tricked down his cheek and he dashed it away with the back of his other hand.

She dug into her handbag and pulled out a packet of travel tissues, handing one to him. He wiped both eyes. 'Sorry. I'm such a soft idiot.'

'No, Rob. There's nothing wrong with you. Anyway, you say you didn't support your mum. But did anyone support you? It doesn't sound like it, much. Didn't you have any friends to help you through it?'

He blew his nose, and then shifted round a little, to face her. He sighed. 'Not really. It was the timing, you see. It happened on the Friday of the weekend I was due to leave for Uni. I didn't go, and nobody would have expected me to under those circumstances; they said I could join when I felt better – sort of compassionate leave, I suppose. Only I ended up putting it off, and putting it off, until …' He played with the tissue. 'But the thing is, all my friends were starting Uni, and off they went. Well, of course they did. I had one really good mate, Simon. If he'd been around, I think he'd have helped me, a bit. But there was just my mum. And she wasn't coping all that well with her own feelings.'

'But what about afterwards, when your friends came back for holidays? Didn't they look you up, come and visit you, take you out?'

He shrugged, and gave a dry laugh. 'No. In fact I reckon they went out of their way *not* to see me. Even Simon. I was out one day near Christmas that first year, doing some shopping with my mum in the town centre, and I spotted Si, walking toward us. He saw me, and I waved.' A grim smile crossed Rob's features. 'He crossed the road and dashed into the nearest shop. It was like I

191

was contagious. Like he might catch murdered-parent syndrome from me.'

'Oh, Rob,' Rachel said. She put her arm around his shoulder. 'You poor thing. I suppose in those days they didn't have bereavement counselling? But even so …'

'Ah well,' he said. 'It's all water under the bridge now. No point dwelling on it.'

'No, I don't think so. Maybe you *should* talk about it, Rob? Perhaps it's not too late to do that now.'

'Maybe,' he said with a sigh. 'Hey, I'm keeping you from your friends. I'd best go,' He gave her a big smile. 'You go back to your party. I'll get off home.'

She reached out and touched his face. 'Do you really think I'd let you go off on your own now, Rob Handle? I'd only be worrying about you.' And thinking about you and wishing you hadn't left, she thought. 'To be honest, I don't really feel like going back.' She stopped. 'Hey, how are you getting home?'

'I'll walk,' he said. 'It's a nice night.'

'Well, in that case, I'll walk with you. My flat's on your way. You can be the chivalrous gentleman, and keep me company. That's if you don't mind?' She stood up.

'Why would I mind? It would be my pleasure,' he said, standing. 'But I'd worry that I'm keeping you from your fellow performers and your adoring public.'

I'd much rather be with you, she thought, realising that it was exactly how she felt.

Rob was studying her face. 'Are you sure you want to leave? You're not just being kind?'

'No. I'm more than happy to go. Come on.'

THIRTY

The pubs were beginning to turn out as they made their way towards Rachel's flat, but plenty of people were still about: groups of young men laughing and shouting football chants on their way to the nearest curry house or kebab van to assuage their beer-fuelled hunger. They passed another group, of girls on a hen night, making even more of a racket than the men, their scanty night club outfits, hair extensions and fake tans set off by diaphanous fairy wings and plastic tiaras.

The streets became quieter the further from the centre they walked. Neither of them broke the silence until Rob did, to ask how Rachel had been planning to get home had he not been with her.

'You wouldn't have walked home on your own, would you?'

'No,' she replied. 'I'd have phoned for a taxi. I'm sure there'd have been someone to share it, or somebody would have given me a lift. How about you? It's quite a hike from my place to your part of town.'

He smiled. 'I'll walk. I enjoy it these days anyway, as long as it's not raining. The exercise is good for me. I spent too many years not doing any at all.'

'You look like a different person from the one who came along to be interviewed, Rob. How much weight have you lost?'

'Well, I've never weighed myself, to be honest. I would guess a couple of stones. Maybe more.'

'Wow,' she said. 'That's very impressive.'

'I've had to buy new clothes three times since May, when I started. That's the downside. Dieting can be a costly business.' They both laughed.

'Well, I've never really had that problem,' she said. 'If anything, I was the opposite. My mother thought I was anorexic at one point, when I was about eighteen. I wasn't, or course. Just skinny. I'm positively chubby now.'

He looked at her. 'No, I wouldn't ever describe you as that. You're just right.' Perfect. He was glad the darkness of the streets hid his blushing cheeks.

'Right,' she said, as they reached a side street. 'This is me. You can leave me here if you like, Rob. My flat's in that building just there.'

Rob looked where she was pointing. He didn't like the look of the alleyways and dark cubbies she'd have to pass to get there. 'No way. I'm taking you to your door, Miss Jenkins. I wouldn't be doing my job as your escort properly, otherwise.'

She smiled up at him. 'You really are being the gallant hero. Okay then.'

They walked on, and she stopped outside the front door of a red brick building which must surely, in the past, have been a private house, but showed signs now of disrepair.

Rob hesitated, at the door, not sure how to take his leave. Should he just say goodbye? A handshake seemed a little too formal, and a kiss on the cheek inappropriate. After all, she was still his boss. But he couldn't help feeling they'd passed some sort of crux in their relationship, and were now a little more than just supervisor and subordinate.

He didn't have to make the decision, because Rachel was putting her key in the lock, and when the door was open, she said, 'Can I offer you a coffee or something, Rob? It seems a little ungracious to let you go off home now, after you've seen me home safely.'

He was the one in her debt, for making her leave her party. Had she done it to be polite? And was she still just being kind? He searched her face. Perhaps it was wishful thinking, but her eyes seemed bright, her face eager. Should he? If he did, it would delay the moment he had to go home and face the bear.

'That would be nice,' he said. 'Just for a while. I won't outstay my welcome.'

He followed her through the front door and up the concrete staircase, onto a landing with two doors leading off it. Just as they reached the door on the left, the opposite one opened, just a crack, and then an inch or two wider, and Rob just made out the features of someone watching, before the door was quietly closed again.

Rachel looked where he was looking, and pushed her own door open. 'That's my neighbour, Bill. He's so nosy. I sometimes think he must camp out behind that door, day and night,' she said in a low voice.

Rachel ushered him into a corridor with two doors on the left, and another on the right. At the far end was a colourful, sparkly bead curtain in iridescent blues and greens. The curtain tinkled and swished as it brushed his head and shoulders when he followed Rachel through it. On the other side of the beads was a small but brightly decorated kitchen. Rachel pulled out one of the two stools underneath the breakfast bar. 'Take a seat. Tea, coffee? I've got some Ovaltine, I think. Or a glass of wine?' She pulled open the door of the waist-high fridge. 'Or ... lager, if you like.'

'I'll have whatever you're having,' he said, sitting on the stool.

'Tea, then,' she said, and filled a jug kettle, then switched it on. She took a pair of matching bone china mugs decorated with butterflies from hooks under the wall cupboard, put a tea bag in each, and then pulled out the stool on the other side, and sat opposite Rob.

He looked around the kitchen, suddenly lost for words. 'Nice place you've got here,' seemed too lame, and he could hardly talk about the weather, but his shyness had driven all possible conversation topics out of his head. He searched his brain, and thought of the incidents leading up to this moment.

'How long have you been singing?' he asked.

'Well, I started singing properly at school in Swansea. We used to do a musical every year at the end of the summer term, and I always signed up for them. Then I joined an am-dram group when I left school. We did things like *Oklahoma* and *Carousel* and *Cats*.'

'So you had to learn dances too? I don't think I could do that. I have two left feet.'

'Yes, that's why I prefer *FLOATS*. They may have changed their name, but they're still primarily a Gilbert and Sullivan society. I can learn dances all right as long they're not too complicated. There's usually some choreography involved in our shows, but never very much, and it's always easy to pick up.' She got up to make the tea.

'My dad was a pretty good dancer, from what I can remember,' Rob said.

195

Rachel brought the two mugs over, and set one down in front of him. She cupped her hands around her mug, and looked at him as if she were trying to decide where to take the conversation.

'I think you were right, before,' he said. 'It probably would do me good to talk about my dad. Not just about what happened to him, I mean, but about *him*, before it happened. I think that was part of the problem – I was scared to talk to my mum about him in case she got upset, and I didn't have anyone else to talk to.'

She nodded. 'Well, I imagine that's what bereavement counsellors do, isn't it?' She smiled. 'I'm a good listener, Rob, if you wanted to talk to me about it.'

He smiled back. 'That's very kind. But I wouldn't want to bore you to death, or make you all depressed.' His mind strayed to the bear again. He might be doing a lot of talking about his dad before long.

'Rob,' she said, 'What exactly happened? You know … when he was—Do you mind me asking?'

'No, I don't mind.' Although telling anyone at all was a first. He put his mug down, and traced the shape of the butterfly with one finger. 'He was on the train on his way home from a conference in London.' He looked up. Rachel was listening intently. 'He'd been there overnight because there was this posh black-tie dinner at the end of the first day. He phoned my mum from the station, to say he'd just missed a train because he got chatting, but he was going to have a quick drink and then get the next one. Imagine that, Rachel. Something as simple as that can change a whole life. Well, three lives, I suppose. It's difficult not to wonder, if he hadn't missed that first train …'

'Did they catch whoever did it?'

Rob sighed. 'No. There were a couple of lads, or maybe men – depending on which witnesses you believe – acting suspiciously on the train. Some people came forward after an appeal the next day. He was still alive when he was discovered, a couple of stops past Fleesham. It was a slow train, so they reckoned, afterwards, that whoever it was could have got off anywhere between London and here.

'Oh dear. Like looking for a needle in a haystack, then?'

'Yes. And back then, they didn't have CCTV on the stations, or anything like that.'

'Did they have any idea what the motive was?'

'Well, it seems to have been robbery. His wallet was missing. Though they didn't take his overnight bag.' He picked up his tea and sipped it. 'The wallet wouldn't have had a lot of money in it. He never carried much cash. He'd paid for the conference and the hotel in advance, and his train ticket. He didn't even have any credit cards. And people didn't have iPhones or Blackberrys in those days – or any mobile phones, unless they were really well off, which my dad wasn't.' He rubbed his chin, and looked at Rachel. 'I wondered afterwards why they picked on him of all people. And I reckon it was because of the suit.'

'The suit?' Rachel asked.

'My dad was always very smartly turned out, you see. He didn't have expensive tastes, not really. He didn't buy lots of gadgets, you know, hi-fi or a flashy car or a camera, or anything like that, but I think he was a bit of a dandy at heart. Perhaps that's one of the reasons he enjoyed doing his shows so much. You know – dressing up in fancy suits and that?' Rachel nodded, and he continued. 'When he started working, he promised himself he'd save up to buy a proper bespoke suit, but not one from his own company – a really good one from a Savile Row tailor. And he did. In fact, as soon as he'd paid for that one, he started saving up for a second and then a third, so he could rotate them, and have one at the dry cleaners, one to wear, and one sort of on standby.' He clasped his hands around the mug. 'They were practically identical – all dark blue – except for very slight variations in the shade. I still have one of them. It's still wrapped in the plastic from the dry-cleaners, and the date on the ticket is two days before … Anyway, Mum was going to get rid of it, but I pinched it and put it in my wardrobe. It's beautiful. Even someone who didn't know what they were looking at would realise it was something a bit special – that it wasn't something bought off the peg from Burton's or Marks and Spencer.'

'So, you think, because he was dressed like that, he looked as if he might have been well-off?'

'It's possible, isn't it? Perhaps I'm wrong. Just looking for the reason they chose him.'

'I suppose that's natural,' Rachel said. 'So, were there any witnesses, any evidence left behind?'

'They found a ginger hair on my dad's suit. And one of these lads or men the witnesses talked about had longish red hair.'

'So this was, what, the mid-eighties?'

'Eighty-six,' Rob said.

'Were they able to check DNA in those days?'

'Yes. It hadn't long been possible. They also found a cigarette end. It was a non-smoking carriage. Back then, they still had some that weren't, of course. But my dad didn't smoke, and it was the only one they found in there, so the police thought it might be significant. Anyway, the DNA from that matched the hair. It's all locked away in a police lab or whatever, I suppose. They told us, if whoever it was ever gets arrested for another crime, they'd be able to link it up to my dad's case. But it's been twenty-three years now. I doubt they'll ever find anyone if they haven't by now. Who knows, the murderer might be dead, or have emigrated, or anything.'

'Do you think it would have made a difference to you – you know, the way it affected you – if they'd been caught?'

He looked at Rachel. 'Do you mean I went into … hibernation, or hiding, or whatever you want to call it, because the killer was still on the loose?' She didn't answer, just looked at him. She'd make a good counsellor, he thought. 'Yes. Probably. Makes me sound a bit of a wimp, doesn't it, though?'

'Hmmm … Survival instinct, perhaps? Maybe it turned into this phobia because of the lack of support. I don't know, Rob. You hear about people becoming agoraphobic over much less, don't you?' He nodded. 'Anyway, if the police have it on their computer, he could still turn up in the future. You hear about those things happening all the time. Wasn't there one on the local news a couple of weeks ago? Some guy was arrested for dangerous driving, and ended up being convicted of a thirty-year-old murder.'

'Yeah,' Rob said. 'But we'd have to hope this one committed another crime first. It makes me feel a bit strange, because it's like wishing misfortune on another innocent person.'

Rachel looked at Rob. 'You're really rather sensitive, aren't you? I would think it's almost inevitable that he will. If he's a violent person, it's amazing he hasn't already.' She stifled a yawn. He'd forgotten what a busy day she'd had. She must be exhausted.

198

He stood up. 'I'd better go. It's really late. Thanks for the tea,' he said. 'And the sympathy.'

She laughed. 'You're welcome. Thanks for the company.' She walked him to the front door.

'Well,' he said, feeling suddenly awkward again. 'Bye, then. See you on Monday.'

Without warning, she took his hand, rather as he had taken hers a few hours ago in the park. And held it. And smiled up at him. His hand trembled slightly, and he squeezed hers to try and stop the shake, and felt hers was shaking, too. They gazed at each other, frozen in the moment. Then he reached out and touched her cheek. So soft, her eyes so gentle, her pupils so large. She moved her hand up to her face to join his and moved closer. Then she was in his arms, and his lips were on hers.

The kiss was gentle, hesitant, as if neither were sure the other meant it, and then her arms draped round his neck and her hands moved to the back of his head, pulling him closer.

He pulled away first and looked deep into her eyes. They were shining. He thought his must be too. The look in her eyes made him giddy. 'Wow,' he said. And kissed her again. God, her lips were so warm and soft and she tasted scrumptious.

They stood in front of her doorway, just holding each other, not wanting to let go. Rob broke the embrace first. 'I must be dreaming. How could someone like you like someone like me?'

'One of many reasons,' she said, stroking his hair, 'is that you have absolutely no idea how gorgeous you are.' Her eyes twinkled at him. 'You really don't, do you?'

His eyes widened. 'Me?'

'Well, there's nobody else here,' she said. 'I think I liked you from the day I interviewed you.'

He looked around him. 'I'm going to wake up in a second and I'll be in my bed.' With that bear looking at me.

She hugged him close again, and then kissed him. 'It feels real to me,' she said. 'But I think you'd better go – before I get accused of harassing an employee.'

'Oh,' he said, smiling into her eyes. 'Miss Jenkins, you can harass me any time you want.' And then they were laughing, and hugging, and kissing again.

'Rob?' she said.

He looked at her. 'Yes?'

'What brought you out of hiding?'

He thought of the bear. 'Oh, you'd never believe me if I told you.'

'Well, I'm very pleased it happened, whatever the reason,' she said.

THIRTY-ONE

Rob floated home on a cloud of bliss. What a day it had been, full of frights and revelations and tears and joy. And he still had to confront Paddytum.

Could he even call him that any more? It would seem wrong.

He had so many unanswered questions. He didn't think he could face any more tonight – excitement or trauma, or anything else. Besides, his head was full of thoughts of Rachel.

He let himself in and crept up the stairs. He considered not putting his bedroom light on in the hope Paddytum wouldn't talk to him. Rob didn't know if he could trust himself to keep quiet, but he wanted to wait until morning. He was too tired, and too emotional, to face it now.

'Did you enjoy *The Mikado*, Robert?' the bear said, and for the first time, he heard the voice for what it was. He admired him. It must have been difficult, he thought, staying in character for such a long time without slipping.

'Yeah, it was really good. The cast was excellent. And Rachel was fantastic.' Rachel *is* fantastic, he thought, and beautiful and gorgeous and—

'Did you go to the after-show party? Is that why you're so late?'

'Yes,' he said. He turned on his side, so he didn't have to look at the bear, and pulled the duvet up to his chin. 'I'll tell you all about it tomorrow. I'm dead tired.' He suddenly felt a mixture of emotions towards this thing he'd thought was just a talking teddy bear: gratitude, fear, love, and not a little anger. He closed his eyes, and tried to think of Rachel instead. Eventually he drifted off to sleep.

Rob returned to his room after breakfast next morning. He'd sat at the dining table, answering his mother's questions about his night out, with half a mind on the subject. He knew he had to face Paddytum, or whatever he was supposed to call him from now on, and the sooner, the better.

He sat on the bed, face to face with the bear, and came straight out with it.

'You're my dad, aren't you?' He clamped his jaws tight on a nervous giggle that threatened to escape at what he'd just said. To a teddy bear.

He waited. There was no reply.

'I know you are. That's why you couldn't perform in front of Deirdre, because you knew she'd recognise your voice. Even though you were putting it on. And have been since you started talking to me.'

Still nothing.

'I know why you chose Frederick as a name, too. If you didn't want me to suss you out … Dad—' He stopped. It felt weird saying it out loud.

'I think I wanted you to know.' Rob shivered at the sound of the voice he'd heard every day for the first eighteen years of his life. 'But I probably needed for you to work it out for yourself.'

Rob sat looking at him. He couldn't talk. Even though the voice confirmed what he'd guessed, he needed time to take it in.

'So,' he said, finally, 'Are you … a ghost, or something?'

'I suppose I must be,' his father's voice said.

'So you're not Paddytum, then.'

A laugh. 'No, of course not. Toys can't talk. I am, sort of, *attached* to the bear, though.'

Rob thought. 'But you haven't been in him the whole time. Since you …'

'Since I died, no. How did you work that out?'

'Oh, a couple of things. You didn't know anything about my driving lessons, for one thing. I was so traumatised by those that you couldn't possibly have forgotten them if you'd been around at the time.'

'Bad, were they? You must have been as nervous as me, when I tried to learn.'

'So, when did you …' Rob fished around in his mind for an appropriate word, 'start to … occupy Paddytum's body? And, for that matter, where were you before that? Were you in some kind of heavenly holding room, waiting to be sent back to earth to … sort my life out? And anyway,' he said. 'Shouldn't I be able to see you?'

The voice of his father gave a low chuckle. 'One question at a time, lad,' he said. 'I think you've been watching too many films. I managed to find my way back home only about six months ago, and for the first two of those I didn't say a word. I was frightened to. I didn't want you to recognise my voice. I thought it'd send you even further into your withdrawn state.'

'But you thought it'd be perfectly okay if I thought my teddy was talking to me,' Rob said archly. 'As long as it was a different voice. Great thinking, Dad!'

'It was a considered decision, Rob. It broke my heart to see you like that. When I first arrived, I thought you must be on holiday from work, or something. When I realised it was how you'd been for years I had to do something. But I didn't know how. Nobody told me how to handle this.'

'Okay, so where were you for the twenty-odd years before that?'

'On that train for most of it. The place I died. I believe, from what I've learned, that we only ever stay behind if we are taken by force. If we have unfinished business.'

'Like trying to find out who killed you, you mean?'

'Oh, I know who killed me. His face is there in front of me always. I shall never forget it. I just don't know his name, or where he is now.' He paused, and Rob opened his mouth to speak, and then closed it again. 'I was tied to the train because it was where I died. And I was also tied to it because I didn't want to leave it, in case he came back. I needed to see him again. What I didn't know was what would happen if I ever did.'

'And did you? See him again?'

'Never. I saw the police, questioning regular passengers, for a few weeks afterwards until they ran out of enthusiasm or leads. I saw some I learned were regular commuters, talking about what had happened, wondering which carriage it had happened in, and saying how it could easily have been them. Until they tired of the subject. It wasn't long before I was old news. I learned a lot, Rob riding that train, day after day, morning, noon and night, for over twenty years. I saw love, and laughter, and wisdom and stupidity. But I never saw my killer again.'

'So why did you leave it? If you were, like you say, tied to it?'

'The train was decommissioned. Replaced by a newer model. The non-corridor kind. Much safer. It would have been better if I'd been travelling on one of those that evening. It trundled off to some dilapidated rail yard, and, when they started breaking it up, I found I was able to leave. I followed the track until I reached home. It was the only place I'd wanted to be, all that time.'

'That makes sense, I suppose. Was it hard to get here?'

'It felt strange. *I* felt strange. Disconnected. Vulnerable. It wasn't pleasant. A ghost, a spirit, whatever you want to call it, needs to be attached. To something of meaning. That's why I chose your bear. It meant something to both of us. Being attached takes away some of the pain.'

Rob frowned. 'Pain? You mean, from being stabbed?' He didn't like the idea of his father being in pain all these years.

'Oh no, Rob. That didn't hurt. Even at the time it didn't hurt much. It was like a hard thump on the chest, and then it ached for a bit, but not a great deal, and then I went numb and it didn't hurt at all. I'm talking about emotional pain. Like a deep, desperate longing. For what has been lost. For the grief of my loved ones to end.'

Rob was silent. Then he said, 'Well, I doubt it ever will, completely. It would mean we'd forgotten you, wouldn't it?'

'No, but your pain, yours and your mother's, might not have been so bad if the person who inflicted it had been found and punished.'

'So was that was why you stayed?'

'I did think that for a long time. But I now think there was a different purpose for my staying.'

'You mean me?' He didn't need an answer, really. 'I'm just so ashamed I let myself become what I was when you found me.'

He sat, thinking. Why me, though, and not Ma? She was the one his dad was closer to. Should he tell his father Maureen had turned against him, and why? He couldn't ask about the mysterious Debbie. Not now, when he'd only just been reunited with him. Rob couldn't bear the idea that he might go away again. Not yet.

'So, what happens now?' he said, more to himself than to his father.

'I have no idea. Now you know who I am, perhaps I will go wherever it is I'm supposed to go. I don't think I have any control over it.'

'One thing I know – we can't carry on doing Story Time now. It wouldn't seem right. Oh! Except that I've said we'd do this thing next Saturday. A charity thing. The Fun Day.'

It was several seconds before the reply came. 'I'm not sure we'll even be able to, Rob. Now you know, you might not be so receptive. We could try. If it doesn't work, you'll have to think up an excuse. Again.' He paused. 'But I want it to be the last time.'

'So do I,' Rob said. 'By the way, how difficult was it to keep that voice up? It must have been like being on stage, non stop, for the last three months.'

'It wasn't easy. There were times I almost slipped. It was my Ko-Ko voice, you know. That's why I couldn't do it in front of Deirdre.'

'I thought it must have been.' He told his father about his conversation with Deirdre. Was it only yesterday? It seemed like days ago. 'Was that right, what she said about you always wanting to play Frederic? Is that why you chose the name?'

'That, and the fact that it used to *be* part of my name. But, oh, son, how I envy you that voice! Did you really not know you could sing?'

Rob laughed. 'How would I? I never sang a note after … you went. I had no reason to.'

'And now? You do?' Rob heard a smile in the voice.

He thought back to last night, and saying goodbye to Rachel. 'Oh yes. I think I might.'

THIRTY-TWO

Now he knew what he knew, he felt impossibly awkward around his mother. He felt as if he was keeping something from her, which, of course, he was. But how could he possibly tell her what he knew now any more than he could have told her Paddytum had started talking to him?

It's all right, though, Ma, because he's turning my life around, he thought with a wry smile. She'd never have believed that, any more than she'd believe his father was in his room, talking to him as if he'd never gone away. It was hard enough for Rob to get his own head around it, never mind expect his mother to take it in. It didn't prevent him from feeling guilty, though.

Perhaps if she were able to hear the voice herself, it would make a difference. His dad said he'd tried, but failed to make her hear. Was it something to do with the suspicion she'd harboured all these years? Was he blocked out because she'd blocked out his memory? Perhaps he should, after all, try to get to the bottom of this 'Debbie' business. He didn't like to ask his dad. He realised that he hadn't really known the state of his parents' marriage, though his memories were of a loving relationship, full of affection and jokey banter. His parents had often cuddled up together on the sofa, and held hands when they went out anywhere together. Rob liked to think he'd have noticed something in his father's demeanour if he'd really been cheating on her. Should he ask him? It was a problem he'd thought about late into the night.

He walked to work on Monday morning, still troubled by it. But there was something else as well. What if his father didn't leave, and was 'attached' to the bear now for the rest of Rob's life? Just when Rob was starting to believe he had a future now. Would he be expected to share that future with his father's ghost? Or the alternative – to leave him behind in the house with Maureen, with whom he couldn't communicate?

There was no point in worrying about all that now. So far, all his father had done was good. He had to believe it would all work out. As he came closer to the library, another worry took over, and drove thoughts of his father away.

Rachel.

He had to work with her now. Of course, it must be more difficult for her than for him. They should talk about it. Neither had said anything on Saturday about seeing each other again. He laughed. Of course they would be seeing each other again – every day, Monday to Friday – but as far as *seeing each other* again was concerned, who knew?

What if she thought Saturday night had been a mistake? What if it had been part of some post-show euphoria and she avoided him like the plague, cringing in embarrassment? The closer he came to the library, the more he convinced himself she'd be regretting it. Oh, it had seemed real and wonderful at the time, but what if he was deluding himself. He stopped outside the side entrance and sighed deeply, almost afraid to go in.

Face the music, Robert. He smiled to himself. Strange that Paddytum hadn't completely gone away now his father had been unmasked. That was definitely *his* voice. He knew it wasn't really there. But the voice, and the persona his father had created, had become so much a part of his life over past few months, that he suspected he'd hear it, at moments of crisis, forever. It was Paddytum's legacy.

He took a deep breath and went in. Marjorie stood behind the counter, sorting through a pile of CDs. She barely gave him a glance over her bifocals. There was no sign of Rachel. Was she hiding in her office, too embarrassed to face him? Carole emerged from the corridor leading from the staff room. She spotted Rob, and winked at him. Heat flooded his face. Had Rachel said something?

Carole sidled up to him. He looked down. She was beaming. Marjorie regarded them both with a puzzled stare, and then shrugged and went back to her CD sorting.

'Rachel wants to see you in her office, Rob.'

He froze. Was this it? Was she going to tell him his services were no longer required? For behaving inappropriately on Saturday night?

207

'Don't look so worried,' Carole said. 'Go on. Don't keep the boss-lady waiting.' She winked again, and gave him a push.

He stood outside Rachel's office, quaking in his size 11 shoes, feeling even more nervous than he had the day he was interviewed. He steeled himself. *Have courage, Robert.* He rapped lightly on the door. No reply, but he heard the scrape of Rachel's chair on the floor, and footsteps, and then, she was at the door, looking up at him shyly. She looked happy.

'Come in,' she said, going back to the desk and sitting. He took the chair opposite; perching on it, still expecting something terrible was about to happen.

'First of all, Carole knows. I told her ... about us.' So there was an 'us' then? Rob's heart soared. It had been real, and Rachel didn't regret it; at least, if her expression was anything to go by. Her face was flushed, her eyes shone. She looked, well, exactly how *he* felt.

'She knows? When did you tell her?'

Rachel sighed, and took his hand across the desk. 'Rob, I was in such a state of confusion yesterday ... after ... you know.' He squeezed her hand and nodded. He didn't think he'd ever stop smiling. 'I rang her, and we had a long chat, about ... things. I knew if I didn't tell someone I'd wouldn't be able to hide it. And Carole was the obvious person. She likes you, *and* she can keep a secret.'

'What did she say?' He wondered why Rachel hadn't phoned him, if she was so worried. But perhaps it made more sense not to discuss ones affections with the object of them at such an early stage. He was new to all this. He had no idea what women discussed about their love lives.

'Oh, she was pleased. She said she'd known for ages that ...' she grinned, 'that we "had the hots" for each other, as she so delicately put it.'

Rob chuckled. 'She's very perceptive, isn't she?' He frowned. 'But why were you in a state, as you say? You weren't upset about it, were you?'

She reached out and stroked his hand, and sighed. 'No, upset's the wrong word. Just ... uncertain. Because we work together. It's not ideal. It might ... affect things.'

'I know,' Rob said. He swallowed. 'Look if it's going to be difficult, and you want to forget—'

'I wondered if I should look for another job,' she interrupted, 'In fact I started thinking about it days ago, after I realised I had … feelings.' Rob's heart did a little jump.

'Oh, no,' he said. 'That wouldn't be right. If anyone should look for something else, it ought to be me. After all, I haven't been here long.'

She shook her head. 'No, Rob, this is the first proper job you've had. If you leave after such a short time, it'll be difficult to get another. I did think about a transfer for you to another branch – even try for a more senior role, but that would be difficult as you don't drive.'

'Well, I could learn. I did have some lessons years ago. It didn't work out, but that's not to say I couldn't try again. Or I could just get up earlier in the morning. They're all within busing distance, aren't they?' He moved to her side of the desk and pulled her into his arms. 'So, what did Carole think you – we – should do?'

Rachel played with his shirt collar, and looked into his eyes. Her gaze made Rob feel warm all over. 'She said wait and see. She didn't think it would be a problem unless we allow it to become one. What do you think?'

'Do I think I can control myself, you mean?' He grinned. 'Keep myself from molesting you in the store room, or grabbing you for a quick snog behind the Crime and Thrillers?' He blushed at the thought it conjured in his mind, but couldn't suppress a laugh. 'Yes, I think I can probably keep a rein on my animal urges, Miss Jenkins.'

Rachel stared at him and then burst out laughing. 'Rob, you're terrible.' She took a deep breath. 'Well, that's all right then. Now, the next question is … do you fancy going for a drink with me? Tonight?'

He cupped her chin in his hand, and smiled. 'Thought you'd never ask.'

That evening, he met her at the *Bunthorne Arms*, a little pub close to her flat. He had kept out of her way as much as possible at work, and she'd managed to avoid him too, but it was inevitable that they made occasional eye contact, and when they did, they exchanged a guilty smile.

In the pub, they sat close together on a squashy sofa, not talking much, and just enjoying the closeness. Rob still couldn't quite believe this was happening. At the end of the evening, he walked her home again, and went in for a quick coffee, before kissing her goodnight.

He met up with Rachel every evening that week. He'd go home, have his dinner, and then go to her flat. Most nights they just snuggled up on her sofa together, watching DVDs or talking.

It was unspoken, but neither of them rushed to take things any further. For one thing, Rob was too shy – afraid of his own lack of experience with women, and Rachel must have either sensed this or was, at heart, an old-fashioned girl, who was happy to wait until the time was right.

On the third evening, he'd just reached the bottom of her stairs when he heard heavy footsteps behind him, and turned, to see a man standing there. He would have looked more menacing had he not been swaying slightly and grinning.

'Evening,' Rob said. The man was a Goth, or an Emo, or a Punk – he wasn't sure which, but he looked a little too old to be any of those things. Rob eyed his raven hair – the red roots were in dire need of retouching.

He opened the front door, and stepped outside. The man followed.

'Are you all right?'

'Depends,' the man said, still grinning. 'I just wanted to make sure your intentions towards my little songbird are honourable, like.'

Rob turned. 'Your songbird? Do you mean Rachel?'

'Who else? Of course Rachel!' the man said, lurching towards Rob, and throwing an arm around his shoulder, sending them both off balance so that Rob had to grab the railing of the steps to keep from falling. 'She sings, y'know. Got a bloody bee-ootiful voice, she has, my little sparrow. I hear her singing them old songs, in her flat. Makes me nearly want to cry, it does. That's why I call her my little sparrow, y'see.'

Rob recoiled from the blast of ethanol-laden breath Rachel's neighbour blasted in his face as he spoke, wondering if sparrows were known for their tear-inducing song. 'I know,' he said. 'She has a lovely voice.' He slipped out from under the man's arm. 'And yes, my intentions are, seeing as you've asked, entirely honourable.'

'Well, guv, they bleedin' well better had be, or you'll have Billyboy here to answer to.' He leaned into Rob again, lowering his voice, but sadly, not the alcohol content of his breath. 'Killed a man, I did. Long, long time back. Over twenty years ago. But that's not to say I wouldn't again, anyone hurts my little sparrow.'

'Oh,' Rob said, backing away. 'Well, er, um, thanks for the advice. You needn't have any worries on that score, mate, er, Bill. I've no intention of hurting her.'

Bill looked at him, and nodded. 'Good. Just looking out for her. Lovely little thing, isn't she? You're a lucky man, that's all I can say.'

'Yes, I am,' Rob said, and started off towards home. 'Very lucky.'

'What would you like to watch tonight?' Rachel asked, the next night.

'Oh, I don't mind. You choose.'

'No, I've chosen all of them so far.'

To be honest, he was so happy just to be with her he didn't care what they watched or what they did. He went to the bookcase where she kept her DVD collection and looked through the titles. He slid a box out from a group of DVDs with plain white covers, and read the back. 'Are these *FLOATS* shows?'

She went over to him. 'Yes. Ron, our stage manager, records the dress rehearsal each year. Do you want to watch one?'

'I wouldn't mind. Perhaps I should familiarise myself with them, if I'm going to audition.'

Rachel beamed. 'Really? Oh, Rob, that would be brilliant.'

He grinned, and kissed her on the nose. 'Hold on, I'm only thinking about it. So, which one would you recommend?'

She looked through the cases and pulled one out. 'I think you'd enjoy this one. We did it last year.' *The Sorcerer*. She put it in the machine and they settled back to watch, Rachel occasionally mouthing the words of some of the songs.

'Wow,' Rob said, after the comic lead had sung his first song, *My Name is John Wellington Wells*. He picked up the remote and pressed Pause. 'Can I see that again, Rach?'

She laughed. 'He's good, isn't he? Actually, you don't need to. He does it again, straight after, as an encore. It's even faster this time.'

Rob gaped. 'Faster than that? What is he; a robot?' He pressed Play, and sure enough, John Wellington Wells repeated the song, at what seemed to Rob to be double the speed.

'I'm gobsmacked at that,' he said over the thunderous applause coming through the speakers of Rachel's TV. 'However does someone learn to do that? I mean, how can anyone move their lips and tongue that quickly without all the words getting jumbled?'

'It's difficult, but it's not impossible. I've sung Patter songs myself. You have to sort of learn all the words of the song, and sing it slowly, over and over until you're word perfect, and then you can concentrate on gradually getting faster and faster. It's like most things; the more you practice, the better you get at it.'

'Well, I'm pretty sure I could never sing that fast, even if I practised it for a year. Wait.' He stopped, looking worried. 'I wouldn't have to do one like that, would I, if I join?'

Rachel shook her head, smiling. 'No. It's not very likely. It's nearly always the comic lead who does patter, and that's always a baritone part. There are occasional duets, but off the top of my head I can't think of any where the tenor has to sing a Patter song.' She grinned. 'So you can't wriggle out of it that way.'

'Deirdre was saying, the other night, my dad was really good at them,' he said.

'Yes, I've heard that about him, too. Well, you probably could learn to do it then, Rob. Maybe it's in the genes.'

He chuckled. 'I seriously doubt it. I get my words tangled up when I'm just talking, never mind singing.'

On Friday, Rachel gathered the staff together in the early afternoon to talk about the arrangements for the Fun Day. Carole, Marjorie and Rachel would be in at the normal time, to open up and set out tables for the stallholders. There would be four in all: a woman who made her own jewellery, a popular local artist, a wildlife photographer who was trying to build up a portrait business, and a face painter, the latter despite Marjorie's initial protest that the children would get paint all over the books. Carole pointed out that this was unlikely to happen unless they actually went and wiped their faces on them.

Rob wasn't needed until around 11am, and they agreed on just two story sessions, using books for both. He would do one with Frederick, for the toddlers, and then he and Rachel would do a second one, without the bear, for the older children. Rachel had suggested they read a Roald Dahl story, taking turns in speaking in different voices for the characters.

The thought of doing this without the bear filled Rob with trepidation. He had doubts even about being able to get through the first part, now that he knew what he knew. He'd just have to do his best.

That evening, he asked his father if he still wanted to go ahead with it. 'I don't want you to if you feel awkward about it. Goodness knows, I do!'

'It should be fine if we're using books. Can you manage the second part without me?'

'I'll have to. The big kids would think it's babyish, me using a bear as a prop. And perhaps … it'll be good practice. I'm thinking of auditioning for *FLOATS*. If I get in, I'll have to get used to performing. And as Rachel said, if I can survive in front of children, it'll be easy in front of grown-ups.'

When Rob arrived next day at ten to eleven, the Fun Day was in full swing. The face painter had her table set up close to the entrance, and had a small queue of willing customers including, Rob saw with amusement, Archie. All round the library were children with colourful freshly-painted faces: dogs, and rabbits, and scary-looking lizards, with a brace of Draculas chasing round the semi-circle of chairs set up in the Children's Library. He went over to Rachel, carrying the bear. His father hadn't spoken the whole way there on the bus, and Rob wondered if he were as nervous as he was himself. He'd not used his old Frederick voice

213

at all since Rob had unmasked him a week ago, so Rob hoped he would still be able to do it.

He took his seat while Rachel announced brightly that Story Time was about to start, and painted animal faces, eager for the session to begin, soon surrounded them. Among the familiar faces of his Tuesday crowd, just about recognisable under their paint, Rob saw a few he hadn't seen before. He hadn't yet told Rachel he wouldn't be bringing Frederick along any more after this session. Still, he thought, if the one for the older kids went well, he might even be able to carry on doing Story Time without a prop.

Some of the Tuesday mums smiled and waved at him as he waited to start, and then Rachel picked up the first book. Rob felt, with relief, the familiar tingle in his jaw, and soon they were in full swing, Frederick's voice as lively as ever. And then, about halfway through, Rob noticed the tingle weakening and, after a second in which Rob faltered halfway through a word, he recovered, and read the words in the book himself, doing, he thought, a passable imitation of the Frederick/Paddytum voice.

He's letting go, Rob thought. He's making me fly solo. As Rachel closed the book, she looked over at Rob, her expression questioning. Then she turned to the children and asked, 'How about some songs?' As they sang, Rob considered what had just happened. Was his dad preparing him for something? Was he planning to leave?

As the last few children wandered away with their parents, either into the main library, or towards the front door, Rachel turned to him. 'Are you okay, sweetheart?' she whispered. He felt a warm glow at the endearment. It was the first time she'd used it here, at work, but was a measure of her concern. 'You sounded a bit different.'

'I'm fine. I was just … experimenting – with the voice.'

She looked at him. 'Actually, I preferred it. It sounded more like you, less stagy. Fancy a quick coffee before I call the big kids over? I don't know about you, but I could do with one.'

'Good idea. I need to put Frederick away, anyway.'

They were halfway there when Rachel stopped. 'Oh, hi Mick,' she said, to a good-looking man standing at the desk. He was about Rob's age, and slightly shorter, with straight, floppy hair which looked as if it had been highlighted to within an inch of its life, and wore a cream linen jacket and a gold neck-chain.

'Hello, my Welsh beauty,' the man said, flashing a toothy grin at Rachel. He loped over to her and draped an arm around her shoulder, stroking her cheek with his thumb. Rob felt as if he'd been kicked in the belly. The man gestured at the decorations with a hand adorned with heavy gold rings. 'What's all this tarting-up in aid of? You having some kind of party?'

'It's our Fun Day,' Rachel replied. 'Feel free to look around at the stalls. We have some nice things for sale.'

Rob didn't like the way the man was looking at Rachel. He didn't like it one bit. He seemed to be scanning every inch of her. Rob's hand clenched on the bear's arm.

The man saw him looking, and his eyes narrowed. 'Haven't I seen you somewhere before, mate?'

It was a struggle for Rob to ungrit his teeth. 'Maybe. I work here in the week.'

'Nah, I only come in Saturdays. To see my favourite librarian. Oh, and to take mum out for her lunch. It's her Saturday treat.' He looked down at Paddytum. 'Bit too old to be playing with teddies, aren't you, mate?' He looked up into Rob's face, sneering.

'Rob, this is Marge's son. Rob uses the bear for Story Time, Mick. ' Rachel said. 'Frederick's very popular. He reads stories to the children.'

'Really? Is it battery operated?' Without warning, he reached out a ring-laden hand, to grab Paddytum from Rob's grasp. Rob stepped back. The hand stopped in mid reach.

The scream came from nowhere, and froze Rob's blood. For a moment he thought it was him, screaming out loud, because his jaw was tingling again. He felt a dull ache in his chest. But then he realised the scream was just in his head. He looked at the man's hand, and it was if a camera flash went off in his head. The blood drained from his face into his aching chest. His legs went weak.

The man rolled his eyes, as he said, in a scathing tone. 'Calm down, matey. I'm not going to take your teddy bear away from you.'

But Rob had seen something just before the man lowered his hand. A freckled hand, the back of it covered in sandy hairs. And tattooed across the knuckles, crudely, in faded blue, was a name.

DEBBY

THIRTY-THREE

Rob rushed into the staff room and sank down onto one of the sofas. He looked into Paddytum's face, as if it could tell him what he wanted to know. Before he had a chance to say anything, Rachel rushed in and sat beside him. She put her hand on his arm.

'Rob, what is it? What's wrong?' She touched his cheek. 'You're white as a sheet.'

I don't know, he thought. I need to ask him. I need to be alone. With my dad.

'I … I'm fine.' Rob tried to hide the shake in his voice, and clasped the bear tightly to stop the one in his hands. 'I probably need something to eat. I didn't have breakfast.' Alhough he had. His chest still hurt: a dull ache just below his ribs. His mind raced and he kept seeing the tattoo as if it was burned on both his retinas. DEBBY. Debby. *Debby*. His mind flashed back to his first conversation with Deirdre. Is it *Bizzie* or *Bizzy?* Spelled with an *IE* or a *Y?* Or is it *Busy? Bee You Ess Why.*

Why.

Was that tattoo the last thing Eric saw, as he slumped to the floor of the carriage?

'I need some fresh air, Rachel,' he said. 'Do you mind? Can you manage the second session on your own?'

Her face was full of concern. 'Do you want me to come with you?'

'No. No, I'll be fine. It's … It's a bit hot in here today, that's all.'

'Are you sure?' She wrinkled her brow. 'Was it Mick? Do you know him, Rob? Was it him that upset you?'

'No, I've never seen him before in my life,' he said.

'Because he's harmless, really. I think he has a soft spot for me, since he did that work in my flat. There's always a bit of banter, but he's a nice enough bloke.'

Rob was torn between leaving so he could talk to Paddytum, to his father, and staying here so Rachel wouldn't be alone with the man, Mick. He didn't like the idea of him being anywhere near

217

her. He shuddered as he thought of that arm round her shoulder. But she wasn't alone.

He bent to give her a kiss on the cheek. 'Look, I think I'll go home. Can I come round to yours, later? You're still closing early today, aren't you?'

'Yes. Two o'clock.' She looked worried. 'You sure you'll be all right?'

'I'll be fine,' he said. The tingle in his jaw was fading, and so was the ache in his chest. But he could still hear the scream.

He slipped out through the side door, to avoid seeing Mick.

Rob walked fast. Halfway home, he was tempted to take the bear out of his rucksack, and ask his father if he was all right, but he just got home as quickly as he could. He caught sight of his face in the hall mirror as he entered the house. His mother was still out, and for that he was grateful. He didn't want to have to explain to her why he looked so pale, and so rattled.

Up in his room, he put the bear on the bed.

'Dad?' he said softly. 'Are you there?'

'Yes,' came the quiet response.

'It was him?'

'It was him. Wait. How do you know? You never saw him.'

'I knew when I saw the tattoo. Debby. The guard told Ma at the funeral that you were saying that name, over and over when he got to you. "Debbie. Why." Only, you weren't *asking* "why", were you? You were trying to tell someone it was Debbie spelled with a "Y".

'I'd forgotten that tattoo. How could I forget? I said that name, over and over, as I waited for someone to find me, in case I forgot before the police – or someone – got to me. I felt myself fading out, so I just kept repeating it. Debby. Y. It seemed really important that I make sure they knew about the tattoo. They call them distinguishing marks, don't they?

And what a misunderstanding that tattoo had caused. How much anguish it had caused his mother. He wouldn't tell him. He'd had enough of a shock.

'Hold on, Rob. Did you say someone told your mother? Did she think—' Too late, Rob thought. 'Is that why she never talks about me? Why she took all the photos down?' Rob nodded. 'But

I'd never, ever have done anything like that. How could she think it of me?'

'Well, perhaps we can find some way to tell her,' Rob said. Goodness knew how, though. But there was another issue to deal with first. 'So ... what do we do now? Are you absolutely sure it was him? No, of course you are. It's hardly likely there'd be two people with that same tattoo. And he looked as if he was a redhead. Before the hairdresser got to him.'

'It was his eyes, too, son. There was rage in them, and I saw it again today.' There was a silence. 'I don't think there's anything we can do, Rob, is there? It's not like you can go to the police and say, my work colleague's son murdered my father twenty-three years ago. Oh yes, sir? How exactly do you know this? My teddy bear told me.'

'No,' Rob said, with a wry smile. 'It might be somewhat difficult for them to take that seriously. It'd be me they'd lock up, instead of this Mick. But what about Marge? She has a right to know what her son did.' Rob put his hand up to his forehead, feeling the start of a headache. 'Dad, this is awful.'

'I don't really see how you can get Marge involved in this,' his father said.

'Well, she is already, isn't she? Accidentally.' He had a thought. 'Dad? Perhaps Rachel could help us.'

'How?' His father sounded exasperated. 'How would you even begin to tell her about all this? She's a lovely girl, but I think even she would have a job to take you seriously if you told her about me ... who I am.'

'The alternative is ...' Rob tailed off.

The alternative was far worse, Rob knew. To let this man remain free, at large, like he had all those years, unpunished for taking a father away from a family. Taking *his* father away from *him*. Not to mention the aftermath. And who knows if he hadn't done something like that since? Or might do in the future?

'I can't see any other way,' he said, finally. 'We can't tell Ma. It would freak her out too much. And we obviously can't go to the police. But Rachel ... she might even be at risk. He's been to her flat. Good grief, he must have spent hours there when he was doing that electrical work. What if he decides to go round there and tell her he wants to inspect his work – make sure it's all

219

working properly. I saw the way he looked at her. I have to tell her. Who knows, she might just believe it.' Of course, it's far more likely she won't, he thought. And then I'll lose her.

He looked at his watch. Two o'clock. Rachel would just be leaving the library. If he set off now, he'd get to her flat just after she arrived home. He was terrified at the thought of what he must do. 'I'm going to tell Rachel.'

'Rob, I really don't think that's a good idea.'

'Sorry, Dad, I have to.'

THIRTY-FOUR

Rob rang Rachel's bell. She took so long to come to the door he feared she hadn't arrived home yet, and he felt a mixture of relief that he could put it off, and disappointment that he'd psyched himself up for nothing. Eventually, the door opened and she stood there, wrapping her hair, turban-like, in a blue towel.

'Sorry, Rob,' she said. 'Just had a quick hair wash. Come in.' She pulled the towel off and her hair fell in damp waves onto her shoulders. 'How are you feeling?' She studied his face. 'You're still a bit pale.'

'Rachel, I need to talk to you about something.' He took a deep breath. 'Can we go and sit down?'

'Oh,' she said. 'You sound serious.' She led the way into her living room, and sat on the sofa. He didn't sit beside her. This would be more difficult sitting close to her. He took the armchair next to the sofa, and perched on the edge.

'Rob?' She looked worried. 'What's wrong? You're making me nervous,' she said.

He took another deep breath. Where the hell should he start? 'That makes two of us. I'm terrified,' he said with a half smile. 'I'm afraid you're going to think I'm nuts.'

'Go on.' she said. 'Try me.'

'Well. How can I say this? Oh, bloody hell, Rachel, this is so difficult.'

'Just say it, Rob. I'm sure you're worrying over nothing.' She leaned forward, her hair falling forward in dark, wavy fronds. He could smell the sharp scent of her shampoo: something fruity and sweet.

'Well, you know you asked me the other day what brought me out of my rut? The one I'd been in since my dad died.'

'Yes?'

'Well ... it was my dad. Only, I didn't know it was my dad. I thought it was Paddytum.'

'Paddy who?' She looked puzzled.

'Well, that's what I used to call him, you see. But he told me his name was Frederick now.'

'Sorry, Rob, you've lost me'

'That may be the case if you don't believe what I'm about to tell you. I'm so afraid I *will* lose you. But I swear what I'm about to say is the truth, however strange it's going to sound.'

'Just tell me, Rob. I don't have any idea what you're talking about.'

So he told her. Everything that had happened since the day Paddytum started to talk to him. He told her how the bear had made him get off his backside and start exercising, how he'd told him to stop eating fattening rubbish, how he'd encouraged him to look for a job, and then stopped him from cancelling the interview at the library. He didn't dare look at Rachel; he sat with his hands clasped in front of him, staring straight ahead. He told her about Paddytum's suggestion that he use him as a prop for Story Time, when he'd accidentally spilled out of the bag. 'It was completely out of the blue. He just thought of it on the spot.'

At the edge of his field of vision, he saw that Rachel's position had shifted. She was no longer leaning toward him. And her legs had shifted a few centimetres away from his.

'Carry on,' she said. Her voice sounded flat.

He told her about his suspicions, after bumping into her in the park, that the bear was actually the ghost of his father, and how they had been confirmed after talking to Deirdre. And finally, he told her the story of the mysterious Debbie, and about the tattoo he'd seen on Marjorie's son's hand.

'And he has red hairs on his hand, too. My dad says it was definitely him.'

Rachel didn't say a word when he finished talking, and Rob was still afraid to look at her. Finally, she said. 'Oh, Rob.'

He looked over at her. And his heart dropped like a stone. The look on her face was not one of understanding; it was not one of sympathy; it was a look of disappointment.

'You don't believe me, do you?'

'Did you really expect me to? I mean, be honest. What an absolute load of rot! I don't know whether to throw you out or have you sectioned.' She looked at him hard. 'What I don't understand is … what is the motive behind this little fairytale of

222

yours? Is it jealousy? Is it because I told you I thought Mick fancied me, you now see him as some kind of threat?'

'But he might be!' Rob said. 'He's a murde—'

'Stop!' She put her hand up, palm outwards. 'I don't know what you're getting out of this. I think you must be seriously disturbed. Talking teddy bears. Ghosts. Murderous electricians. What next? Is Marjorie an alien? Is Carole ... a ... a ... zombie?' Her face was red. Rob sat, looking at her. Misery flooded his heart. He'd ruined everything. His dad had been right. He should have listened to him.

He stood up, slowly. 'All right. I'll go. I'm sorry, Rachel. It's true, but I don't blame you for not believing me. Shit, I mean, I wouldn't believe such a mad story, either. I still have trouble getting my head around it myself. But I promise you I am not lying. I mean, why would I?'

Rachel just sat, not looking at him. 'I don't know, Rob. You tell me.' Expressionless.

'I'll let myself out.' He walked a few steps into the corridor, and then turned round. She hadn't moved an inch, was still staring ahead. 'I'm sorry,' he said. And then more quietly, 'I love you.'

And then he was gone.

THIRTY-FIVE

Rachel sat for a full five minutes after she heard the front door close, just staring at the blank screen of the television. Then she became aware that her hair, still wet, was starting to drip onto the towel draped around her shoulders. She shivered, but not with the cold. She stood and went to the window, standing slightly to the side so she would not be seen if Rob were out there looking up. There was no need. She watched as he turned the corner, walking with his shoulders slumped.

She went to her bedroom, took the hair-dryer off the top of her chest of drawers, and plugged it in. Taking a round brush, she started to blow-dry her hair, playing the dryer across the thick strands as she brushed in long, rhythmic strokes.

She stared at herself in the mirror. What a difference from the happy face she'd seen there just this morning when putting on her make up. She was glad her mascara was waterproof, because she knew tears were not far away. Angry tears, not sad ones. Oh, who was she fooling? She was angry with herself more than him. He was just to be pitied. The poor man must surely be deranged. Who the hell did he think he was, expecting someone of her intelligence to believe such a ridiculous story? How bloody dare he? 'Oh!' She tugged at a tangle, yanking the brush in frustration, and finally throwing it down and switching off the dryer. She wanted to scream.

She'd thought, finally, she'd found someone she could trust. Someone who seemed to think the same way she did. After she'd caught Paul cheating on her, she'd sworn off men altogether, and then this sensitive, sweet man had come into the library, had come into her heart, and stolen it. Yes, he was childlike, perhaps, and she'd liked that, but this ... this load of rubbish he had come out with now was not what she had bargained for at all. She felt her hair. One side was dry and the other still damp. Who cares, she thought, suddenly devoid of energy. She lay down on her bed, not caring that her soggy hair would make her pillow damp, and closed her eyes.

She lay there for half an hour, trying hard not to think about Rob. But, inevitably, her mind drifted back to him. What about work? How could she possibly see him every day after this? Mind you, she'd managed to keep her distance from him during working hours all week. Could she carry on like that?

And what about Story Time? Well, she would have to tell him his and Frederick's services would no longer be required. The children would be disappointed, no doubt, but they'd get over it. They'd managed without Rob before he came along, and they would again.

Are you sure he wasn't telling the truth, though? A little voice began to nag in her head. He sounded earnest enough, didn't he? Yes, but if he actually believed it, he's obviously deluded. He might even be dangerous.

I promise you, I'm not lying. I mean, why would I? He'd sounded so sad, defeated, beaten. Yes, why would he? How could anyone come up with such a fantastic story? She had to give him credit for imagination. She reminded herself that she hadn't known him very long. Perhaps he lived in a fantasy world, and had been dreaming up these stories in his room ever since his father's death – some kind of psychosis brought about by grief. There had to be an explanation for why he'd never had a job. He might even have been sacked for something like this in the past, and managed to cover it up.

Oh, Rachel, you can't be that bad a judge of character, can you?

Oh, she'd been daydreaming too, for sure, this past week. Part of her had loved the thrill of their secret relationship – well, secret from everyone but Carole, anyway. But she had really thought Rob might be 'the one'. It had felt so *right*. If she admitted it to herself, she had seen herself being with Rob for good. A three-bedroom semi in a nice part of town; he would eventually be promoted and she would take a career break – like Carole – to look after their two gorgeous musically talented bookworm children. Yearning for the patter of tiny feet.

Perhaps that was it. Her biological clock ticking away and leading her up the garden path to a totally unsuitable relationship.

'The patter of tiny feet.' she said out loud. 'What an idiot you are, Rachel Jenkins.'

She suddenly had the feeling she was missing something important. What if it was true, as absurd as it seemed? A ridiculous thought, and anyway, there'd be no way to check his story.

Patter.

She sat up.

The patter of tiny feet. *Patter.* Rob had said he couldn't possibly sing a patter song, but—

She picked up the phone, and looked at the list of staff phone numbers she kept by her bed in case she couldn't get in because of illness, as she was the only key-holder. Rob's name was at the bottom of the list.

She dialled the number, her hands shaking as she pushed the buttons, far from sure this was the right thing to do. A woman answered.

'Hello, Mrs Handle? Is Robert there, please?'

'Yes, he's just this minute walked in. May I ask who's calling?' She had to strain to hear her. Softly spoken, like her son.

'It's Rachel.'

'Oh,' she said. 'Is that Rachel from his work? I've heard so much about you.'

I wonder what. She waited.

'Hello?' Tentative, unsure.

'Rob. Could you come over tomorrow?'

A long pause. 'Um ... yes, of course. What time?'

'In the afternoon. Around one o'clock?'

'Yes. That's fine.' A pause. 'Rachel?'

'Yes?'

'Why?'

She was the one who paused this time. 'I'm not sure,' She sighed. 'Rob?'

'Yes?'

'Bring Frederick with you.'

Rob had been sure when his mother had handed him the receiver that Rachel was ringing to tell him not to bother coming in to work on Monday. He still didn't know she wouldn't tell him that tomorrow. Except that she could have said it on the phone, and it didn't explain why she wanted him to bring Paddytum. Her voice hadn't given anything away, neither friendly nor hostile.

He hadn't spoken much to his father since he left Rachel's. It was not because he was angry with him – if anything, it was himself he was angry with – it was more that he was beginning to doubt the whole thing himself, and to wonder it he'd conjured the entire thing up in his own head.

The next day, having dropped off to sleep sometime after dawn, he woke at eleven feeling groggy and flat. He wished he could just pull the duvet up and hide from the world.

His mother bustled round him in the kitchen, making him a bacon and egg roll for brunch. 'Are you all right, love? You've been ever so quiet since yesterday.'

'Don't worry, Ma,' he said. He wished he could tell her. But her reaction was likely to be worse than Rachel's had been. There was no point in saying anything until he knew how the land lay.

At one o'clock, he stood outside Rachel's door, carrying the rucksack containing the bear.

Rachel opened the door. She smiled tightly and stood aside to let him in. It wasn't the smile he'd become used to over the previous week, or even the friendly smile to which he was accustomed at work, but a smile nonetheless.

'Come and sit down,' she said, leading him into the living room. He took a seat in the armchair, and waited.

'What you said yesterday was a bit of a bombshell. To say the least,'

He didn't reply. There was nothing to say.

'But I've been thinking about it, Rob. In fact, I've thought of little else.'

'Did you come to any conclusions?' he asked.

'I suppose, the only conclusions possible are that you're either stark raving bonkers ...' she smiled ruefully, 'or a very bad practical joker ... Or ...'

'Or?'

'As completely outrageous and unlikely the story you told me seems to be, I have to consider the possibility that it might be true. After all, as you said, why would you make it up?'

227

Rob's eyes widened. She believed him? Or she might be willing to, anyway. A tiny sliver of hope.

'But, Rob. I have to ask you to prove it.'

Hope slid out the door, leaving him deflated. 'I can't, Rachel. How can I?'

'Is Frederick, or Paddything, or whatever you call him, in that bag?'

Rob picked up his rucksack, and unzipped it, taking the bear out. He hadn't spoken at all this morning. Rob wondered if he'd gone. Or if he'd ever been there in the first place.

'Can *he* hear what I'm saying to you? Your father— God, I can't believe I'm saying this—'

His father spoke. 'Tell her I'm here,'

Rob nodded. 'He just spoke to me, then.' Rachel looked uncomfortable. She looked hard at Rob's face.

'I believe she's going to test us, Rob,' his father said. 'She's a bright girl. I wonder what she has in mind.' Rob couldn't believe it. His dad sounded pleased. Excited, even.

'You remember, the other day, we were talking about Patter songs?' she said.

'Yes.'

'I want you to sing one for me,'

'How? Why— But I don't know any. And anyway, I don't think I could—'

'Exactly!' Rachel said, with the hint of a smile. '*You* couldn't …'

Rob frowned. 'So, what do—?'

'But I *can*. Oh, you clever girl!' The voice in his head was so loud that he looked at Rachel because he was sure she must hear it too.

'You told me that day, that your father was an expert at singing patter?'

Rob nodded. 'That's what Deirdre said, anyway.'

'So, if he can control your voice, like you say he can—'

'I could sing a patter song? But … how would you know I wasn't lying in the first place, about not being able to sing one. I know I might not be doing myself any favours here, but if I was lying about the rest of it, why would you believe me?'

228

'I thought about that, Rob, last night.' She looked at him. 'I don't know why, but there's something that tells me you really *don't* know much about Gilbert and Sullivan. And yes, I suppose you could have learned *one* patter song, to try and convince me. But, if I were to choose—'

'Rob, she's brilliant! If the choice is hers, it makes it very unlikely that you could have learned the very one she happens to choose. Tell her to name her song. Whatever she wants me to sing, I'm game.'

'Are you sure?' Rob said, looking at the bear, and Rachel frowned. 'Sorry, that wasn't for you. I was talking to him. Won't you be a bit rusty, after all this time?'

'Well, there's only one way to find out, isn't there?'

He looked back at Rachel. 'Which song?'

'He said yes?' Rachel said carefully.

'Actually, he sounds pretty eager,' he said. 'I can't say the same for myself.'

Would his own 'vocal equipment' as his father called it, match up to the person controlling it? He thought back to the guy singing on the DVD, rattling off the words rapid fire, and doubted it.

'Okay. The first verse of the *Matter Patter* from *Ruddigore*.'

'The what?'

'It's all right, Rob, his father said. 'I know the one she means. *My eyes are fully open.*'

'Never mind your eyes, let's hope my mouth is.'

'No, that's the name of the song. But it's known in G & S circles as the *Matter Patter*. You'll see why. Or rather, you'll hear …'

Rachel was watching him, bemused, her glance switching from him to the bear. 'Well?'

'He says he'll do it.'

'Ready, son?'

'As ready as I'll ever be.' Here goes nothing, Rob thought, waiting for the tingle. He waited.

His father spoke again. 'It's all right; I just need to go through the words quickly in my mind before I start. It's been a few years, you know.'

'Okay,' Rob said. 'When you're ready.'

229

Rachel gave him an odd look, and Rob shrugged. And waited. And then the tingle came, and Rob's mouth opened.

'My eyes are fully open to my awful situation,
I shall go at once to Roderick and make him an oration.
I shall tell him I've recovered my forgotten moral senses,
And I don't care tuppence-ha'penny for any consequences.'

It started quickly, and gathered speed. Rob's eyes grew wider as his mouth machine-gunned the unfamiliar words out into Rachel's living room. Halfway through, he noticed that his left foot was tapping out the beat, and the beat was getting faster by the line.

'Now I do not want to perish by the sword or by the dagger,
But a martyr may indulge a little pardonable swagger,
And a word or two of compliment my vanity would flatter,
But I've got to die tomorrow, so it really doesn't matter matter matter
matter matter.'

The words flew out, all but unintelligible to him, though he could hear that his diction was perfect, and the singing perfectly in tune. He watched Rachel's face change from a watchful expression, to doubt, to interested attentiveness, to sheer wonder. At the end, his jaw relaxed. Was that the end? It had finished quicker than he expected.

'Does she want me to do the other two verses?' his dad panted. He sounded exhausted. No surprise; Rob felt the same way. He didn't get a chance to ask Rachel. She had risen to her feet, and came over to put her arms around his shoulders.

She kissed him full on the lips, and caressed his neck. 'I'm so, so sorry.' She kissed him again. 'I'm sorry I doubted you. Rob, that was the most amazing thing I've ever heard in my life. Or seen'.

'Charming!' he heard his father say. 'I do all the hard work, and *he* gets the kisses.' But he sounded pleased. Rob grinned.

'What?' Rachel asked.

'Oh, I really wish you could hear what he's saying, Rach,' he said.

'So … does he talk to you the whole time?'

Rob looked down at the bear, played with one of its ears. 'No. Not really.' He grinned again. 'For a ghost, he's really quite well behaved.'

Rachel lowered her voice. 'Are you sure that's what he is, though? I mean, how does he control your voice? I can't say I'm an expert on ghosts but I'd never heard of anything like that before.'

'No, and he doesn't know, either. Or why I can only hear him and not see him. It's strange, isn't—'

'If you two have quite finished rabbiting about me behind my back, shouldn't we be talking about what we're going to do?'

'Oh dear,' Rob said. 'Sorry, Dad. Rachel, he says we need to decide what to do … well, about Marjorie's son.'

Rachel sat down. 'Is there anything we *can* do? I can't tell the police about your suspicions any more than you can, Rob. It all comes back to the source of the evidence.' She leaned over and touched Paddytum's head. 'A ghost – hiding inside a teddy bear. It's hardly … irrefutable, is it?'

'Couldn't we get hold of his DNA, somehow, and get the police to test it?' Rob asked. He knew even as he said it that it was a stupid idea. 'No, they'd still want to know why we wanted them to test it – and what made us so sure it was him.'

'Lets think about this, Rob. Mr Handle recognised him … Sorry, I feel like I'm leaving your dad out.'

'She can call me Eric.' his dad said. Robert passed this on.

'Well, Eric recognised him – was it mainly from the Debby tattoo?'

'He recognised his face, too, but the tattoo clinched it. Didn't it, Dad?'

Rachel put a finger on her lower lip, and gazed into the middle distance, thinking. She turned to Rob. 'And Mick seemed to recognise you, Rob. I wonder why that was …'

'No idea. I certainly didn't know him … Hey! Are you thinking it was because I look like—'

'Well, yes. From the photos I've seen, you're very like him.'

'You have your mother's eyes, though, Robert. And you're taller than I am—was.'

'Not by much though, Dad.' Rachel shot him an enquiring look. 'He says I'm taller, but yes. And my mother's said so a few times recently.' He scratched his head. 'Rachel might be onto something here. Do you think we can use that … to, sort of force a confession out of him?'

'I don't know. Can you make yourself look even more like your dad looked … then?'

'I could gel my hair down. He used to use Brylcreem. And there's the spare suit. It's practically identical to the one he was wearing that day. But it's such a long time ago. Over twenty yea—'

'I remember,' his father said quietly, 'every single word I said to him that evening. Before …'

Rob sat up straight. 'You spoke to him? You never told me that.'

'Well, you didn't ask.'

Rachel was looking from the bear to Rob. 'What's he saying? That he had a conversation with … him? Before he …'

'He said he remembers every word he said.' He paused, as if listening. 'He says it was hardly a conversation. Hang on, are you suggesting …'

'A sort of re-enactment,' Rachel said. 'Could that work?'

'I don't know,' Rob said, looking down at the bear. 'Do you mean talking through me again? One last time.'

'It would be traumatic,' Rachel said. 'For both of you. But, if it gets a result …'

'He says he's willing,' Rob told Rachel. 'He thinks we should try.' He stroked the bear's head. 'I do too. But … how? And when? And where?'

THIRTY-SIX

It was Rachel's idea, and Rob didn't much like it. It put her at risk. After all, she didn't even need to be there.

'But I'll be a witness, then, won't I? Otherwise, it'll just be your word against his.'

'Yes, I know, but it isn't fair, dragging you into this.'

'I'm already a part of it, aren't I?' she said. 'And I can't see any other way of doing it without involving Marjorie.'

In the end, Rob had agreed. Reluctantly. They had talked for hours, discussing all the possible outcomes. Rob had worried that it wouldn't go the way they planned. 'He might just run out of the flat, and then where would we be?' Rob had said. 'And what if he attacks you?'

'Well, he'll have no reason to do that, will he, if he doesn't even know what we have planned?' She hugged Rob. 'Don't worry. I'm sure it'll be fine. We have to try. For Eric's sake. For your mum's sake, too. If he's arrested, it won't take much to link his tattoo to your father's last words to the guard. And once she realises that there was no Debbie your dad was carrying on with, it'll put your mum's mind at rest.'

'I wonder if the guard's still alive, though. He'd have to appear as a witness. And wouldn't it just be circumstantial evidence, anyway?'

'I think we're getting ahead of ourselves here, Rob,' Rachel said. 'We need to cross those bridges when we come to them, not burn them before we even try.'

Rob laughed. 'Sorry. It's one of my problems. I always over-think everything.'

She put a hand up to stroke his cheek. 'Well, in some ways, it's good to be cautious, isn't it? As long as you can be impulsive occasionally.' She smiled. 'Like serenading girls in the park.'

Next day, at the library, Rachel approached Rob while he was re-shelving books. 'Right,' she said. 'It's all set. I phoned him this morning and told him the overhead light in my living room keeps flickering. He's coming round at half past eight tonight. He sounded really eager.' She made a face. 'It turned my stomach. Are you ready for this?'

Rob's insides churned. 'I kind of wish we could wait and do it another time.' He looked away, and then back at Rachel. 'But I know that's just me being a coward. I wish I were as brave as you, Rach. You're so little and I'm so big, yet you're willing to do this. For me. But I know we have to try.'

'Yes, we do. If we succeed, you'll really be free, I think. And then you'll start to believe in yourself.'

'Do you think so?'

'Oh, Rob, I think you could do anything if you put your mind to it. Anyway, I'm all set. I'm almost looking forward to it. In a "want to get it over with" sort of way.'

'So, I'll come round at … what, eight o'clock? Or should we make it seven thirty?'

'Yes,' she said. 'Earlier is better. But I was thinking, after I rang him – I wouldn't put it past him to turn up early and hang around waiting for me to get home. He did that a few times when he was doing the work originally. He knows what time I get in.'

'You know what I could do with? A mobile. I meant to get one sorted out when I started work, but never got round to it. Then you could warn me if he's already there.'

'Good idea,' Rachel said, looking around the library. Marjorie and Carole were both involved in other things. 'Look, I'll lend you mine. I can ring you from my land line to tell you if the coast is clear.'

Rob laughed. 'All right, Agent Jenkins. Why do I suddenly feel as if I'm in a James Bond film?'

She grinned at him, and then looked over her shoulder again. 'It is a bit like that, isn't it. Just call me M. Or is it Q?'

'No, he's the one with the gadgets. You're not telling me your mobile is equipped with a Death Ray, are you?'

She giggled. 'No, but it has an mp3 player if you wanted to fire Abba songs at him.'

Rob snorted with laughter. 'So he can meet his Waterloo, you mean?'

Rachel laughed so hard she had to hold onto the shelves. Marjorie looked over at them, and rolled her eyes in disapproval.

234

Carole grinned at them. 'That was quite good,' Rachel said, when she'd calmed down.

'Thank you. Sometimes I'm so brilliant it's frightening.' He took a breath, to calm himself. He knew his flippancy was due to nerves. 'Right,' he said, his face straight, 'So I'll wait on the corner at half-seven.'

'And bring the suit with you.'

'Of course. And the hair gel.'

'And Freder—Paddytum.'

'Of course. We can't do it without him, can we?'

Rob had tried his father's suit on last night, as soon as he reached home. He looked at his reflection in the full-length mirror on the inside of his wardrobe door, and stood in stunned silence. It brought back a memory of his father setting off for work in the morning, saying goodbye to Maureen with a kiss, and to Rob, in his school uniform, with a squeeze of his shoulder. He was thankful for Rachel's suggestion that he change into the suit at her flat. It might be too much of a shock for Maureen seeing him dressed like this. In the mirror, he saw Paddytum on the bed behind him. 'What do you think, Dad? Will I do?'

'The resemblance is almost frightening. Trousers are a fraction too short, of course. '

Rob looked down. The trouser cuffs rested a little higher than they should, but it was the sort of thing someone would only notice if they were looking for it. 'Well, hopefully, he'll be too busy looking at my face to look at the bottom of my trousers.'

'Your hair will need taming. But then, so did mine. These days I suppose I would have let it stay the way it was.'

He fiddled with a stray lock, and shrugged, and then turned to face the bear. 'How do you feel?'

'I don't know,' he said. 'Frightened. Although it's not as if he can do anything to me now. I'm afraid for you, perhaps. Afraid it could go wrong, and that we're wasting our time.' There was a pause. 'Afraid I'll … break down at having to relive it. Even in speech.'

'Perhaps that's the key, though, Dad. You were afraid. Terrified for your life. But perhaps you have to keep in mind that it's a bit like acting. Because, this time, he can't hurt you. So, act your socks off. Play the best role you've ever played. It'll be

235

method acting at its finest. Do you think … a rehearsal would help? A run-through, sort of thing?'

His father took a while to answer. 'No. Reliving it will be hard enough just once. To do it twice would be unbearable. And … I think it would take away from the impact. No, son. To borrow from the language of the film-makers, this has to be a one-take performance.'

He carried the overnight bag containing the bear, the suit, and his father's glasses downstairs while his mother was still in the kitchen dishing up their meal, and tucked it in the corner of the front porch. The last thing he needed would be for her to see what he was carrying. He just hoped she'd have no reason to go to the front door before he left, and he kept his ears open for the doorbell. It would be a real pain if a couple of stray Jehovah's Witnesses or a double-glazing salesman scuppered his plan.

'Everything going well with your girlfriend, Robbie?' Maureen asked, as she lifted a chunk of beef to her lips.

'Yes, fine,' he said. His mind whirled with thoughts of the ordeal ahead of him – and Rachel and his father – and he was in no mood to chat. Would tonight be life-changing? Best not to think about it. Just keep your mind on the goal, Rob, he thought.

He kissed his mother goodbye and snatched up the bag on his way out. On the bus, he sat with his hands clamped tight around the handles of the bag, shaking his head several times to push negative thoughts away. In the bag, the bear was silent.

He stood on the corner of Rachel's road twenty minutes later, the bag at his feet, and as soon as he saw Rachel's Yaris make the turn, the butterflies started swarming in his abdomen. Her eyes met his, briefly, through the windscreen, but her face was expressionless. He looked at his watch. Twenty-five past seven. He took Rachel's pale blue Samsung phone out of his pocket, his eyes going first to the little block of bars indicating the signal intensity. Four bars. Then five, then down to four again. So far, so good.

The phone rang within minutes, playing a snatch of an Abba song, startling him so he almost dropped the phone in his attempt to answer it. He registered the words, 'Home calling' on the display.

'Hello?'

Rachel's voice was hushed. 'All clear, come on up. Front door's on the latch.'

He picked up the bag, and walked quickly to the building.

Seconds later, he was pushing open her door. She pulled him into the corridor and put her arms around him in a hug. 'Hi. You okay?'

He nodded against her shoulder. 'If I were to tell you I'm not nervous it'd be a lie. Well, actually, it wouldn't be. Nervous doesn't even begin to describe it.'

'I know,' she said, standing back and looking at him. 'Me too. Do you want to do it another time? You can always leave your costume and props here.'

He sighed. 'It's tempting, but I'm afraid if we don't do it now, I'll just chicken out again the next time, and the next. He looked down at the bag in his hand. 'And I owe it to ... him.'

'Fine, let's go,' Rachel said. 'You can change in my bedroom.' She opened the door to the right, and stood aside to let him in.

When Rachel had left him, he quickly stripped off and pulled the other clothes out of the bag: the suit, a white shirt and a navy tie. He slipped off his brown shoes to change his trousers and then put them back on. His dad's shoes had been black, but this was a minor detail. Then he gelled his hair, keeping an eye on the alarm clock on Rachel's bedside cabinet, his heart racing as he saw how much time had slipped past already. Finally, after straightening the tie and running a comb through his newly gelled-down hair, he looked at the effect in Rachel's dressing table mirror. 'You'll do,' he said. He looked inside the overnight bag, into Paddytum's black, glassy eyes. 'Right then, Dad,' he said. 'Here goes nothing.'

'Thanks for the vote of confidence,' was the reply, but there was a hint of a laugh in the voice. 'Good luck, Rob.'

'Same to you,' he said. 'Let's go.'

He carried the bag into Rachel's living room. She'd moved the sofa so that it faced the door. Rob touched his gelled hair, which was set so hard it felt like plastic. However did people use this stuff? He just wanted to wash it out. Brylcreem must be worse, though, like having permanently greasy hair.

237

Rachel followed him into the room. 'Wow, look at you! You look so different.' She fingered the fine wool fabric of his lapel, and ran a hand down the sleeve. 'It's a lovely suit. I can see why he was so fond of it.' She glanced toward the door. 'It's almost time. You'd better sit down.'

Rob positioned himself on the sofa, and lifted the bag onto his lap. He put his hand inside it, making sure it was in contact with the bear.

'Dad,' Rob said. 'Did you have your jacket on?'

'I think so,' the voice said. 'I put it back on as we arrived at the last station before Fleesham. And the bag was on my lap, too, like you have it. I was ready to get off at the next stop.'

Rob nodded at Rachel. 'We're set.' He took a deep breath, and tried to relax.

Rachel stepped over to him, and kissed him on the lips. She gave him one last look up and down. 'Rob. Glasses.'

'Oh God, yes,' he said. He'd slipped the spectacles into his top pocket in the bedroom, so that he could see properly to walk to the living room. He put them on, and everything immediately blurred. He blinked, and looked up at Rachel over the top of them. She giggled, and clapped a hand over her mouth.

'Sorry, you reminded me of Marge, doing that. Can you see all right in them?'

'Well enough. I don't suppose it makes much difference how well I can see.'

The doorbell rang. Rob froze, and Rachel's hand, on his shoulder, started to shake slightly. Rob tightened his own grip on the bear's head, while reaching up with his other hand to squeeze Rachel's fingers. He turned his head to kiss her fingertips.

'Be careful,' she said, and tiptoed away, closing the living room door on him.

Rob listened. He faintly heard the door open and Rachel greeting Mick, and then muffled footsteps along the carpeted corridor, as Rachel said, 'Go in, Mick. Would you like a cup of tea or coffee?'

'Coffee would be good,' he said, 'Unless you have anything stronger?' Rob fixed his eyes on the door handle. It turned, and then stopped, as he heard Rachel's voice again. Rob heard the shake in it. 'I might have some beer in the fridge.'

'Magic. Yes please.' The handle turned again, and the door opened.

Mick stood in the doorway, in a T-shirt and jeans, a tool-belt slung around his waist. He froze at the sight of Rob on the sofa looking at him over the rims of the glasses.

'What—' Mick said. 'Who—'

Rob felt the tingle. He was ready for it – had expected it from the moment the door opened. Nevertheless, his father's own voice, coming out of his mouth, gave him a jolt which felt like electricity.

'*Sorry, you can't smoke in here, son. This is a non-smoking carriage.*'

Mick blanched, and looked behind him, at the open doorway. Even with the blood pounding in his ears, Rob wondered where Rachel was. And he thought for a second the man was going to turn and run, but he simply turned back, and peered at Rob. He said nothing, and stood as though paralysed.

'*I'm sorry, aren't you going to tell me not to effing call you "son" because I'm not your effing old man and you'll effing do what you effing want?*' The voice was sardonic, almost an echo of the one Rob had first heard in his head. '*Excuse me not quoting verbatim, but I'm a gentleman, and there's a lady present, so I'm paraphrasing, of course, but wasn't that your cue to pull out your little knife.*'

Mick looked around him again. 'What knife? What are you talking about? It wasn't me, mate. You must be confusing me with somebody else.' He narrowed his eyes, and looked more closely. 'Hang on! You can't be that bloke; he was a lot older than me. What's going on?' He took a step forward, and Rob's heart juddered, and began to hammer in his chest. He hoped he wouldn't need to stand, because he knew his legs wouldn't support him.

'*Bloke? What bloke, Mick?*' his father's voice said, through Rob's throat and lips. '*Oh, do you mean me? The one you stabbed? Even though I gave you my wallet? Can you remember, Mick, how I pleaded with you?*'

Mick's eyes were wide now, petrified, as Eric's voice continued, and Rob's heart thudded louder as he realised he was beginning to stand, that Eric was forcing him off the sofa to stand on legs made of foam rubber, and lean towards the man.

'*Please. Take the wallet. Take my bag too, if you want. You can keep the wallet. I'm sorry there's so little in it. I don't carry much cash.*' Mick was backing away, his legs against the armchair, almost climbing backwards onto the seat. All the time, Eric kept talking, and Rob heard the panic in his voice and it almost brought tears to his eyes, and it just carried on, unrelenting, '*Please! Just take them and go. Don't do this. I have a wife. A son. They love me. They're expecting me home. Please, I beg you.*' The voice rose, and then stopped abruptly.

And then Rob saw that the man who, he now had no doubt, had killed his father, was not looking at his face any more. He was looking at his hand. And he realised that as he stood up the bag had slipped, exposing Paddytum. He stood, panting. Waiting.

'Hey. You're him. That bloke from the library. What is this, then? Some kind of sick joke?'

His face was a mixture of anger and confusion. Rob took a step toward him. He felt the tingle again, and this time he fought it.

He murmured, 'Dad. Let *me*.'

Mick took a step back, toward the doorway. 'Who are you?'

Rob advanced, still holding the bear. 'You killed my father, you little bastard. You took a good man away from his family. You broke my mother's heart and you ruined my life.'

Mick shrank back just as Rachel appeared in the doorway, holding her phone to her ear. Mick saw Rob's gaze shift, and his hand darted to the tool-belt.

'Rob, watch out, he's got a—'

As he spotted the object in Mick's hand, Rob's arm was gripped with a force that raised it up, still holding the bear tightly by his head, and he watched as Mick's hand thrust up and towards him. He heard Rachel's half-gasp, half-scream as the shaft of the screwdriver sank deep, deep, into Paddytum's belly.

Rob reached out with his other hand and shoved him on the forehead, hard. Mick stumbled and fell backwards; landing sprawled on his back on the floor.

'I didn't mean it, mate. I didn't want to do it. You have to believe me. I'd do anything – anything to take it back. I'm not like that any more.'

Rachel said, coldly, behind him. 'You are. You just tried to stab him.' She looked at Rob. 'I called the police. They're on their way.'

Mick turned his head to look up at Rachel. 'But I didn't do anything. Except stab a teddy with a screwdriver.'

'And you just confessed to his father's murder. Didn't he, Rob?'

'Yes, he did. Overcome with remorse, Rachel, wasn't he?'

Mick struggled to his feet. 'No! No I didn't! You can't pin that on me. I'll deny it.'

'Fine,' Rachel said. 'I'm sure the police will believe you over the two of us, won't they, Rob? They'll find it a complete coincidence that your DNA was found at the scene of his father's murder.' She stopped. They all heard the sirens, getting louder and then stopping abruptly.

Mick stood and darted to the door, and Rachel stepped out of his way. They heard the front door slam open, and running footsteps.

'It's not worth chasing him, Rob. I told the police he might run. I gave them a description.' Rob was inspecting the screwdriver jutting from Paddytum's abdomen.

'It's not a big hole,' he said. 'I'm sure my mum can sew it up.'

'Better not touch it, Rob. In case the police need to use it as evidence. Hang on ...'

They went to the front door, and listened.

'Got 'im. Officer. Running out of my little sparrow's flat.'

Rob and Rachel looked out onto the landing, where Mick was pinioned face down on the floor, with Bill sitting on him.

THIRTY-SEVEN

The police left, taking the screwdriver away with them in a plastic bag. They'd held Mick on the landing while Bill crowed about how he'd served in the Falklands in '82 and had even killed a man, and how nobody messed with his little sparrow and got away with it.

'Of course my prints are on it,' Mick cried, as they marched him away, his hands cuffed behind him. 'It's my screwdriver. I use it every day. You'd be better arresting these two. They're in collusion. They planned all this.'

'I'm sure we can sort it all out at the station, sir,' the police sergeant had told him as he led him away. Rob and Rachel gave brief statements.

Rachel closed the front door after the police left, and came back to sit with Rob on the sofa. 'I'm willing to stick to the story about the confession, Rob. In court, I mean.'

'You don't have to lie for me.'

'It wouldn't be lying. He practically did confess, didn't he?' Rob was lightly touching the hole in Paddytum's abdomen. A tiny puff of white was poking through. 'I'll sew that up for you,' she said.

He looked at her. 'Thanks. He saved my life. Probably.'

'Is he still ... here?'

'Dad, you mean? No. I didn't think he would be after all that physical stuff. He'll be gone at least until morning. Maybe even lunchtime.'

Rachel took the bear off his lap. 'Rob, are you sure he's not gone for good this time? I mean, he doesn't need to stay now, does he?'

'I don't know. Maybe not.' He picked up Rachel's hand, and held it. 'I just get the feeling he's not, though. He didn't say goodbye.'

'Perhaps he had no choice. Perhaps he was just sort of ... whisked away.'

Rob hadn't even considered the possibility that he might never speak to his father again. Tears pricked at his eyes. 'I hope not. I need to thank him. For everything.'

The next morning a police officer called round to speak to Maureen, and told her a man was helping the police with their enquiries into her husband's murder. 'I'm sure your son will tell you all about it, Mrs Handle.'

He'd returned home late last night. Rachel had told him to stay off work today so he'd be home if the police called round. He hadn't been able to face telling Maureen at breakfast, although she was curious as to why he had the day off. He'd been about to tell her when they arrived.

After they'd gone, he told her his and Rachel's version of the story: Mick had seen Rob in the library on Saturday and had been struck by the resemblance to the man he'd killed. Racked with guilt, he had gone round to see Rachel, to ask her advice. And when he'd seen Rob was there, he'd confessed. Because, Rob explained, the crime had weighed on his conscience all these years.

Maureen didn't look convinced. 'So why has he changed his story, then? The police say he's denying it. And they said he tried to stab you. Why confess and then do that?'

'Well, he's a crazed killer, isn't he, Ma?' Rob said, inspecting his nails. 'Who knows how his mind works.' The police hadn't missed that their story was a little contradictory, either, and Rob knew it would all be down to the DNA evidence now. And the police sergeant had confirmed that DNA would be taken, because of the attempted assault charge.

He told Maureen about the tattoo.

Her face slowly changed, from hope, to realisation, to sorrow. And she wept. 'All those years, when I thought ... Oh my poor dear Eric, I'm sorry. I should have known. Oh, I do wish I could tell him.'

Rob put his arms around her and looked towards the stairs. 'He knows, Ma. I'm sure he knows.'

His father didn't wake until the afternoon. He asked if there were news. Rob told him about his talk with Maureen. 'Good,' he said.

'Rob, I don't think I'll be here much longer, son. I feel as if … as if I'm only halfway here now.' He sounded calm, unafraid.

'Last night, Rachel wondered if you'd already gone.'

'Ah yes, Rachel. She's a wonderful girl. Just promise me one thing.'

'What?'

'That you will not call any of your children George Frederick.'

Rob laughed through his tears. 'We won't. Except, maybe the girls. I wish you didn't have to go. I'll miss you.'

'You'll be fine now, Robert. You don't need Paddytum any more.'

'Oh, I think part of me always will.' He picked up the bear and hugged it, imagining the face of his dad. 'Thank you. For being such a good father. For helping me.' A tear dripped onto the top of the bear's head.'

'Oh, it was the least I could do.'

Downstairs, the phone rang, and Rob wiped his face as he went to answer it, leaving Paddytum on the bed. It was the police, telling him Michael Hackett had been charged with the murder of Eric Handle in 1986. He thanked them and passed the news to his mother.

When he returned to his room, he knew, without even picking up the bear, that his father had gone.

EPILOGUE

Six years later.

Five-year-old Georgia Handle looked up into Nana Maureen's eyes as she tucked her into her big girl bed. Her baby brother Eric had a travel cot set up in Nana's room.

'Can you sing me a song, Nana?' she said. 'Dada always does.'

Nana gave her cheek a little pinch and said, 'Oh, darling, I wish I could, but you wouldn't like the sound of my voice. I can't sing to save my life, sweetie-pie. Never could.'

Georgia looked puzzled. 'But Mummy can, and Dada can. Why can't you?'

'Some people can sing, Georgie, and some can't. I'm one of the ones who can't. I could read you a story, though, if you want. Daddy packed some books for you, didn't he?'

'Can Paddytum listen, too?' She hugged the bear close. He was one of the best things about coming to stay with Nana; that, and sleeping in Dada's old bedroom. And she liked looking at all the pictures Nana had, all over the walls of her house, of Grandad Eric. In the photos, he was on a stage, dressed in funny clothes and wearing odd make-up, or a wig, or a moustache. He looked like he would have been a lot of fun, and Georgia thought it was sad that he'd died such a long time before she and Baby Eric were born.

Maureen opened one of the picture books Rob had packed in Georgie's little pink suitcase on wheels. It was the book Georgia liked best, the one about the owl babies. 'Is Paddytum sitting comfortably?' Nana asked.

Georgia giggled. 'Yes, and I am too. Nana, could Grandad Eric sing?'

'Oh yes,' she said. 'He was a wonderful singer.'

'Poor Nana,' Georgia said. 'You're the only one, then.'

Maureen smiled. 'Don't worry, sweet. It doesn't worry me. I'm good at other things.'

As Maureen read the story, Georgia thought about her mummy and daddy. They were away for the weekend. Dada had been working hard at college, which was like a very, very big

245

school – much bigger than the one she went to. And now he'd finished and didn't have to go any more, because he was going to be a teacher. He wouldn't be working at the library like he used to, on the days he didn't go to his college school, but Mummy still worked there sometimes.

Maureen finished reading, and closed the book. 'Do you want the door open a little bit, Georgie? So you can see the light on the landing?'

'No, Nana, I'm a big girl. I don't need that. I've got Paddytum. He'll look after me.'

Maureen smiled. 'I'm sure he will. Night night, lovey.' She kissed Georgia on the forehead, and, as an afterthought, kissed Paddytum's head too. Then went out, closing the door.

'Night night Paddytum.' She sometimes talked to Paddytum when she stayed here.

And, sometimes, she thought he spoke to her, too.

The publication of this novel was funded by pre-orders. The author and publisher extend their gratitude to the following people:

Marc Aucoin
Nick Bouton
Zaina Budaly
Julie Cairns
Catherine Cargill
Jason Clifford
Mike Cook
Roseanna Cooke
Barnaby Eaton-Jones
Rachelyn Farrell
Andy Frankham
Jean Gilmore
Jackie Howland
Tracy Hickson
Brad Jones
Marianne Kavanagh
Kate MacKenzie
Chris McIntyre
Andrew Montgomery-Hurrell

Dina Moreth
J G Muir
Cathryn Mullen
Tamsyn Murray
Dulcinea Norton-Smith
Charlotte Perry
Angela Peters
Jordan Rockerbie
Eric Rountree
Thomas Ruane
Ana Cristina Simon
Michele Smith
Jonty Stern
Eileen Stonock
Will Thaggard
Danielle Tjoelker
Treena Westwood
Ruth Wheeler
Maria Wood

Also from www.hirstpublishing.com

Cemetery Drive
By J.T. Wilson

J T Wilson
Cemetery Drive

Death, it's a once-in-a-lifetime opportunity.

Alexa cheated death today. Well, at least that's what she was told, but how can you tell, if the Grim Reaper doesn't show up? Lucky she's got Robbie really, who'll go out and confront Death for her, even if it means going to the furthest corners of the world and killing himself in the process. And given Robbie's suicidal anyway, everyone wins. Zan's having a bad day. Death's best employee, he's been collecting souls since the day he died, but today one wasn't there for him to collect, and that means a soul's achieved immortality and a serious threat to his job security. Now he's got to hunt that soul down and return it to the afterlife before the universe is torn asunder, before the fabric of space-time is destroyed and more importantly, before his boss finds out. Featuring steampunk package holidays, demon summoning, sex, violence, casual drug use, possessed technology and technomagic of a universe-threatening nature.

Also from www.hirstpublishing.com

Tales in Dark Languages
By Cynthia Garland

Geoffrey Midori is a magician and raconteur - a purveyor of ancient tales, lost arts, and dark secrets - and he is having trouble sleeping. His nights are plagued by vivid dreams, bouts of sleepwalking, and a strange sensation that he is not alone in the dark. He takes a break from his travels with a caravan of performers to visit friends, only to find that their daughter is having troubles of her own. She has come of age, and is exhibiting certain specific traits from a vilified race that was exterminated centuries ago - traits that elicit fear and suspicion from those around her. When the authorities come to investigate, Geoffrey takes her on the run. Aided by his companions in the caravan - a soothsayer, dream interpreter, medicine showman, astrologer, and strong man - he must use his fragmented knowledge of ancient mythologies to unlock the secrets of the dead races - all the while battling his own demons and keeping one step ahead of the agents who are pursuing them.

Also from www.hirstpublishing.com

Lemon
By Barnaby Eaton-Jones

Spencer was an insignificant Data Input Operator and this
suited him fine. However, when he is mistaken for someone
actually significant, due to a mix-up by the Post Office, then his
life becomes complicated. By complicated we're talking murder,
sex, violence, car chases, beautiful women, and an annoyed fat
cat (both of the feline* and big business variety). Spence didn't
like complicated things and he was as far removed from being
James Bond as Shakespeare was from being a hack plagiarist.

A week in Spence's life usually consisted of nothing more than
dull, repetitive, time-wasting tedium. But, not this week. This
week was going to be different and Spence wasn't going to like
it one little bit.

* Just to add some extra zest to this 'Lemon', you can read all
about Spence's love-hate relationship with his feline nemesis in
'Eric's Tale' at the end of the book.

Also from www.hirstpublishing.com

Fates, Flowers
By Matthew Waterhouse

Sara Smith is one of the most monstrous characters you can
hope to meet. She lives in Greenwich Village on Life Insurance
courtesy of her late husband, but she has fallen into a dreary
routine: work in a card shop by day, where she is the rudest
sales clerk imaginable, and weary evenings passed in the same
cellar bar night after night with the same old people. But when
she meets and seduces a gorgeous boy called Steve, she has no
idea what she is getting herself into.
Neither has he. Neither will you.

Also from www.hirstpublishing.com

Flight Risks
By Douglas Schofield

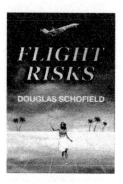

Basel, Switzerland, February 2001 : Fifty-six years after the end of
World War Two, Switzerland's bankers finally agree to release
21,000 dormant accounts left behind by Jews who died in the
Holocaust. Claims from the victims' heirs pour in from across the
world...

New York and Washington, September 2001 : The Twin Towers fall.
The Pentagon burns. Western democracies scramble to meet a
deadly new threat...

Victoria, Canada, October 2001: For legal secretary Grace Palliser,
the post-911 media circus is just background noise. Grace is too busy
with the unholy mess she calls her life. But when she stumbles on
evidence of a vast international fraud, her life gets a whole lot
messier. Framed for murder and desperately searching for the
evidence that will clear her, Grace flees across the continent to New
Orleans, then to the Florida Panhandle, and finally to a small island
in the northwest Caribbean. Hot on her trail is a corrupt former cop
with a simple assignment - to Kill Grace Palliser.

Also from www.hirstpublishing.com

Amusements, Carousels and Candy Floss on Sticks
By Brad Jones

Meet Bernard Stint. A marriage guidance counseller from Hendon, North London. A rather meek and mild man whose idea of a fun day is sitting at the local transport depot collecting bus numbers. Wife, Angela. Son, Sam. Bernard's life is turned upside down one day, when arriving home from work, Angela announces she is leaving him in favour of a muscle-bound fitness instructor. Realising he can't counsel himself when his own marriage breaks up and losing his job shortly afterwards for drunkenly assaulting Angela's new man, Bernard decides a new life beckons. Somewhere new. Somewhere miles away. Closing his eyes and putting a pin in a map of the UK, he moves to the sleepy north-east town of Lympstone-on-Sea. There he meets Melody, newly arrived from Southern Ireland, a music hall style singer who plays to an nearly empty pier theatre most nights. Can Bernard build his new life and revitalise Melody's flagging stage act? Will success and fortune prevail? Will Bernard and Melody fall for each other in this land of amusements, carousels and candy floss on sticks

Also from www.hirstpublishing.com

Look Who's Talking
By Colin Baker

To many, Colin Baker is the sixth Doctor Who; to some, he is the villainous Paul Merroney in the classic BBC drama The Brothers. But to the residents of South Buckinghamshire he is a weekly voice of sanity in a world that seems intent on confounding him. Marking the 15th anniversary of his regular feature in the Bucks Free Press, this compilation includes over 100 of his most entertaining columns, from 1995 to 2009, complete with new linking material. With fierce intelligence and a wicked sense of humour, Colin tackles everything from the absurdities of political correctness to the joys of being an actor, slipping in vivid childhood memories, international adventures and current affairs in a relentless rollercoaster of reflections, gripes and anecdotes. Pulling no punches, taking no prisoners and sparing no detail, the ups and downs of Colin life are shared with panache, honesty and clarity, and they are every bit as entertaining and surreal as his trips in that famous police box... for a world that is bewildering, surprising and wondrous, one need look no further than modern Britain, and Colin Baker is here to help you make sense of it all, and to give you a good laugh along the way.

For teenage readers, from www.hirstpublishing.com

All Aliens Like Burgers
By Ruth Wheeler

Young, polite and intelligent Tom Bowler has barely ever ventured out of the small English town where he grew up. So when he applies for a job in a fast food restaurant at a "local" service station during his gap year he is rather surprised to discover that the vacancy is in fact based on Truxxe, a planetoid stationed between local galaxies Triangulum and Andromeda. Hes surprised further still to find himself becoming friends with a purple alien and that he has strange feelings for his android supervisor, Miss Lola. Tom soon discovers that Truxxe has many hidden secrets - just what makes it so special? And why is its terrain so rich and varied that it can be used for fuelling such a diverse variety of intergalactic spacecraft? What are the Glorbian space pirate brothers Schlomm and Hannond plotting? And just what is it that they put in those burgers?

Find Hirst Books on Facebook

Get regular special offers, promotions, all the latest news, and connect with our authors.

And if you've enjoyed this book, why not enter a short review on the Paddytum page of our website?

www.hirstpublishing.com